ALSO BY C D MAJOR

Writing as Cesca Major:

The Silent Hours
The Last Night

Writing as Rosie Blake:

The Hygge Holiday
How To Find Your (First) Husband
How to Stuff Up Christmas
How To Get A (Love) Life
The Gin O'Clock Club

The
Other
Girl

C D MAJOR

THOMAS & MERCER

Text copyright © 2020 by C D Major
All rights reserved.

Published by Thomas & Mercer, Seattle

www.apub.com

Amazon, the Amazon logo, and Thomas & Mercer are trademarks of Amazon.com, Inc., or its affiliates.

ISBN-13: 9781542021814
ISBN-10: 1542021812

Cover design by Emma Rogers

Printed in the United States of America

The Other Girl

To Naomi – for endless cheerleading

Prologue

I'm Edith.

    I'm a patient.

    I'm a loony.

    I'm a woman.

    I'm innocent.

    I'm guilty.

    I used to be someone else.

    I'm a victim.

    I'm a villain.

    I lie.

    I tell the truth.

    Whatever I do it always ends the same way.

    I'm Edith.

    I'm a patient.

    I'm a loony.

Chapter 1

NOW

Seacliff Lunatic Asylum, 8 December 1942

There's smoke, shouting, steps: the whole building is awake and shrieking.

It's the middle of the night. They are locked in. The keys are on the other side of the doors, the locks on the outside of the shutters. If they call out, will someone hear them? If they pummel at the wood with their fists, can they force their way out?

They stumble, the smoke makes them cough, makes their eyes sting, fills them up.

The heat is already unbearable. Why is no one coming?

Someone is crying, someone is hiding in the corner, someone still thinks she's in her nightmare. Someone has dropped the thing she was holding.

Their bodies press together, all trying to reach the windows, to break out, to breathe in the cool night air. There are voices outside, faint, calling out, shouting instructions. The women pull at the shutters, claw at the wood. At one of the windows, someone is free.

There is more wailing; the smoke billows. The women can't see. They feel along the walls and huddle together. As far from the flames as they can get.

There is no time. No help.

The fire is everywhere. Screaming.

The whole building is scorching, searing . . .

Chapter 2

BEFORE

Summer 1927

Mother is bent over, clipping the pink roses with her big scissors. I am sitting on the rug on the lawn, Mrs Periwinkle is opposite me and I am pouring her tea. Mrs Periwinkle has both her eyes, not just one like my doll from before. She is cleaner too, with a creamy face and two pink circles for cheeks. Mother says I have to be careful not to spill the tea on my white dress, but she is being silly as the tea can't really spill.

It is quiet at this time of day, nothing moving down the road, no rumble of carts or motor cars passing. I can hear a fantail in the trees. I like it here the best, sitting near the orchard with the honey pear trees, away from the other side of the garden and the churchyard with the crooked gravestones that you can see through the gaps in the fence. The church is huge, the spire always showing us where home is when we walk or get the motorcar back.

Father is in his study writing a sermon. Tomorrow is when he will stand up at the front of the church and everyone comes to listen to him talk. Before bedtime I am allowed to see him in his study and he has started to read to me from the Bible. I like the other book Mother has with the pictures of the ladies in tall cone hats and long dresses best, but Father says I need to know the scripture and I don't say anything about the other book because I don't want to make him angry.

Father is very important and lots of people stop and tip their hat and say hello to him when we walk around Dunedin. I like it when he wants me to go with him to see the people he calls parisners and it is just us together. Mother and I make visits to the parisners too and she tells Mrs Clark to make the biscuits with the walnuts on top to take, and Mrs Clark huffs as she bends over the separator and wipes her floury hands on her apron but she makes the biscuits, warm on my tongue with the insides all soft.

Mrs Periwinkle has asked for more tea and I pour it out as I talk to her. She is wearing a blue dress with two petticoats underneath and I make sure they are neat around her. I hope she is not too hot; there are hardly any clouds today. She always wears her matching hat and her large blue eyes are wide, above a small red mouth. I tell her about the new ribbon Mother bought me for my hat and about how when we were in Dunedin we saw a man with only half a leg. I always have to tell her things because I don't have anyone else to tell any more. I think of a silhouette in the bed next door to me, a sleepy smile across the narrow gap: she always listened. I miss sharing my bedroom.

Mother has stopped snipping the roses and the big scissors are lying in the grass nearby. The edges look sharp, the sunlight flashes on the silver surface. I feel my fingers twitch as I look at them. I'm not allowed to touch. I look back at Mrs Periwinkle. Sometimes I want to snip her hair off.

Above the house a trail of smoke leaves the chimney. Mrs Clark is inside by the coal range and we are having the soup in the big shiny saucepan. She let me help her knead this morning: the dough was sticky and stretchy and didn't smell like bread. I like the smell better when it is cooking.

Mother has picked something up, her back to me, and I open my mouth to ask her how soon it is until the soup is ready. Nearby the fantail chirrups.

Mother turns and I see what she is holding. It is a large, grey rock and suddenly I am pushing backwards on my hands and I don't care about my white dress. I feel my eyes go big and round as she walks towards me. My skin goes cold and I can smell the sea, sharp in my nose, feel the damp sand clinging to my tunic, hear the waves.

'Edith, can you run inside and—' Mother stops then.

My chest is going up and down, up and down. I'm still crawling backwards on the grass. Away. He had walked towards me like that.

'What's wrong, Edith? Are you unwell?'

I can't stop staring at the rock in her hand.

'Edith?' Mother has her head tilted to the side.

'No, no, no, no.' My voice is high and loud. The fantail soars away.

'Edith.' Mother stops.

I take little breaths, my ears full of the crashing waves. 'That was what he hit me with.'

Mother frowns, two lines in the middle of her forehead. 'Edith, don't do this. Why do you . . . ?' She takes another step.

'No.' I tremble. 'Don't. Stop. He hit me, he hit me over and over.'

Chapter 3

NOW

Declan was alone in the room with the policeman, the man's stomach spilling over too-tight trousers, a button missing from his waistcoat. Declan poured him a glass of water. The policeman sniffed it suspiciously, then left it sitting on the side by the jug. Licking a fat finger, he turned a page in his pad.

'You a doctor here, then?'

'One of the junior doctors, sir, yes. I started a few weeks ago.' Declan sipped at his own glass. 'My first job,' he added, thinking of how relieved he'd been to tell his father when he'd received the offer.

The policeman grunted and looked around the small room: the two wooden stools, the medicine cabinet in the corner, the iron bed frame, leather shackles dangling from it.

Declan heard the footsteps, glad not to have to search around for something else to say. He'd been up all night, since the alarm was raised just before midnight, trying to help. His brain was sluggish and his throat felt thick, clogged with the night's horrors.

The door opened and the second woman was ushered inside. The second of only two survivors. From a building housing thirty-nine women.

Declan hadn't seen this patient before, but that wasn't surprising; there were hundreds living in the main building. She was clutching a nurse's arm, still dressed in dirty nightclothes, a shawl thrown over her shoulders, her thin frame bowed forward. Someone had wiped her face but the soot marks still streaked her neck, a smudge remaining on her right cheek. Her curly hair, unbrushed and loose, fell down her back. The policeman pulled on his belt as he watched her sit on the stool.

The nurse left with a curious glance back, part of the drama, the whole place crawling with talk of what had taken place just hours earlier. Declan shifted in his seat, an uncomfortable straight-backed chair reminding him of chilly school classrooms. His pad rested in his lap. He was taking notes for Doctor Malone, who was still busy talking with the fire chief in the grounds. As Declan sharpened his pencil, he noticed the young woman watching until the neat curl of shaving fluttered to the floor.

The policeman launched right in, no introductions, just straightened and began his questioning.

'You are Miss Edith Garrett,' he said, checking a note in his pocketbook.

The woman said nothing, still staring at the shaving on the floor. She looked younger than her twenty years. Declan glanced at the brief information he'd been given: Edith Garrett, an in-patient for almost fifteen years. Her hands met in her lap, one resting on top of the other.

'Miss Garrett, you were a resident in Ward Five, is that correct?'

Were. Declan noted the past tense with a heavy heart.

The policeman continued as if she had responded, 'Can you talk us through the events of last night?'

The woman remained silent, her brown eyes not flickering from the spot.

The policeman sighed, frustrated perhaps by another unwilling patient; the first survivor hadn't said a word either. 'At what time did you notice that something was wrong?'

Wrong: what an understatement. Declan swallowed, seeing again the wooden building lit up with livid orange flames, the noises that he knew he would never forget, and then, worse perhaps, the silence from inside, just smoke and smells and . . .

Edith looked up at the policeman, her mouth lifting a fraction. Was she even listening?

The officer bent his head forward and down, raised his voice. 'Can you tell me how you came to be outside the building?'

Declan watched the patient blink, a strange half-smile forming.

The policeman stood up, threw Declan a look, as if he were complicit in this rebellion. His voice became even louder, the words sped up. 'All the doors and windows had been locked at the last check, so, Miss Garrett, how was it that you came to be outside?'

Her smile was gone. She tipped her head a fraction to the right, reminding Declan of a rifleman he had once spotted: the fragile bird with brown feathers flecked with ochre, so still, a twitch of its head as it searched amongst the leaves at its feet.

The policeman cleared his throat, shifted his weight. 'Miss Garrett, I must prevail upon you to answer.'

She didn't. The policeman breathed through his nose, the clatter of a trolley sounded somewhere in the corridor outside, the rattle of metal, a male voice called to someone. Declan fidgeted in his chair, pencil poised.

'Miss Garrett, need I remind you of the terrible incident that has happened here?'

The question led to nothing more from the woman. Declan attempted to catch her eye. She twisted a little on her stool, looked right at him, her eyes round, brows raised, as if she'd just woken, as if she'd just noticed him there. Then, as if he had said something

10

pleasant, her face broke into a different smile: wide, a row of straight teeth, eyes creased. Declan sat upright, struggling with an appropriate response, the confusion knitting his eyebrows together.

'Miss Garrett, if you could please talk us through last night. We are putting together a timeline of events.'

She turned towards the voice then, as if she'd only just noticed the policeman, too, despite the fact he was enormous, his frame squeezed into the space between the hospital bed and the cabinet.

'Last night.' She repeated the two words. Declan was surprised by her voice, suddenly in the space: strong, clear.

'Yes, you were found outside at' – the policeman flicked back through the notes, squinting at his own scrawls – 'around 1 a.m. How did you get outside? When did you get out?'

'She got out too.'

'I'm sorry?'

'Martha.'

'Miss Anderson, yes, we were just speaking with her.'

Declan recalled the mute woman who had been in the room moments before. It hardly qualified as a conversation.

'She got out too,' Edith repeated.

'Yes, we know that.' The policeman gritted his teeth, the words pushed out between them.

'I saw her. I—' She stopped abruptly, screwed her eyes shut.

Declan wondered what she'd been about to say.

Edith changed tack, talking with her eyes closed as if back there, reliving it all. 'I climbed out of my room, there was so much smoke. So much. I felt along the edge of the window; the shutter, it was broken. They hadn't fixed it, you see.'

'You climbed out? Of what? A window?' the policeman checked.

Edith's face cleared, eyes opened again. 'The window, yes, they hadn't fixed the window,' she said. 'I'd told Bernie but . . .'

11

She became distressed very quickly then, her face collapsing.

'She was upstairs too. Bernie,' she whispered.

Declan watched her eyes darken as she repeated the name, fingers worrying at thumbs until she grasped her hands together in her lap. 'She's gone. She's gone.' Repeating those two words she started to gently rock on the stool, back, forward, back.

She scooped forward, picked up the curl of pencil shaving from the floor, clutched it to her chest in both hands as if it were precious. 'She's gone.'

Bernie. He had a patient called Bernadette. Young, shy, gentle. He felt a terrible slice of fear course through his chest.

'She's gone.'

He stared at Edith, aware his face mirrored the distress on her own. Then, without warning, her mouth gaped open and she began to laugh, slowly, her head tipped back, her neck on show, tidemarks of soot highlighting the creamy skin beneath. The laugh, hiccoughed and strange, merged with tears in her throat, became sobs that shook her whole body.

'Gone.'

The policeman turned away from her, muttering under his breath. Declan reached into his inside pocket and pulled out a handkerchief, held it out to Edith. She scraped back her stool, the sobs stopping as abruptly as they had begun. The handkerchief in his hand hung limply in the gap between them.

He pulled back, off-kilter, placing it back into his jacket pocket beneath his white overcoat. Shouldn't have done that. Doctor Malone told him not to get in the way. He heard footsteps, a command from outside the room. One tear rested on Edith's cheekbone, marking a clear trail through the smudge. Her expression was passive again, brown eyes now dulled as she turned towards the noises too. He realised he was holding his breath.

Doctor Malone appeared in the doorway then, almost obscuring the young nurse standing behind him, just a thumbprint of soot on her pristine white hat, a strand of sandy hair escaped, needing to be pinned; her eyes rimmed red, a smile plastered on too late as she looked at Edith.

'Ah, Detective, how are we getting on here?' Doctor Malone's voice hadn't changed despite all the events of the last few hours. Brash, confident. As if he were checking up on the weather. His large, grey moustache twitched as he waited for a response.

The policeman looked at him, then back at Edith, and grunted.

Doctor Malone eyed the girl on the stool. 'Edith, you can finish up here. Nurse Shaw will take you off, get you dressed.'

Edith nodded quickly, the knuckles on her hands growing white as she clasped them together.

Doctor Malone looked across at Declan. 'Doctor Harris, we'll catch up shortly. I need to go and see the pathologist, see what we can do about the bodies. Then we'll need to discuss today's routine – as you can imagine, it is awry.'

'Yes, sir.' Declan stood, pushed his glasses up the bridge of his nose. He glanced at Edith, hoping she hadn't listened to the senior doctor's crass description. He was surprised to find she was watching him with lowered eyes as he put his pen away, the movement clumsy.

The nurse quickly crossed the room and placed a cloak around Edith's shoulders. 'We'll get out of the doctor's way, won't we, Edie. Go and have a bath.'

Edith remained in her chair, eyes still on Declan, head tipped to the side again: the rifleman.

'You're the new doctor,' she said.

Declan cleared his throat.

'You talk to the patients; you make them better.'

Declan couldn't help the slight puff of his chest. He hoped that was true; certainly he'd had some recent success. His thoughts strayed back to Bernadette, and his body drooped. How awful.

The nurse placed an arm under Edith's shoulders, lifted her to her feet. 'Come on, Edie, come now.'

'She told me,' Edith was saying as the nurse moved her awkwardly to the door, Doctor Malone standing aside. 'She told me he had made her better.'

Declan watched her leave, a deep sadness stealing over him once more.

'There was a fire,' Declan heard her say in a matter-of-fact voice as she was led away.

'I know, Edie.'

'There was a big fire. Everyone was burnt.'

The nurse didn't respond to that.

As the policeman spoke to Doctor Malone, Declan moved to the open doorway, watched her leave. As if Edith felt his eyes on her she turned to smile at him, lifted a hand.

'I got out,' she called back to him.

'I'm glad,' he heard himself saying. 'I'm glad, Edith.'

Chapter 4

THEN

Three months earlier

Edith followed Deputy Matron out of the dayroom to the toilets at the end of the hall: patients were never allowed to go alone. They walked in silence, only the sounds of their footsteps on the stone floor. There was constant prattle in Edith's head though: comments on the dormitory, bedding, whether the black-and-white caterpillar was still there, whether it was mutton that day, where the doctors lived when they didn't live here and would the patients go on an outing to the flicks soon? Some days felt the same, as if she had lived them all before; talking helped.

She couldn't talk too much to the doctors in case they said she was lying, and you couldn't be sure the nurses wouldn't tell them things too. It was better to say things that made them smile, give her the red pills and tell her to go back to the ward. When she was little she hadn't known how to do that; it seemed everything she said had got her sent to the white room. And she'd been louder then too, not able to keep the things in her head inside.

She used to talk to Patricia the most; she had been there since they were both little girls. Although sometimes Patricia had got angry, turned the same colour as her bright-red hair and shouted at Edith, calling her Fred and telling her to get lost. But other times she had let Edith rest her head in her lap and stroked her hair and told her about her family trips to their crib by the sea with the dunny on the beach and her grandmother who wore long black dresses and refused to go bathing. Edith had loved it when Patricia did that. She would close her eyes tight and imagine she was back home in her bed before she came here and Mother was moving her soft fingers gently through her curls.

Patricia didn't do any of that any more; she'd been moved to another ward last month after the episode with Donna. Edith had seen her once since, in the dayroom, but they'd made her stand next to the nurses' station for getting over-stimulated, so Edith couldn't talk to her. Edith had been safer on the ward when Patricia had been there. Now she had to be alert: always ready.

She wasn't completely alone; she had Bernie still, at least. Bernie was smaller, and more than four years younger than Edith. Fifteen was what Nurse Shaw told them; she could do the adding. Bernie had long, dark-brown hair the colour of the trunk of the big tree in the garden. Edith stayed with her as much as she could. It was better not to be on your own. Patricia had been on her own when it happened.

Deputy Matron stopped outside the dank, sour-smelling room. Only one bare bulb was working, but it wasn't quite dark enough to hide the dripping spots on the ceiling, the plaster peeling. The cleaning gang hadn't visited with their mops today. There were watery footprints on the floor, dirty smears. Deputy Matron wavered, refusing to move inside and sit on the wooden stool against the wall, ushering Edith past her as she remained in the doorway, one hand up to her mouth. Five toilets stood in a line; none of the cubicles had doors.

Edith stepped into one. She wanted to wipe the yellow droplets from the rim of the seat but didn't want Deputy Matron to be angry with her for dawdling. She lowered her undergarments and sat down, a tiny gasp as her bare flesh hit the cold enamel, feeling the spots of liquid on her skin. Deputy Matron stood only a few feet away. Edith always wished there were doors.

She heard her laugh first: sharp, distinctive. Edith's head snapped up. Then suddenly there she was outside in the corridor walking with Martha and Nurse Ritchie: Edith could make out her dark hair cut in a wonky line below her ears, the short fringe. Edith drew her knees together, leant over, desperate to cover herself, feeling everything freeze inside her.

Donna.

Had she seen where Edith had headed? Was that why she was here now?

She prayed she wouldn't notice her in here, that she wasn't heading to the dunnies. The footsteps got louder until she could sense someone right in front of her open cubicle. She slowly lifted her gaze. There was Donna, looking down at her, her left eye snapping open and shut, a tic; Martha, a step behind, her thin face pale as she too looked at Edith.

'Well, well. Hi, princess,' Donna uttered.

'Get on, ladies,' Deputy Matron called and Donna smirked and moved to the cubicle next door, scrawny Martha on the other side. Edith looked desperately at Deputy Matron, grateful suddenly for her nearness. What could Donna do here? Surely she was safe?

There was a cough, a rustle. Deputy Matron and Nurse Ritchie were talking to each other in the doorway now, not looking into the room, and that was when Donna and Martha began to whisper

17

things. Disgusting, frightening things they were going to do to Edith. Their threats floated under and over the gaps of the cubicle, swirled around her, so quiet Edith might have imagined they were only in her head.

She couldn't move. Their words made her want to wash herself, wash them away.

'Bloody hell, Edith, take your time,' Deputy Matron snapped.

Edith remained where she was, waiting for the two women either side of her to flush, to leave. She couldn't stop the trembling in her legs, couldn't do anything but sit there exposed.

The nurse's eyes swivelled to her now. 'Get up.'

Martha pulled on the chain and left, waiting nearby. Finally another flush and Donna walked back out, not looking at Edith until she reached the doorway, fishing something out of her pocket. Whatever it was couldn't be seen by the two nurses and Edith felt a small cry lodge inside her. It looked like a key, one of the keys the nurses kept on the big silver hoops. One of the keys that might open any door inside the ward: her door.

Donna could get things. She got cigarettes from Franklin the attendant. Soft slippers from one of the nurses. Now she had a key. Donna grinned at her, all her uneven teeth on show as she stepped outside.

'See you back on the ward, Edie,' she called, Martha's laughter echoing off the stone as they moved back down the corridor, Nurse Ritchie joining in as if they were all friends.

'You reckon I've got all day, Edith?' Deputy Matron shouted from the doorway.

Edith hated it when the nurses raised their voices. She'd spent years trying to avoid angering them, knowing if you did the wrong thing it could be made a lot worse. Worse than loud voices. Much worse. 'I'm sorry, I'm sorry,' she repeated, her undergarments bunched around cold ankles, her bladder still full. Edith stood up, pulling at her clothes.

'You reckon I won't punish you for wasting my time, I'll . . .' Deputy Matron was still talking as she turned and marched away, as Edith fumbled with the fastenings and raced to catch up.

Edith followed Deputy Matron back down the corridor towards the ward, her bladder swollen and uncomfortable. Had Donna really got one of the keys? Should she tell Deputy Matron? Edith felt her throat close, the panic balloon inside her. She had been warning her since Patricia left, her last plaything, that she'd find her way to her. Was this it? Was she no longer safe?

They were heading to the ward. She would tell Deputy Matron; she would listen to her, she wasn't one of the nice nurses, but she was fair. It had been years since she'd been in trouble. They might listen, might not punish her.

'Deputy Matron,' Edith breathed, her steps quick.

'What is it?' Deputy Matron kept walking.

'Did you see?' Edith continued. 'Donna, Deputy Matron, Donna,' she stuttered, 'she's got a key. It's to my room, I know it . . .'

'Don't spin a yarn, Edith. Patients don't have keys.' She rattled her own silver hoop as they moved past the window of the dayroom and around the corner.

'I know she has, Deputy Matron.' Edith could hear her voice rising. They were nearly back on the ward – if she could convince her, if they could search her . . . 'Please, please I saw it, she'll use it . . .'

Deputy Matron stopped stock-still then, Edith almost barrelling into her.

'Are you raising your voice at me?'

'I . . .' This was her last chance. She swallowed, tried to control her voice. 'She'll use it to get to me, please.' The last word came out as a strangled cry and Edith stepped forward: too close.

'She will do no such thing, Edith. Get back behind me.'

Edith could see the door to the ward just ahead; she was running out of time. She could hear her own breathing, heavier.

'Do I have to report you to Matron for dawdling and delusions?' Deputy Matron's voice was low, dangerous.

'No.' Edith just stopped herself reaching out her hands to grip her. 'I'm sorry, it's just, I saw . . .'

'I don't want to hear any more of what you saw. Get back behind me.' Deputy Matron didn't believe her; Edith could see it in the curl of her lip.

Edith swallowed the rest of the words, nodding furiously. 'It was nothing. I'm sorry, Deputy Matron.'

'I've got enough to be doing today without this.'

'Yes, Deputy Matron.' Edith scuttled behind her as she marched to the end of the corridor.

'Get inside. Keys? Honestly.'

She unlocked the ward and Edith was through. She didn't look up, didn't stop, just raced through the dormitory, alert to dark hair, a wonky fringe. She clattered down the staircase, ignored a voice calling out her name, swept into her own room, pulled the door shut behind her, rested her back against the wood, closed her eyes.

She could hear the noises from the floor above, the women moving in between the beds; a break before lunch. She pictured Bernie up there somewhere in the big dormitory, sharing the space with nineteen others. Edith tried to calm her breathing, her chest lifting and falling too fast. The need to piss overwhelmed her and she rushed to reach for the chamber pot under her bed, pulled at her clothes again, squatted over it.

She looked up sharply. Had she imagined the door handle slowly turning? She placed a hand on the floor, righting herself in the squat, all her senses straining to feel something. She had always felt her room was safe, locked at night. When she had first been moved she had lain awake in the dark, not used to being alone, too scared to sleep in case a monster got her.

Now she was older it wasn't monsters she feared.

Chapter 5
NOW

Declan held his handkerchief up to his face, but the flimsy cotton was powerless to block out the stink of it. It was horrific, the rows of lumpy sheets, the flakes of ash dancing in the breeze like a macabre snowstorm.

Doctor Malone was striding ahead, deep in conversation with an elderly man across from Dunedin who worked in the mortuary. Declan lingered behind them both, unable to stop looking at the shapes around him, remembering these were the bodies of the women he'd heard crying out only hours before. Declan closed his eyes for a moment, his empty stomach churning.

The wooden ward was reduced to blackened stumps, the frame barely intact; twisted remains of small tables, iron bedsteads. What had housed thirty-nine women twenty-four hours before was now nothing more than a sticky, dripping mess. The firemen and volunteers had done well to stop the fire spreading to the main building, but no one had been able to get inside quickly enough. They said the women had suffocated. The damage was so great the fire chief said it would be hard to identify where it had begun. You couldn't even see the separate rooms in the outbuilding, make out the walls, imagine what it looked like before it became this smoking, charred wreckage. Declan thought back to Edith smudged in soot, grateful at least that she had got out. And then he thought of Bernadette, and stared at the sheets: Bernadette under one of them.

The people moving past him were carrying buckets, towels, sheets; handkerchiefs tied around their faces. Behind them the imposing main building soared in the background: the central tower, turrets, thick stone immune from the devastation. There was a low murmur of voices, faces peering through the bars of every window at the scene.

He couldn't imagine the fear, what it must have been like to have been trapped inside. Had they all realised at the same moment? Did they claw pointlessly at the doors and windows that could only be opened from the outside? What pain had they felt? Declan turned his back, skin clammy, as he gulped at the air; the winding driveway, iron gates, the sea beyond. Greens, greys, blues: calm.

Doctor Malone was alone now, his forehead wrinkled as he stood looking up at the main building of Seacliff, at the enormous stone blocks, soaring turrets and slate roof. 'Thank God it didn't spread,' he said, hands on his hips. 'This building.'

Declan felt his hands trembling and stuffed them in his pockets. Yes, other patients had been saved, but it had been too late for so many.

'I hadn't come across the girl this morning before, the woman. What has she been diagnosed with, sir?'

'Woman?'

'Edith, sir, one of the patients who got out.'

'Edith Garrett,' Doctor Malone confirmed. 'Oh, schizophrenia, been here since she was an ankle-biter.'

'And Martha?'

'Martha Anderson, only been with us a couple of years or so from what I remember. She's in on an insanity charge.'

Declan's eyebrows lifted. They often had patients transferred from the prisons; he wondered what her crime had been. He thought back to the policeman's exasperated shout as she'd sat there saying nothing, the chilling stare Martha had given him.

'They were lucky,' Doctor Malone continued, 'to get out. The rest . . .' He faded away, swallowing, his large Adam's apple lifting up and down. It was the most emotion Declan had witnessed from the older man all day. 'An awful business. Awful.'

Declan nodded, hopelessness flooding him, desperate to be of assistance. Edith's earlier words reminded him he had helped other patients. Perhaps he could help her. 'I did a module at the university, with Professor Bates. We were looking at examples of battle fatigue, men who had suffered a great shock, and I was wondering if I might meet with the two survivors in the next few days?'

'See them?'

'Yes, if that would suit you, sir, I would be keen to try to help them. I imagine they might display some of the symptoms of having been through a traumatic ordeal. Certainly they both seemed affected, as you would expect.'

He thought back to Martha: her silence boiling but contained, and Edith with her shifting expressions, her ill-timed laughter, her choked sobs. How could they not have been impacted by surviving such a terrible night? Perhaps this was how he could play a small part.

'That probably won't be necessary, Doctor Harris. They're my patients, after all, and Edith has had some recent troubles. We need to manage what they say carefully – it might be delicate . . . the chief superintendent is concerned. Well, we will see . . .'

We will see felt like a small opening. Declan fell silent, determined to raise the question again.

'And the cause, Doctor, of the fire? Someone has mentioned a previous problem with the building. The foundati—'

Declan wasn't prepared for the sudden grip on his arm as Malone's hand trapped his wrist.

'We don't need you to be asking questions like that. It's bad enough the staff are . . .' He released Declan's wrist, suddenly aware, perhaps, of Declan's wide eyes. 'No need to concern yourself, Doctor,' Malone said, voice suffused with false cheer as he moved away towards the front of the building where a motorcar swung into view, men stepping out, adjusting bowler hats, smoothing jackets.

Declan stared after him. As he moved back through the side of the building he was grateful to leave the ruined ward behind him. The asylum was buzzing with an unsettled energy. The patients were fretful, rumours rife amongst them and the staff. Everyone had seen the smoke, of course; some had been awake to see the flames, and others had heard screaming, shouts from inside, from the trapped women. Everyone was asking what had happened, how it had happened, the narrative shifting and spreading like the fire.

The dayroom was frantic; the staff had already had to intervene with various patients. One of the men on Ward Two had throttled another patient for laughing about something and a female hysteric had been removed in the middle of a violent outburst, when she had continued to shout 'FIRE' until the other patients started crying or yelling at her to stop. Perhaps Malone was just wanting to keep the peace. Yet something about the way he had gripped his arm when he'd questioned how the fire began made him wonder.

The nurse from the interview that morning, Nurse Shaw he recalled, was walking towards him, wheeling a trolley, her shoes squeaking on the stone floor of the corridor. Declan paused for only a second before making up his mind.

'Nurse Shaw,' he called as she passed him.

The faint clink of silver on the trolley as she stopped.

'Oh, I'm sorry, Doctor Harris, I wasn't paying attention.' She jerked her head up, swiping at the loose strand of hair still poking out from her hat.

He looked at her. 'It's all right, I didn't meant to startle you. I was just wondering where we keep the patients' records for Ward Five?'

Her face fell immediately as he said the words, and he recalled her red-rimmed eyes from that morning.

'In the main building. It's all so dreadful, isn't it?' Her pale eyes already had a thin film over them, fresh tears about to fall. He noticed then her blotched skin, the ball of tissue in her fist.

'It's terribly grim,' Declan agreed. 'Would you like me to help?' He gestured at the trolley.

'That's kind of you. I mustn't. I should get on; we're so busy this morning and Nurse Ritchie told me off for being a drip . . .' She covered her mouth with a hand, her nails neatly clipped, as if she'd only just remembered who she was talking to. 'She's right, of course,' she added, 'but I can't stop thinking about them all, locked inside, not able to get out. We've been so short since the start of the war and I wonder if we had more . . .' Her voice was getting higher, faster, and the tears that threatened were now falling with abandon. 'I'm sorry,' she sniffed, pushing the tissue under her eyes.

Declan reached into his pocket, glad of the freshly laundered handkerchief. He passed it to her and Nurse Shaw took it with a wordless nod.

'You're not being a drip,' Declan reassured her. 'You've every right to be sad.'

Her face lifted a little.

'Come on, reckon I can help you with that trolley. Just point me in the right direction and then you can show me where the records are kept.' He used the voice he had recently adopted with patients and Nurse Shaw seemed marginally soothed.

They moved down the corridor together, passing rooms that Declan had yet to discover, an endless web of offices, locked cabinets, supplies, corridors leading to different wards. The scale of the building never failed to impress him; it had been the largest building in New Zealand when it was first built in 1877. His father had been pleased he would work in such a prestigious setting, at least, even if he wasn't quite a *real* doctor.

'We're here,' Nurse Shaw said, handing him back his handkerchief.

'Keep it.' Declan smiled.

She pocketed it with a quiet thank you.

They moved inside and she led him across to a filing cabinet, showing him where the keys were kept, a small bunch inside a blue glass vase. 'The current patients are in here. The numbers on the front relate to the ward, but people do move around and sometimes you might have to look at a previous ward. It depends how long they've been here, whether they get regular treatments. Doctor Malone keeps historic records in his office. Are you looking for someone specific?'

'Edith Garrett and Martha Anderson.'

The nurse nodded silently, the tears threatening again. 'Thank God, at least, Edie . . . thank God. It's one good piece of news from the night.'

She moved across to a filing cabinet that had a five engraved on a small plaque. 'You'll find the most recent notes in here. I know Martha arrived two years ago – I'd only been here myself for a month or so. She was very unpredictable in those early days; it wasn't hard to imagine her doing what she did to her husband. Some say that she might have, maybe, well . . .'

Declan was barely listening, already pulling open the filing cabinet and moving to the letter 'G'.

'. . . that might just be gossip.'

'And Edith?' He found a faded tan-brown folder and drew it out, placing it on the desk behind him.

The nurse looked wrong-footed for a moment before continuing. 'Edie? Edie's been here for years; she's grown up here by all accounts. Since she was a little girl. She's a lovely girl is Edie. Despite what's been happening recently,' Nurse Shaw continued, before Declan could interrupt to ask more. 'She's always thinking of other people. Oh.' A hand went up to her mouth, and the eyes filled. 'Bernie.' She whispered the name.

'Bernadette.' Declan nodded sadly. 'She was a patient of mine.'

Nurse Shaw looked at him. 'Oh, Edie will be devastated. She and Bernie were so close. Edie was like an older sister to her.' Something seemed to break then and she crumpled in front of him, the sobs getting louder.

Declan touched her shoulder lightly. 'Can I get someone?' he asked.

Nurse Shaw shook her head. 'I'm sorry,' she said, dabbing at her eyes. 'It's just I keep remembering who was . . .' She couldn't finish the sentence and Declan understood. Thirty-seven women. He could smell the smoke on both of their clothes, following them through the labyrinth of corridors, trailing behind them.

There was a distant voice and it was a moment before Declan realised it was calling out a name. Nurse Shaw straightened in an instant, looking at the door, as a faint 'Nancy' reached them. She pressed her eyes with the palms of her hands and stood up, smoothing her skirt. Declan looked over her shoulder at the door. 'Do you need another minute? I could distract them.'

'No, no, I'll be fine.' Then, in a firmer voice, 'I need to be busy, to stop thinking about it all and help. I need to go.' She went to move away, the tiniest lurch before she stuck a hand out and balanced herself on the desk. Then, swallowing, she made it to the door, a hand moving to her hat, tucking the errant strand of sandy hair back inside.

'Thank you, Doctor,' she said. 'I hope you find everything you need.'

Declan nodded at her once, feeling strangely older than his years when hearing his title. Only a few weeks ago he had been a medical student in Dunedin, the slightly disappointing son of a celebrated physician. Now he was Doctor Harris: a figure of authority. He turned back to the filing cabinet.

He found a file with Martha's name on it: the familiar heading on the medical notes, the stamp of Seacliff, the dates typed below. There were court documents and a photograph, slightly faded, the scalloped edges yellowed and curling. He traced his finger over a woman he didn't recognise: rounded face, dimples in both cheeks, clutching the hand of a little boy tucked into her side. What had happened to her? He thought of Martha leaving the policeman's interview earlier, all hollowed cheeks and angles, the silent fury. So different from the woman in this picture. He rushed through her notes, aware of the other file on the table that drew his eye, his fingers itching to reach for it.

Edith. What was it about her? The way she had tilted her head, perhaps, the intelligence he thought he glimpsed in her gaze? Something about her small, sad smile, the way she had jumped from one emotion to the next, the last look as she'd been led away. Something intrigued him. He straightened the papers carefully with two hands, the folder not as weighty as he had expected.

He dragged a seat across, lowering himself into it, trying to trace her story. There was her original admission form signed by her father, a pastor, and her mother, of no occupation. A brief confusing statement from Edith herself: comments about her family, her house by the sea, an older brother, a nasty incident – someone had hit her – and beneath it Malone's diagnosis of multiple personality disorder. Then the notes skipped a number of years, leaping to some that were only a couple of months old: an increased paranoia, talk of hearing things in the ward, ramblings about a friend called Patricia, a new drug she'd been given, a suggested round of EST. Seizing a pencil Declan scribbled some of the information down, secreting the paper in his pocket, knowing Doctor Malone would not take kindly to him removing her file.

Declan checked through the folder again, the chronology incomplete, the notes like reading a one-way conversation. The last page was a report from Matron on an incident that had occurred in the women's dormitory between Edith and another patient. A note was attached with a paperclip to the top of it and Declan reeled at the words, forgetting the rest of the file.

He reread the small note over and over again, his throat dry.

'Leucotomy being considered: patient to be observed.'

Chapter 6

BEFORE

Mother and I are visiting Mrs Boone in town. She's been ill and Father has asked for everyone to pray for her in the church. Mrs Boone is very old and she has a house that you can't see behind big high hedges that Mother calls 'macrocarpa'. It has a stone driveway and a man who doesn't speak opens the door and lets us in. It smells of the polish Mrs Clark uses when she cleans our bannisters.

Mrs Boone is sitting in a high chair with a rug over her body and she can't stand up when we go inside and sit opposite her. There's a fire and the room is hot but Mrs Boone doesn't seem warm, even under the rug. The man brings in a tray with a silver teapot and a sponge cake with currants and he hands me a plate with a slice on. My hands are all slippery from the heat and I forget to say thank you and Mother looks at me but it's too late.

The fruitcake is dry and a bit almost sticks in my throat. Mrs Boone doesn't eat her cake.

Mother asks her how she is coping and Mrs Boone's voice is crumbly like the sponge and she has to stop a lot to get air in. The man doesn't come back and I wish he would and could open a window. Mother is telling Mrs Boone about the Dunedin fair and

Mrs Boone nods her grey head just once. Then Mother talks about the pretty flower arrangement and it is when I look up at it on the mantelpiece that I see the photograph.

Next to the flowers in a glass vase is a photograph of a woman and a boy at the seaside. I think it is Mrs Boone when she was younger as her hair is sort of the same, a curl almost covering one eye.

'Sea, sea.' I point, eyes round, my legs kicking up as I speak.

Mrs Boone follows my finger, a small smile making the lines on her face even deeper. 'Arthur, my boy,' she whispers.

'I miss splashing in the sea,' I say.

'Don't be silly, Edith, you haven't been in the sea.' Mother carries on talking about the flowers, her voice louder, her eyes flicking to look at me.

I can't stop staring at the photograph, imagining all the colours even though the picture is just black and white. The blues of the big sky and water, the yellow of the sand, the soft pink of the inside of the shells. Like the picture of the sea in my bedroom in my old home, with the boats in. I had loved the sea when I was a big girl.

'There were penguins,' I remember.

Mother and Mrs Boone stop talking. I can hear Mother's breath leave her body in a whoosh. She says something quietly under her breath to me. I don't hear it. I used to think everyone was like me. That everyone had lived before. When I first said some things, Mother didn't get angry.

'Penguins in the sea,' I go on.

There is a moment's silence and then Mother laughs and tells Mrs Boone that I have a 'colourful imagination'. I don't know what that means. Mrs Boone says her son had liked the sea too. Mother is trying to look at me, her eyes round, not leaving my face. I look away, eat my cake, the sponge dry in my mouth, remembering the feeling of the sand between my toes, the sound of the waves as they pushed ever closer, the big row of rocks opposite the cave where the penguins would lie, jump, dip, the blue feathers clear when the sun was out.

The cave.

I think I might start crying, sitting on Mrs Boone's sofa with the dry cake in my mouth. I can feel tears push into my eyes and look hard at the plate and the crumbs until the tears go away. But my chest aches when I think of the sea, hear my old mother's laugh, louder and lower than my new mother's, as she splashes her swollen red feet in the sea, looks at me over her shoulder.

The cave hadn't been scary then.

'Chase me, slowcoach.'

When we leave I can't help looking back at the mantelpiece, at the photograph, suddenly desperate not to be in Mrs Boone's house that smells of polish in Dunedin but to be back running along the sand barefooted in my old tunic, dodging the water as it sweeps in, hearing my old mother's laugh as I chase her.

Chapter 7
NOW

Declan slept fitfully, dreaming of flames consuming his bed, hearing others screaming for help, scratching hopelessly at the walls either side, the floor, needing to escape the searing heat, the stench of burning wood, fabric, flesh. He woke in the dark, reaching immediately for the glass of water by the bed, shaking a little as he raised it to his lips, imagining ash in his mouth as he gulped it down.

He rested back against the iron frame, his hair sticking to his forehead, trying not to be drawn back there. He closed his eyes and it was Edith's face he conjured. The small smile as she tilted her head: something in her expression. He wondered where she was sleeping, imagined her in a narrow-framed bed like his own. He shifted on the sagging mattress.

Through a thin crack in his curtains he could see the night sky, thin clouds unable to dull the spattering of stars. He thought of Edith's rambling admission notes and the twenty-year-old patient he had encountered, something niggling at him. Multiple personality disorder – was it really true?

Then there was the note attached to the report. What had Edith done to warrant being placed on the list for a leucotomy? An operation that altered the frontal lobe, one that could settle a volatile patient but sacrificed their intellect and personality, sometimes robbed them of their life. Declan lay there remembering the studies: facts and figures, not real people.

He felt a sliver of hope that it wasn't too late: that he might be able to appeal for her case to be looked at more closely. Often patients were observed for a while, watched for their suitability. He still had time. With that tiny comfort he slipped back into sleep.

Overnight the mood of Seacliff had altered. Adjusting the leather satchel on his shoulder he wound his way down the stone steps from his small room in the eaves, catching glimpses of the grounds through the high, narrow windows, the iron-grey sea beyond, careful not to trip on the uneven steps, the stairways always full of shadows. An unseasonable wind moaned outside, but aside from this noise he was aware of a strange silence that hung around the place. Unlike the hysterical jangle in the air yesterday, today it seemed that the whole building was spent: exhausted and unable to maintain the fraught atmosphere.

He walked past nurses and attendants in the narrow corridors, most of whom he didn't recognise, the open doorway of the patients' filthy toilets speeding up his steps. The window of the dayroom showed it was empty of patients: a stained carpet, some squares of rugs, an assortment of different chairs, wooden, cushioned, most needing attention, a nurse arranging beakers and jugs on a flimsy pine table.

He nodded at Matron, a formidable woman almost as tall as Doctor Malone, her height exaggerated by the white hat that stuck out like wings on either side of her head. She gave him a curt nod as she passed. 'Good morning, Doctor.'

He was nearing his office when he saw her, sitting in one of the high-backed dusty pink armchairs at the end of the corridor. Her head was turned away from him and she was staring out of the lead-lined gabled window, alone. One hand on the armrest, clutching it, her curly hair loose. He approached her, pausing for a moment, worried he would startle her.

'Edith,' he said in a quiet voice.

The head twitched to one side.

'Edith,' he repeated, moving to crouch down next to her. 'How are you?'

She turned slowly to him, her eyes dragged away from the window and the gardens beyond. She was clean now, no trace of the soot that had coated her skin the previous day. Her cheeks were flushed, her brown eyes warm. He found himself staring at her features, opening his mouth, forgetting what he had wanted to say.

'Are you quite well?' he stumbled. 'Do you need anything?'

He noticed a mole on her neck, a mark on the smooth skin.

'No, Doctor, thank you.'

Her voice was soft as she answered, her whole demeanour calmer than in their first meeting a few hours after the fire. Declan wondered briefly which pills she might have been given.

'Did you sleep well?'

'I did, thank you, Doctor. I slept in Ward Three, in the main building. I share a room now. Audrey snores a little, but I don't mind.' She added the last bit in a rush, her voice higher.

Declan laughed at this, too quickly perhaps, too loud; she flinched at the noise, her head pressed into the pink velvet. He thought back to the policeman yesterday, the sudden smiles, the jerk of her head, the changeable mood.

She twisted her body towards him. 'I won't say anything about it though, I won't complain.' She seemed uncomfortable in the seat now, her chest rising and falling a little faster. 'I don't want to be any trouble. Matron said . . . I don't want more treatment.' She said the last bit quietly.

He had read in the file that she had undergone electric shock treatment only recently after an incident with another patient in the dormitory. Declan wanted to calm her. 'I'm sure there's no need to worry about that.'

She didn't reply at first, her slender neck simply turning once more to stare back out of the window. 'I often worry about that, Doctor.'

Declan swallowed, a foreign feeling of helplessness. What could he really promise? He thought of the note in her file; was she even aware of her fate?

'At some stage I imagine you might benefit from talking about the recent event,' Declan ventured, leaning forward, distracted suddenly by her scent: citrus and something else. He was still wondering at it when she replied.

'I'm not sure,' she said, with a momentary bite of her bottom lip.

Declan tried to find the right words, wanting to persuade. 'It might be of benefit; you've been through quite an ordeal.'

Was she listening? he wondered, staring up himself at the view beyond: the stretch of lawn, a man pruning the flowerbeds nearby.

'I did talk to Doctor Malone about the possibility of seeing you myself for some sessions in the future,' he admitted, hoping she would look at him, that he might make a connection.

'I think I would like that,' she said, her eyes not leaving the window.

Declan nodded, a small relief. 'Right. Good, that's good. I'll set something up with Doctor Malone.'

Would the older doctor agree? Had he been too hasty to make the promise? He felt an ache in his thighs from crouching so long and went to stand up.

'You won't make me have the treatment, will you?' She asked it in a rush, twisting around, her hand shooting out to grab hold of his arm.

He was startled by the strength of her grip. 'No, I . . . no, Edith.'

'Even if I said things . . . said the wrong things . . .'

Declan frowned at the words, looking at her hand on his arm, her creamy skin, tiny white dots on one nail. 'I . . . no, Edith, no, you couldn't say the wrong thing, there is never a wrong thing.'

The grip loosened slightly but she kept her hand there a fraction, on his arm. Declan paused before gently lifting it and placing it back on her armrest.

'Oh good, that's good,' she said with a small sigh, nestling back in the chair once more.

Declan straightened as a green delivery cart trundled past the window, heading for the driveway to the main gate, the noise on the gravel making them both turn their heads to watch it pass.

'I like it when they tidy up, make everything better,' Edith said, pointing to the man pruning nearby. 'They're lovely, aren't they? The grounds. Bernie and I would walk around them; I love the flowers.'

'It's a beautiful place,' Declan said, knowing this was a half-truth. Seacliff was beautiful; it could be a castle from a fairy tale if you didn't know it was an asylum. But something about its remote location, its removal from the rest of the world, sitting on this exposed cliff, the patients living so far from civilisation, had always given it a Gothic air. 'You have a pleasant morning, Miss Garrett,' Declan said, taking his leave.

'Thank you, Doctor; you also.'

He felt a small glow as he moved away from her, gratified she seemed pleased at the thought of meeting with him. He must persuade Doctor Malone; he had made a commitment to her. Glancing back, he could see her staring once more out of the window, seemingly oblivious to the bustle of the asylum around her, curling a loose tendril of hair around a finger. He found his mind straying back to the details of her face and then he cleared his throat and moved back down the corridor in the direction of his office.

Chapter 8

NOW

From the window in his office Declan could just make out the charred edges of Ward Five. He was back there, reliving that night. A blackened shutter hung at an angle. He had a sudden image of Edith pushing her way out of a window, feeling the relief of the cool night air, taking a gulp of it. He reached for his coat and cast his eye over his diary. He was due to see a patient, a new arrival, in fifteen minutes. He had some time, he thought as he headed for the door, and this was important.

'Come in,' Doctor Malone called imperiously from inside his office.

The room was much larger than Declan's own office but crammed full of filing cabinets, bookshelves, heavy wooden furniture and the man himself. Declan pulled at his collar. A stuffed bird, a breed of hawk perhaps, sat on a top shelf, casting its gaze around the room as if at any moment it might decide to leave its spot, swoop down and capture something soft in its claws. Declan stared at it as Doctor Malone cleared his throat, sitting back in his leather chair, his hands closed together in a steeple as he peered over them.

'Take your time, Doctor Harris, please, it's not like we are under immense pressure to keep this place running, to stop the police scurrying into every nook and cranny, calm the staff, stop the damn rumours and look after the patients.'

Declan started forward, hands up as he appealed to his superior. 'My apologies, of course, thank you for seeing me. It's a small matter, something I mentioned to you yesterday. I was hoping to arrange a time to see Edith, sir, and . . .' He paused, reddening, realising he had forgotten the other patient's name. 'And M . . . M . . . the other survivor.'

Doctor Malone huffed, his moustache bristling, 'Edith and Martha. No, no, Doctor Harris, I don't think that is a good idea. Only this morning I saw Martha, who became extremely distressed after more questions; I had to recommend she be sedated, and Edith Garrett has been volatile in recent weeks. Matron sent me a most disturbing report about her recent violent behaviour . . .'

Declan wondered again at the unassuming girl in the armchair: volatile, violent? He had seen no evidence of that in his dealings with her. It made him all the keener to meet with her. He wondered then whether to admit what he had read in her notes, that she was being considered for the leucotomy.

'I wouldn't want to distress them further, sir, I was just hoping to be of some help, to offer assistance after the ordeal they have lived through . . .'

Doctor Malone's moustache twitched with impatience. 'There's no need. You stick with your own patients, Doctor, leave those two to me.' He went straight back to scribbling at his desk, the upside-down inky scrawl illegible, as if he didn't expect a response at all.

He looked up one more time, Declan just standing there uselessly. 'Yes, Doctor?'

'I . . .'

'What would be worse, Doctor Harris, do you think – if there was some evidence the building was unsafe, or arson?'

'I . . .' Declan repeated, unable to concentrate on the question, reeling from the blunt rejection of his request. He had promised her.

'No matter. Neither outcome is desirable.' Malone was back to scribbling. 'But arson makes more sense, does it not? These patients, unstable at the best of times, and the superintendent is concerned that the enquiry might conclude that the building, the staff are at fault and we can't have that . . .' Malone seemed to be almost mumbling to himself at the end.

Declan pushed a hand through his hair. What was Malone hinting at? Arson was a serious crime; did he imagine a disgruntled member of staff? An accident? A patient?

Doctor Malone looked up at him and sighed. 'I can see you are still loitering, Doctor Harris. I really am incredibly busy, as you must surely be too, and I would kindly remind you we have all experienced a terrible tragedy and need to get on with things, keep up our normal routines. It won't do to be late or upsetting arrangements.'

'No, absolutely, sir, I do understand that, it's just . . .' Declan found the request sticking in his throat. He thought back to Edith sitting in the dusty pink armchair, remembered her voice lifting when he had offered his help.

He opened his mouth and, as if Doctor Malone had known, was instantly cut short. 'If that's all, then best be getting on.'

'Just one session perhaps, to run alongside your own time with h . . .' The words were quiet and tailed away as Doctor Malone dropped his pen, leaving drops of ink on the page.

The older man's voice was ice-cold. 'Doctor Harris, I have expressed my reasoning to you and I don't feel the need to repeat myself. It is a no; my patients will stay under my supervision and you will continue to go about your day, seeing the patients that have been assigned to you. Do I make myself clear?'

Declan took a breath, trying to summon courage from somewhere inside him.

'I would hate to have to report to your father that we've started off on such a dreadful footing,' Doctor Malone added, still not looking up, the words intended to sting.

Declan had always wondered how he had got the job at Seacliff, whether it had been down to him or his father's reputation, his acquaintance with Doctor Malone.

'I . . .'

'Have a productive day, Doctor Harris.'

The sentence was final. Doctor Malone picked up his pen and then, after a moment, took the paper he was writing on and balled it into his fist. 'I'll be starting it again,' he said, an angry glare towards Declan.

'I'm sorry, sir.' The words tumbled out; Declan was already backing towards the door, a hand reaching behind him for the handle.

He felt a momentary swell of relief as he found himself back in the corridor, and then shame stole over him as he retraced the route back to his office. Where was his fight?

Perhaps he was wrong to think he could help, he reasoned; he was only out of medical school a few months. Doctor Malone had years of experience. He tried to push away the doubts in his head, remembering the note in Edith's file, the course that Doctor Malone had set for her, a feeling of unease nudging him. Volatile. Violent.

If only he hadn't seen her that morning; if only he hadn't promised. He cursed ever stopping by that faded armchair.

He was staring at nothing when there was a knock at his door and Nurse Shaw blushed as she stepped into his room. 'Charlotte's waiting outside, Doctor,' she said.

He stared at her, nodding dumbly, not really taking in the words.

'I'll tell her to come in, shall I?' Nurse Shaw asked him, with a small frown.

'Right . . .'

Nurse Shaw took a step forward. 'Is everything satisfactory, Doctor?'

Declan inhaled loudly through his nose, brought himself back to the small square of room, taking in Nurse Shaw, her concern, the smell of antiseptic, the tick of the clock. 'I'm sorry, of course it is. Charlotte. Absolutely. I'll see her now.'

Nurse Shaw nodded. 'Very good, Doctor,' she said, turning to leave. She had a hand on the smudged brass doorknob. 'And I just wanted to thank you, Doctor, for yesterday. I'll return your handkerchief, of course.'

Declan didn't register the words, still lost in thought.

'Doctor.' She hesitated.

'Yes, good.' He didn't mean to sound so curt.

He saw her shoulders fall. 'I'll fetch Charlotte, then.'

Declan reached for the folder on the desk in front of him, opened it on the first page, scanning all the information about the woman he was about to see. He tried to read her notes, familiarise himself with her case, but the photograph secured with a paperclip to the front page blurred. Her face swam before him: her straight hair suddenly curly, her bare neck suddenly sporting a mole just below her ear, her brown eyes deep and warm. He slammed the folder shut as someone stepped inside the room, as Charlotte moved to sit in the seat in front of him. He rolled his shoulders, coughed, forced himself to concentrate; to do his job.

Chapter 9

THEN

The dormitory was practically empty; only Bernie and her, and Deputy Matron sat on a stool at the other end of the room with Joyce, lying still in her bed, back from treatment. Joyce went to the white room a lot; they didn't like her slapping the walls with her fists, but even when they got angry and shouted at her to stop she didn't, so they took her away. Joyce was next on the list. She had heard Deputy Matron tell Nurse Shaw. Deputy Matron nodded at Edith but she looked away quickly, not sure what the nod meant.

Bernie was straightening her sheets; she did that often, so Edith was lying on the floor. Bernie's grey cat Misty was curled up in a box underneath the bed and Edith was lying on her stomach looking at her, staring at the small black mark on her ear.

'Do you think cats have dreams?' she asked.

Bernie continued to smooth and pat the pillow. 'Perhaps.'

Edith twisted her head to look at her. 'What do you think they dream about?'

Bernie paused, the corner of a sheet bunched in her hand. 'Fish and mice and someone tickling their stomach.'

Edith twisted back, cupping her face with a hand. 'I'd like to be a cat,' she announced. Misty looked well fed and content. And Misty could leave rooms whenever she wanted.

Bernie stopped again, smoothing her pillow with one hand. 'I wouldn't.'

'Why not?' Edith sat up.

Bernie blushed a little. 'Cats are always alone.'

Edith didn't answer. That didn't seem a terrible price to pay. Cats were safe, so it was all right to be alone.

'You can sit here now,' Bernie said shyly, as she looked down at Edith on the floor.

Edith scrambled up and dusted herself off before sitting. Bernie stood watching her as she got comfortable, two of her fingers tapping at something imaginary on her leg.

'Come on,' Edith said, holding out two hands. 'You too.'

It was relief on her face as she took them and sat down next to Edith, as if she had needed permission.

'Give me Misty,' Bernie said.

Edith looked at her dumbly, then remembered Misty was the cat's name. For ages, months, they'd called her 'Cat', but then Bernie had shouted that everyone should have a name and it was wrong. So they called her Misty.

Edith scooped her up from beneath the bed, fur tickling her arms as she handed her across. Bernie held her against her chest, rubbed behind her ears. There were loads of cats in the building and they always belonged to someone somewhere. Malcolm told Edith they'd got rid of them all once, but the mice had come back and so now they let them stay. Not that Misty seemed capable of catching a mouse; she spent most of her days nuzzling Bernie, winding herself round her legs, purring on top of the bed.

Edith wondered where Misty had come from, if Misty had anyone who missed her. Or if she was like them.

It was only when she looked up and noticed Deputy Matron wasn't there that she felt a swilling feeling in her tummy. They were alone. Bernie hadn't noticed yet but Edith was already up on her feet again. 'We need to go.'

It was too late. She saw the shadows on the corridor wall through the thick pane of glass in the door. She knew it was them.

They stood in the doorway, silhouetted. Bernie looked up, made a noise. Misty fell from her lap and scampered beneath the bed as if she had picked up the change in her mistress's mood. Edith darted her eyes left to right, hoping Deputy Matron might be back soon. Joyce was still sleeping. You always slept a lot after treatment, so long it was as if you might have dreamt it all.

Bernie started to hum; she did that a lot now around Donna.

Edith sat down, resting a hand on Bernie's leg. 'Stop,' she whispered.

Bernie didn't stop humming but it was quieter, much quieter, like she was trying to keep it only in her head.

Donna stepped into the room; a quick glance around and then a look as if she couldn't believe her luck. Her left eye opened and shut quickly as she moved inside, calling over her shoulder at Shirley and Martha, who followed her.

'I thought I could smell piss and I was right.' She held her nose deliberately and Shirley and Martha copied her, laughing, their voices filling the room. No one came.

Donna paused by Joyce's bed, looked down at her, lifted the edge of her blanket. 'Poor little Joycie,' she said in a babyish voice.

Shirley and Martha clucked next to her. For a moment Edith thought they'd lose interest, choose Joyce instead. Once they'd cornered Joyce in the toilets, made her lean right in, flushed her head, telling her that might clean her out. Now, though, Joyce didn't stir and Donna dropped the blanket. Edith felt her whole body clench.

Donna crossed the room now. Edith could feel her close, could smell her: old cigarette smoke, acrid breath.

'Look at me,' Donna said quietly. 'Come on, pretty girl, look at me.'

Edith was looking at her fingers as she clutched her hands together. Bernie was still humming next to her, impossibly quiet.

'Oi,' Donna whispered.

The word forced Edith to swallow; she couldn't ignore her any more. She licked her lips and slowly looked up. Donna's eye twitched, and Edith noticed one pupil got bigger for a moment. She had the same dark-brown eyes as her hair, with tiny flecks of green in them; yellow teeth. Her short wonky fringe was sticking to her forehead.

Donna's voice changed again, louder now, directed half over her shoulder, a performance. 'Why're you staring?'

Edith wasn't sure what the right answer was. She kept looking at her, not able to blink, to move.

'You like me, don't you?' Donna suddenly grabbed at Edith's right hand, tugged it towards the space between her legs. 'Hey, Martha – she likes me.' She pressed herself against Edith's hand, made moaning noises as Martha laughed, before turning her eyes back on her. 'Ugh, what are you doing, don't touch me.' She pushed Edith's hand away as if she had been the one to reach for her. Laughter: spittle landed on Edith's top lip, but she didn't reach up to wipe it away. Martha made a low whistle, like Edith had heard one of the attendants do when Nurse Shaw walked by. Nurse Shaw had very long legs and a pretty pink mouth. Edith could feel Bernie shifting next to her on the bed.

The other two women stood in the small gap between the beds, blocking the view from the door of the dormitory. Edith looked sideways, saw Shirley's hand reach into her pocket, pull out a hand-kerchief. Shirley was enormous, about twice the size of Martha.

She was always dabbing at the back of her neck, the short curly hair damp when she climbed upstairs or walked from the dayroom to the dormitory. She hadn't always been fat. Edith heard Nurse Hall, who left to get married to a man in the kitchen, tell Nurse Shaw that Shirley had once been thin but then she started to eat everything, even the paper in the dunny. Her skin was tightened out; she didn't have wrinkles like Donna, but Edith thought they were about the same age.

Donna leant down so her face was on the same level. Edith could make out the dots on her nose, the tiny pores in her skin. She was staring so hard she could feel her eyes crossing, Donna's face blurring, her nose and cheeks merging in front of her. Edith was holding her breath, trying not to notice the stale, wet warmth on her face as Donna deliberately inhaled, exhaled, enjoying the closeness. She snapped her teeth together suddenly and laughed as Edith flinched.

Bernie's humming grew louder but Donna didn't seem to be interested in her.

'What shall we make them do?' she said, her voice playful, her eyes not leaving Edith's face. 'Martha, ideas?'

Martha twitched behind them. Edith imagined her pushing her limp blonde hair behind her ear. 'Ooh.' She drew out the noise. 'I can't decide.'

Donna rolled her eyes, stood up abruptly. 'Some help.' She turned. 'Shirley?'

Shirley cleared her throat. An interminable wait; Edith could feel the tension stretching. Perhaps Donna would direct her anger at them? You never knew how it would go. Martha hadn't always followed Donna around, not in the beginning.

Then Shirley spoke. 'Give us their pudding at lunch.'

Donna's left eye twitched again. 'Trust you to ask for fucking food. Anyway it's hours off lunch. I mean now, something now.'

She was getting impatient and that never ended well. Patricia had made her angry, impatient like that: not listening to her, calling her Fred and shouting at her.

'Fine, I'll come up with something on my ow—'

'Kiss.'

The word came from Martha.

'You what?' Donna blew at her fringe so the dark hair lifted.

'They should kiss.' Martha's voice was as thin as she was, the only substantial thing about her a prominent nose covered in freckles. 'Kiss,' she repeated, puckering her own lips and blowing a kiss at Edith.

Donna's eye flickered. 'Kiss,' she repeated.

Edith felt her heart pound in her chest. Bernie was staring ahead, absolutely still, as though if she stayed like that she could wish herself away from that bed, that room. Her mouth clamped tight, the humming stopped.

'Hear that, princess,' Donna said. 'Martha wants to see you two kissing.' She wrapped her arms around herself as she said it, puckering her lips and moving her body. Then she was laughing, bright, loud, leaning down. 'Come on then, show us how it's done.'

Martha whistled again, long and low.

Edith's mind had sped up and she wondered what she could do to make it all go away. She felt all three of them encircling Bernie and her. Donna was down at her level again, her eyes shut, her mouth open, her tongue going back and forward. Smack, smack. Edith could feel them all too close, Bernie frozen, Joyce still asleep; no one else coming.

Edith reached out a hand and tapped Bernie on the leg, knowing they just needed to get it over with, that they just needed to do it quickly so all of it would stop.

Bernie didn't move; she had started humming again out loud, as if she couldn't hear anything but the music in her own head.

'Come on,' Edith said, her voice urgent.

'Oh, she's keen,' Donna was calling in a loud voice, as if there were twenty other people watching in the room.

'She wants it,' Martha added quickly, a high laugh.

'Bernie.' Edith tapped again.

Donna shifted her weight from one foot to another. Edith knew this was taking too long already. She didn't want her to lose her temper. She didn't want it to be like when it was Patricia.

'Bernie, please.' Her voice was pleading, and she jumped as Misty streaked out from beneath the bed.

Bernie darted her eyes towards her, humming, still humming.

'What is she playing? Fucking background music? Shut up,' Donna shouted at her.

The words were sudden, so loud in the space that for a moment Bernie was completely silent. Then the humming was louder, more insistent and Edith knew she wouldn't be able to stop now, had seen her like this before and knew she was somewhere else.

'Bernie.' Edith tapped her leg again; she had to try. She could feel Donna's breathing thicken.

It was hopeless. *Dum, dum, dum, dum, dum.* The beats were filling the air around them and Edith knew this wasn't going how Donna wanted.

'Shut up, shut up, sh—' Her voice was getting higher and louder and Edith could feel her own pulse in her head. Reaching across to Bernie quickly she grabbed her face in two hands, leaned forward and kissed her. Lips dry as the kiss clashed, Bernie's face unmoving beneath Edith's palms, just pressed together. *Dum, dum, dum, dum, dum.* Edith kept her mouth on hers for a long time. Hoping this would do.

'Your tongue.' Donna said it quietly, right next to her ear, and Edith closed her eyes and felt her tongue push against Bernie's closed mouth, skin, lips, wet.

51

'Tongues,' Martha repeated delightedly; another whistle.

Bernie started rocking, head shaking, still humming, and Edith let go of her face, felt warmth creep up and through her.

'I did it,' Edith said. 'I did it.'

They didn't laugh or jeer; Shirley looked at Donna to see what would happen next.

'I did what you wanted,' Edith explained, not understanding why they weren't laughing, why it wasn't over. She could feel Shirley and Martha behind her holding their breath and she didn't dare look, didn't dare stop looking at Donna.

Then there was a call from behind them all, footsteps, and Deputy Matron was back in the doorway, holding a glass of water, her voice sharp. 'Ladies?'

Martha and Shirley shuffled along, into the central aisle between the rows of beds: shuffle, shuffle, yes Deputy Matron, no Deputy Matron.

'Haven't you got jobs to be getting on with?'

'Yes, Deputy Matron,' called Donna, her face twisting into a smile that couldn't reach her eyes. Her left eye twitched as she stared down at Edith.

'Well, then . . .'

Donna stayed where she was.

'Do I have to call Matron?'

That got Donna moving. No one wanted Matron in here.

'No, I was just getting a cardigan, Deputy Matron.' Said in a voice dipped in sugar.

She stepped back and Edith felt all her breath leave her in that moment. Bernie was still beside her, humming more quietly now, softer.

Deputy Matron carried the water across to Joyce's bed.

Donna looked down at her with a sneer, a glance at Bernie who was still rocking, still humming. 'Fucking nutcase.' And then she brought her lips together in a kiss. 'You fucking loved it. And soon, princess . . .' She leaned right down to Edith's ear, her breath onions and ash. 'Soon we can kiss in your room.'

A flash of silver in the pocket of her housedress. Her eye flicking: open, shut.

Edith felt her stomach lurch, stood up quickly, squeezed past them, bile in her throat. Left Bernie alone on the bed. Bernie still humming whatever was in her head.

Chapter 10

NOW

Declan was standing, hat held in his hands, head bowed. All around him doctors, nurses, attendants, kitchen staff, gardeners and patients were silent. A sea fog lay heavy on the water in the distance, the light mist a sheen on his face. The chaplain's voice, soft and melodic, ebbed and flowed amongst the crowd, some words snatched away on a breeze. A prayer to one of the women, now spinning up and away above them.

There had been clamouring for an occasion to mark the event, a memorial to those who died in the fire, and they had congregated that morning in front of the main building – the gable roof and the top of the enormous clock tower lost in the mist, the charred view of Ward Five hidden around the corner, out of sight. He'd had to walk past it to get here and a strong breeze still threw up flakes of ash, like fallen leaves: an intermittent reminder.

There were no burials today, but they stood in a semicircle around a single wreath. The fire devoured so much that night that there were still remains to be identified; not everyone would be found. Some families wanted their relatives to be brought back home, what remained of them. Others hadn't come forward and those women would be buried, Declan didn't even know where, once the investigation was complete. Declan wondered if some had died without a soul realising they had gone.

He looked across the way, at Nurse Shaw, tears flowing freely down her cheeks as she muttered an 'Amen'; at Matron, a far-off look in her eye, her stiff, high-necked black dress so unlike her usual attire. Amongst the rows of patients deemed safe to attend, he saw Martha, even more gaunt, staring into the distance, out over the sea as if she couldn't hear the words. Her hair fell down around her shoulders, lifeless and unwashed. He couldn't read her expression but for a moment it seemed she was simply bored.

He scanned the row: faces he didn't recognise, some he did. Charlotte, the new patient who hadn't been here that night, whose family had committed her due to melancholic episodes. She had her eyes closed, fervently muttering the responses. Then next to her he noticed curly hair, arms wrapped around her body, the buttons of her coat done up wrong. With a jolt he realised Edith was looking straight across at him, unblinking, her face caught in a mask of misery. Then, as he met her gaze, a tiny lift at the side of her mouth, an acknowledgement, before she bowed her head like the rest. He found himself doing the same, feeling a heat creep up his neck.

He looked sideways at Doctor Malone who was surreptitiously checking a pocket watch, stuffing it back into his pocket as the chaplain called for a hymn.

Mouths wide, their voices were disjointed and out of tune but the swell of sound made his heart lift a fraction. He sang, trying to raise his own voice, trying to give them all hope.

The chaplain ended with a list of names read out in a slow and careful voice. Declan listened to each one, so many, whispering a goodbye in his head at the name Bernadette. He felt his head swivel back to Edith, an ache as he watched her mouth words, her eyes squeezed shut.

He was distracted then by another name. He had seen Shirley Rowe only a few weeks before, a sad woman who had a compulsion to eat, she explained, to fill the hole inside her. He had seen Doctor Malone about an earlier diagnosis, 'hysteria', which didn't seem adequate.

'She got herself in trouble,' Doctor Malone had explained, 'and there was going to be a baby.'

'Going to be?' Declan ventured, knowing in part what was to come.

'Parents were respectable and couldn't be having that scandal. She had an operation – not here, I might add – but it affected her' – he tapped the side of his head – 'up here.'

'I can only imagine. That sort of operation would be terribly traumatic.'

'Well yes, yes, I'm sure,' Doctor Malone had said, clearly wanting to wrap up their impromptu conversation. 'But that was just the start of things. She began to eat.'

'I see.' Declan thought back to the woman in his consulting room, stooped and sluggish, slowly lowering herself into the chair, wincing as she moved, her calves covered in bandages.

'Not just food, you understand,' Doctor Malone said. 'Everything. Her parents told us she'd been slim, but when we saw her, well, she was enormous, eating paper, clothing. She tried to eat her bedding once; Deputy Matron had to stop her eating the straw from the mattress. An extraordinary woman; quite, quite mad. She became incredibly aggressive when we were forced to restrain her.'

Now as he stood there, listening to her name read out loud, he felt a desperate sadness for a life that had been blighted by tragedy. He would never be able to help her now. He closed his eyes, concerned he was going to be overwhelmed by the emotion, feeling the tears building in the back of his throat. He was relieved when a silence greeted the end of the list.

Seeing Edith at the memorial stirred Declan into action. He returned to his office, removing the piece of paper, the notes he'd made on seeing her file, from his desk drawer. Her most recent round of EST had been administered only a couple of nights before the fire. He searched the words for something he could use to appeal to Doctor Malone.

Declan thought then of the small note clipped to the file, a reminder he was running out of time to help. How long would they observe her before scheduling the leucotomy? With the investigation meaning Doctor Malone was often tied up with the superintendent, it seemed some things had been put on hold; what time did she have?

He must find a way to help. His eyes lit upon the new course of drugs, the amount she was now given. Thinking back to the lectures at his university, he frowned. Pushing the paper to one side he stood, took a breath and moved out of his office, his shoes click-clacking with purpose down the corridor towards Doctor Malone's. This was it. He had read the recent studies, he was coming to things with fresh eyes. He needed to make himself heard.

It was empty, but Declan didn't want to give up now. He headed towards the treatment rooms. The moment he pulled on the door he heard the cries. He had read the studies. Electric shock therapy had its place: inducing a seizure could temporarily calm a violent patient, and regular sessions helped those with severe depression over a course of months. Still, he flinched as a shout wrenched the air; then he saw Doctor Malone heading towards him, a frown on his face, throwing instructions over a shoulder to a nurse trotting to catch up.

The senior doctor stopped in front of him, gave an impatient click of his tongue as he waited for Declan to speak. 'What is it,

Doctor Harris?' he asked, as Declan mouthed soundlessly in front of him.

'I was looking for you,' Declan said after a beat, his earlier bravado leaking away.

'In here, in here.' The doctor ushered him in with an impatient flick of his hand.

'Oh, I . . .' Declan lingered for a moment in the open doorway to the small room beyond. Someone was in there; he could see two bare feet sticking up towards the ceiling.

'Come on, man, I can't stand around all day.'

'Of course, sir.' Declan lurched forward.

The smell of bleach couldn't disguise the powerful stench of urine as he stepped inside. The man was quivering on the table. His wrists were strapped down with thick leather cuffs, a bruise on his right side, pale skin looking starker against the white sheet beneath him. He craned his neck up as they entered the room, eyes rolling, sweat beading on his hairline. Something inside Declan turned over, the academic studies suddenly in the room with him, all the talk of curing now in action, lying in front of him, shaking and whimpering.

'Doctor Harris, why don't you assist me. Nurse Ritchie, we'll take it from here,' Doctor Malone told her as he took the towel she was holding and passed it to Declan.

'I can't stay long,' he said, forced to take the towel from Nurse Ritchie as she left. 'I just wanted to ask . . .'

Doctor Malone wasn't listening. Declan couldn't drag his eyes from the table, watching as Doctor Malone wiped something on the two electrodes attached to a large grey machine set up beside the bed.

'Now, Howard, there's no need to pack a sad every time. You know the drill,' Doctor Malone said, reaching across and placing an electrode on the right side, the pad sticking to the skin on the man's temple. Declan watched as Doctor Malone did the same on the left. Declan knew he would be expected to administer one of these treatments himself, but he had yet to be convinced any of his patients would benefit from it.

'Come on, Doctor Harris, make yourself useful.'

Declan wasn't absolutely sure what he should be doing. The pads were in place and all there was to do was set the amount of electricity to be passed between them. Doctor Malone sighed, reaching over to place a wad of cloth in the man's mouth. Declan felt he had failed some test, meeting the patient's eyes at the same moment Doctor Malone told him to stand back. Declan jerked as the sound from the machine shocked the air, a smell of burnt hair replacing everything else, the man on the trolley arching his back, wrists still pinned, eyes now closed.

'Could be the last one he'll need for a while: stops the fits,' Doctor Malone said, writing something on a notepad as he spoke. 'But the effects don't always linger . . .' He stopped writing and looked over at the patient. 'Shame.'

Declan nodded, trying to concentrate on what Doctor Malone was saying and also trying to remember his reasons for being in that square of room.

Drugs. Edith. The amounts she had been given in recent weeks. A chance to study her care with fresh eyes.

For a moment he pictured Edith lying in place of the patient in front of him.

'I wanted to discuss Edith Garrett.' Declan spoke quickly, hoping the doctor would be too distracted to recall their earlier conversations.

The sharp look he received in return didn't bolster Declan's confidence.

'Doctor Harris, we have discussed your desire to see this patient and, as I think I have already been very clear with you on this matter, I—'

'The drugs . . .' Declan intervened, surprising both of them with his interjection. The doctor was left, mouth flapping, as Declan continued. 'I was hoping to look again at the amounts? And in recent weeks I see she underwent electric shock treatment. I was wondering if perhaps it might be worth looking at a new approach if it did not have an effect?'

'I have looked at a new approach,' Doctor Malone said, his eyes narrowed.

Declan swallowed as he realised the meaning behind the words: the list.

'A softer approach, perhaps. I wanted, with your permission of course . . .'

Doctor Malone grew redder and redder as Declan continued.

'. . . the amount of drugs might be stinting the patient's ability to feel, to process . . .'

Doctor Malone's moustache quivered.

'. . . I have had some success through talking therapies. I know some still wish to pursue a more aggressive approach, but . . .'

A palm went up, fingers splayed, Doctor Malone a deep red. Declan spluttered to a close as he studied the man opposite him. Doctor Malone was practically whispering over the jerking body of the patient between them, Declan straining to listen. 'I do not take kindly to subordinates wilfully going against the things I have expressly forbidden them to do, Doctor Harris.'

He emphasised the word 'doctor', and Declan found himself fading in front of him.

'If you value your position at this hospital, you will do well to be reminded that I am in charge here.'

Declan slumped.

There would clearly be no new dosage, no chance to change Edith's course of treatment. Declan was banned from the very topic in future. He thought of that slight woman standing in the crowd

60

of mourners and with one last gasp pushed on, 'Doctor Malone, please understand I am not trying to go against your wishes, I just wanted to raise a few concerns . . .'

Doctor Malone allowed him to speak, and as the seconds passed Declan could hear strength returning to his voice. It was as if he was a different somebody, feeling his shoulders loosen, his hand movements more exaggerated as he laid down the points he wanted to make. For the first time in his life he felt that he could be the doctor others saw; he wasn't the student or the scared teenager any more. He had qualifications, expertise. He finished his appeal with a flourish. 'I know you have been working with this patient for a number of years and I would love to see if my fresh perspective could now add something. I understand we have very little time if she is to have the operation.'

Doctor Malone waited, hands dropped to his sides, the patient still now, unconscious between them, his head lolling, the wad of cloth half in and half out of his mouth.

'You've really got the bull by the horns, Harris,' Doctor Malone began.

Was that a small smile of respect Declan detected in his older colleague? 'I have, sir.' Declan nodded, his own mouth lifting. 'I am a bit of an evangelical when it comes to psychoanalysis.'

'Psychoanalysis,' Doctor Malone repeated.

'That's right, sir. I had an excellent professor at the university, Professor Bates. I'm sure you would know of his work in that field; he was very convincing.'

'Was he now?'

'Yes, and I saw from Edith's notes that she . . .'

'Her notes,' Doctor Malone said, eyebrows lifting. 'You have been busy.'

Declan nodded once, waiting for the doctor to continue. In that moment he looked down to see the patient leaking urine.

Doctor Malone seemed to see it at the same moment, the small yellow pool forming on the white sheet. 'You didn't insert the catheter,' he commented.

'I . . .' Declan didn't want to break this moment, desperately hoping Doctor Malone was about to agree. He held his breath, watching the senior doctor snap off gloves, throw them in a bin in the corner.

The older man pointed to the puddle. 'You'll be wanting to clear that up.'

And with those words he stalked past Declan, the door slamming shut behind him.

Chapter 11
BEFORE

The doctor has come to see Mother. I'm playing with the cat downstairs, running a cotton reel along the floor and watching her follow it with her eyes, snatch at it with a paw. She has soft, grey fur and when she lies near me her whole body quivers. I like it when she lies next to me: it makes me not think about Mother so much. I don't want her to die like I did.

I remember then his silhouette, black against the bright blue of the sea: so black I can't see his face or his combed-down black hair that he wore in the style all the boys wore then. He had walked slowly towards me, forcing me back, forcing me to scrabble back on to the flat, wet stone, the sand immediately sticking to my fingers.

The doctor is ages and when he leaves I run through to Mrs Clark and she tells me I can go and see Mother now. I run up the stairs and Mother is sitting up on the bed with the four posts and pillows all around her. She pats the bed and I take off my shoes to climb up and sit next to her. I like being in her bedroom with the roses in a vase that make her smell nice, the long peach curtains that go right up to the ceiling and the glass bottles all lined up on the dresser. It smells sweet: flowers and sunshine. Mother doesn't look like she is about to die.

'Are you going to die?' I ask quickly.

'Edith.' Mother's eyes open so I can see all the whites around the blue bit. Then she rests her hand over mine. 'I'm going to have a baby,' she says. She takes her hand away and puts it on her stomach.

I feel all my air whoosh out that she won't die, so I'm not thinking when I ask, 'Will it be a sister like I had last time?' I feel my body grow warm and excited. I think of a laugh: chubby legs, a tiny hand in mine. I'd loved my sister.

Mother doesn't reply straight away but her hand turns all white as she makes a fist on the duvet. 'Not again, Edith.' Her voice is low.

I don't know what she means, 'again'; she has only just told me about the baby.

'Will it be a little baby girl?' I don't want her to be cross, but my head is all muddled.

'You mean like you?'

'Yes, and Mary, my sister.'

'You don't have a sister,' Mother says, looking away from me and out of the window.

'I know, but I did before.'

'Don't, Edith.'

'I always tried to keep her safe, away from him, so he wouldn't hurt her instead . . .'

'Edith.' Mother's voice is different: short, sharp. 'Don't.'

I stay next to her on the bed, biting my lip to stop more words falling out. I can see Mother isn't happy; she won't look at me and she starts pleating the sheet in her fingers.

The door opens and Father walks in, and Mother sits up straight and drops the sheet and says in a too-loud voice, 'I was just telling Edith about the baby. And Mrs Clark is making a lamb casserole for dinner,' she adds.

Father looks confused, as she told him about the lamb casserole earlier, at breakfast.

Mother tells me to get down off the bed now, shooing me with one hand. I leave the bedroom in my stockings, past Father, lots of thoughts in my head now, more questions. I don't want to ask them though, I don't want Mother to be angry with me; I know I need to keep them inside.

Chapter 12

NOW

The days passed, and it was as if she was now everywhere when before he hadn't seen her face. Declan saw her first thing that morning, waiting on a chair outside Doctor Malone's office, her face lighting as he approached, falling as he moved past her quickly, heading towards his office. He paused, back to his own door. What kind of man was he? He shut his eyes, banged his head lightly against the wood before collecting himself, moving across to his desk and fetching the file for his next patient.

All that morning Declan kept returning to the sight of Edith waiting to see Doctor Malone, her curled hair tied back, her face pinched, fingers worrying at her skirt.

Another patient left and a knock came; Declan was far away once more before calling, 'Come in.'

Nurse Shaw appeared, a small cup and saucer rattling lightly as she moved.

'I noticed you hadn't stopped, Doctor,' she said, lowering the tray on to the desk.

'Hmm?'

'Coffee,' Nurse Shaw said quickly as she motioned to the small tray in front of him.

'Oh,' Declan said, removing the pen he'd been chewing. 'Thank you, that's kind.'

She stood in front of his desk as if waiting for something, so Declan reached out and took a sip from the cup, the coffee tepid and weak. She smiled at him and he managed one in return.

'Well, busy as ever,' he said, needlessly picking up some notes from his desk.

'Of course,' she said, stepping backwards. 'I didn't mean to interrupt.'

She had almost reached the door when Declan had a thought. 'Nurse,' he called.

She spun round to face him, two pink spots high on her cheeks.

'You might be able to help me understand something.' Declan cleared his throat, tapping his pencil on the desk. 'You seem rather fond of Edith Garrett . . .' he began, his words slow, carefully selected.

'Oh, I am,' Nurse Shaw said. Then her eyes rounded. 'That is, I know I shouldn't get too close to the patients but sometimes you can't help it when, well, sometimes some of them seem almost . . .' She tailed away.

'Oh, let me be clear, Nurse, I am certainly not criticising,' Declan said, leaning over his desk. 'In fact it sounds as if it is highly beneficial for the patients to form such positive relationships with the people who care for them.'

The pink spots deepened as Nurse Shaw bit her lip.

'I was curious to hear your opinion, Nurse. Would you describe her as a volatile patient? Violent?' Declan asked, unable to forget the recent terms.

A line appeared in the centre of Nurse Shaw's eyebrows. 'Edie?'

67

'Edith, yes,' Declan confirmed, lifting his chin, momentarily concerned she might think it strange he was enquiring again after a patient who was not his. 'She had treatment after attacking a fellow patient. Somebody called Donna Iver?'

Nurse Shaw fell silent, her eyes slipping from Declan's face.

'Nurse?' Declan could feel the hint of a secret, something the nurse was battling to disguise.

'Yes, she did.' It was Nurse Shaw's turn to tread carefully as she spoke; Declan wondered why. 'Edith hadn't had any electric shock treatment since she was a child. She was very distressed to be sent for it, but I wasn't sure . . .'

'Sure of the treatment?' Declan clarified.

Nurse Shaw's head snapped up. 'No, Doctor, no, I would never go against the doctor's recommendations. No, I wasn't sure if Edie deserved it. I wondered whether Donna hadn't . . .' Nurse Shaw fiddled with the collar of her uniform. 'I'm not sure it's my place, Doctor. I don't want Matron to feel that I am questioning her decisions.'

'Nurse Shaw,' Declan said, his voice softer, 'anything you say to me in this room is just between us, I promise you that.'

Nurse Shaw swallowed and nodded. 'Well, Doctor, Edie was having some trouble with her, you see; with Donna. Donna went everywhere with Shirley and Martha and . . .'

Declan felt a lurch of surprise, confused that there was more than the fire that connected the two women. 'Martha?'

Nurse Shaw nodded. 'Martha was very tight with Donna. The three of them were a pack of sorts, I suppose.'

'You make them sound like animals,' Declan said, with a hollow laugh.

She didn't reply for a moment and Declan wondered what the women had done.

68

He had to strain to hear her voice when she next spoke. 'I wasn't sure if Edie started it, if she wasn't set upon. But the other patients all repeated the same story, that she attacked Donna, so there was very little I could say . . .' Her voice moved up a register. 'Sometimes I know I should say something . . .' She started to tug at her collar again. 'But when I do it doesn't always help.'

'It isn't always that straightforward,' Declan said, his own voice soft, thinking then of all the things he had wanted to say to people in his own life. 'Well, Nurse.' He cleared his throat. 'Thank you, that's been very useful.'

'I'm not used to being asked for my opinion. It's very flattering.'

'We are all here to help the patients, are we not?'

'We are.' Nurse Shaw beamed at him, her shoulders dropping.

'And thank you for the coffee,' Declan said, wanting a moment alone to think about what she'd told him.

'My pleasure, Doctor,' she said, the smile widening. She waited another second and when it was clear there was nothing more to discuss, she turned around. 'You'll be wanting to get on, Doctor.'

The door clicked shut and Declan flopped back in his chair. The coffee grew colder, a thin white film forming on the surface as he ran through much of the exchange, the pencil back in his mouth, a habit from his schooldays. Were his instincts correct? Nurse Shaw seemed a sensible sort of woman; she didn't recognise the traits he had mentioned, either. A knock on the door; Declan removed the pencil and sat straighter in his chair as another patient appeared.

◆ ◆ ◆

The day darkened and the gardens outside looked a ghostly blue as he left his office for the evening, the stone buildings in every direction lost in shadows. Stopping to lock and unlock the doors, the keys jangling on their ring, echoing in the stone corridors, he proceeded all the way up to his small, single room with the sloped ceiling and the bare floorboards. Sliding the case from under his bed he headed back out, glad to be busy that evening.

Then, as if he'd conjured her again, he saw her, moving along the corridor ahead of him, headed into the music room too. Declan hurried in behind her, his trumpet case banging painfully against his leg.

The music room gradually filled, people sitting in chairs in a semicircle in front of an empty wooden stage, faded velvet curtains lost in the wings, dust collecting in the corners. The sound of voices grew louder, cases being opened, music stands being righted. One of his patients, Cecil, middle-aged, a rounded stomach, gave him a small, shy wave. Declan was used to seeing him in his office, soothing him as he wept over a second daughter who had drowned, a wife who had refused to discuss it, his attempt to end his own life. Now he was carrying a thin music case, a small smile on his face as he weaved his way to the back row of chairs. This was when Declan was reminded that Seacliff could be a place of genuine rehabilitation; in this room, recovery seemed possible.

He had never noticed that she was a member of the orchestra, too and now he wondered how he had ever missed her. He sidestepped to his usual seat, eyes not moving from her. She held a flute in her hands, resting her chin on the tip of the instrument as others tuned up around her, seemingly oblivious to the intermittent screeches and squeals of violins, cellos, woodwind. His trumpet lay in his lap as he watched her: the expression on her face.

Her eyes weren't really focused on the room, but somewhere else. Declan considered getting up, moving across the room to talk to her; she seemed to be alone, her small frame curled into the chair as if she might disappear in it, the buoyant, brunette head of curls the only thing that prevented it. He thought then of the nurse's words earlier, wondered what had happened between her and the three other patients. He found he couldn't look away, watching as she fiddled with her earlobe, waiting for the conductor to arrive. She studied the sheet music on the stand in front of her, readjusted her flute, head cocked to one side as if she was already listening to the music in her head.

A cough, and the conductor was up in front of them, baton raised: a small, thin man with a shock of black hair, the air of the dramatic as if he were conducting the national orchestra and not the rag-tag jumble of Seacliff residents. They were rehearsing for the annual Seacliff show: patients, staff and relatives invited to this therapeutic evening of entertainment. Declan lifted the trumpet, the mouthpiece, pistons, feeling foreign, as if he were a boy again, learning for the first time.

She was absorbed, eyes half-closed as she blew into the flute. Declan watched her face, travelling down to see her foot move up, down, up, down, her ankle slim. He missed his cue. The notes danced and jumbled in front of him, the correct order just out of reach, nothing making sense that evening.

He finished the last bars and lowered his trumpet, went to close the sheet music. His eyes were drawn back to the same spot. She looked up, catching his gaze, her face glowing from the bracketed light behind her; his trumpet slipped in his grip. He nodded at her, rolled his eyes as someone pushed past him. Her smile grew wider. For that moment it was as if they were in a different place completely, another world: a bar at university or a library or a hundred other places young people meet. Declan felt his cheeks grow hot with the thought, his hands dampening. He reminded himself who she was and his position in the institution. They were worlds apart, but for that moment, in that look, it felt that they were exactly the same.

He found himself sliding along the row towards her, embarrassed as he stumbled over the leg of a music stand, feeling clumsy as she giggled at him in the seat next door.

'Hello, Doctor.'

'Edith, I didn't know you played?'

'Oh, yes,' she said, the flute in her lap now, the lights overhead reflecting on its surface. 'They taught me here. Malcolm bought me this flute, he is such a kind man.'

Declan wasn't sure who Malcolm was but felt an embarrassed swell of emotion when she spoke about him.

'Music takes me away from here,' Edith said, twisting her body towards him. He swallowed, smelling an exotic fruit, feeling an urge to lean further forward, inhale. 'It is all I have.'

She said the last sentence quietly, her eyes drawn down. Declan felt a renewed sense of failure that he hadn't been able to persuade Doctor Malone to let him see her. He could just make out the telltale patch on her temple, hairs burnt to a stub by the recent treatment. Did she know what was going to happen to her? The procedure he seemed powerless to stop?

'I am sorry, Edith, I have been speaking to Doctor Malone but I haven't been able to persuade him as yet . . .'

'I'm sure you've tried, Doctor,' Edith said, her gaze direct now, making him shift on the flimsy chair. Someone dropped a drumstick nearby and Declan started. 'No one can help me,' she said in a small, sad voice. 'I thought, perhaps, after the fire . . .'

'It was a terrible thing, to lose your friends in that way,' Declan said, his voice low, wanting to draw her into a private circle, then aware of the conductor loitering near the door, an enquiring tilt. Declan drew back, cleared his throat. 'I hope you can talk about it with Doctor Malone, or one of the nurses, perhaps . . .'

Edith was nodding slowly, her eyes dimming. Could she feel him pulling away? He got up, looking down at her for a last time.

'And we can talk again, of course,' he added. 'Here. Members of the orchestra,' he said, a strange laugh leaving his mouth.

She looked up at him, a small light back in her eyes. 'I would like that a great deal, Doctor. A great deal.'

Chapter 13

NOW

'Doctor Malone has asked for you.' Nurse Shaw pushed her head around the door, her voice soft in the room. 'I said I'd come and tell you.'

Declan was at his desk, a file in front of him, his pen poised, midway through his notes. 'Asked for me?'

Doctor Malone hadn't consulted with him before. Declan felt a tiny buzz. Was he requesting a second opinion?

Declan sat up in his chair and nodded once. 'Thank you, Nurse Shaw.'

'My pleasure, Doctor,' she said, coming into the room with light steps. 'It was an excuse to return this,' she added, dangling a freshly laundered handkerchief across his desk.

Declan was bemused for a moment before she reminded him, 'It's yours, Doctor – you were kind enough to lend it to me.'

'Of course,' he said, standing, wishing he had a mirror in the room, flattening his hair with the palm of his hand and dragging a tongue across his teeth. He moved his head from side to side, stretching the muscles in his neck before making for the door. 'Thank you.'

He left the room, Nurse Shaw still standing at his desk. His stride was purposeful, brimming with confidence and then, as he rounded the corridor, a less pleasant thought hit him and he stopped dead in his tracks, Doctor Malone's door up ahead. He recalled a time in his schooldays, a summoning to the headmaster's office, and the same sinking feeling washed over him. Perhaps this wasn't a consult after all; perhaps Declan had done something wrong.

At school Declan hadn't got into trouble, would sit reading his book on the low, stone wall of the playground, knowing he didn't quite fit. The other children would race around him as he stared at the words on the page, not wanting to look up; looking up invited danger. Two boys had been prodding something nearby, and Declan peeked over the pages of his book. It was a bellbird, lying on its side, trembling, one wing flapping frantically as it tried to escape.

Then, without warning, they'd stood up; one of the boys had swung a foot back and forward, a flash of black leather, and the bellbird flipped over. Sniggering as Declan yelped, moving to crouch over the broken body, the wing now twisted away at an angle, the dull, tiny eye still open, no more trembling. Before he had been able to do much else someone was hauling Declan away by his ear, the other two boys melting back into the schoolyard.

He received a lashing and carried a reputation with him for the rest of that school year. The teacher hadn't seen exactly what happened but Declan never said a word about the other two boys, reasoning life might be easier that way.

He still had a thin white scar where the cane had left a welt on his skin; another longer one on his buttock after his father had heard and punished him too. As he knocked on Doctor Malone's door and waited for the reply to go in, he thought back to that day in the headmaster's office, his palms up, the agonising sting as the wood met flesh, and felt the same dread creep up on him.

Don't be absurd, he chided himself. Years had passed and he wasn't that boy any more. Was he?

'Come in.' The voice was muted by the heavy wood.

Declan squared his shoulders and twisted the handle.

He'd been expecting Doctor Malone to be sitting at his desk but the office chair was pushed back, the worn leather seat empty. Doctor Malone was standing, resting against the top of the desk, arms folded, stethoscope around his neck and a patient sitting in a chair beside him. Declan didn't need to see her face, recognising the back of her head, the thick curls, in an instant.

'Edi—' He went to say her name, then stopped.

She glanced round, looking like the deer in the lens before the hunter takes his shot.

Doctor Malone was still resting back on his desk watching Declan, an expression on his face that the younger doctor didn't recognise.

'Thank you, Doctor Harris, I wanted you here.'

'Nurse Shaw told me you asked for me,' Declan said, clearing his throat partway through the sentence, mind still racing with possibilities as to why he'd been summoned. Was this it? Was Doctor Malone going to transfer the care of Edith to him? Had he been asked in for a formal introduction to her case? He felt himself swell with hope. He thought of her file, at the number of questions he had, where his therapy might begin. He thought of her sitting in the orchestra, just another person, playing the same tune; something clear and uncomplicated about her.

'I just wanted help with administering the dose. I'm having dreadful trouble with my grip . . .'

Declan slowed the words in his mind as Doctor Malone held up a hand, a sticking plaster on one finger.

'Papercut. Doesn't look dreadful but it's amazing how much it stings. I feel thoroughly debilitated by it.' A bark of laughter.

'Sorry, I don't understand . . .'

'I thought a man like yourself could help with the correct dose and application. I've got it all here, prepared.' Doctor Malone waved a hand towards a tray on a trolley to the side, and Declan followed his gaze. 'Nurse Shaw just brought it in. So if you could . . .'

He'd been brought here to administer the very drug he had queried. Was this a test? How was Declan expected to react?

He looked again at Doctor Malone's face. His voice had sounded soft, jovial, but his eyes were watchful.

'I . . . insulin would . . . I . . .'

'Come on, Doctor Harris, we don't want Miss Garrett to be left waiting around for you to finally wake up, do we?'

Declan was transported back to the orchestra practice: the sad statements she had made, the lucid way she had spoken to him.

'I was hoping, perhaps . . .' He should say something, remind the older doctor about his concerns.

'It's a simple task.' Doctor Malone cut him off, steel in his voice now. Declan was clear why he had been brought here. This was a test, a test to see that Declan would do his bidding.

Declan fell silent, pressing his lips together as if that might stem any other words. What could he do? Malone was his superior; he couldn't defy him without risking his job, his first job. And yet.

They stood staring at each other in the silence, just the tick of the carriage clock on the mantelpiece. Edith hadn't moved or made a sound but as Declan acquiesced, he thought he heard the tiniest murmur; a whimper.

He moved across to the trolley as Doctor Malone watched, picking up the needle from the square of cream cloth it was resting on and filling the syringe with the right amount.

'Need to prepare Edith for the new treatment. Finally a cure, Edith, after all this time.'

Declan swallowed, almost returning the syringe. He shouldn't do it; it was wrong.

Then he stepped across to the chair Edith was sitting on and sank down, knees bent, so he was at her eye level.

She didn't look at him but allowed him to take her hand. It was cold as he turned the palm towards the ceiling. He held out her arm, the creamy flesh exposed, faint marks from previous needles that had been administered in the crook of her arm.

'This might sting,' he said softly.

She turned her head, eyes staring at the bookshelf to her left, the stuffed hawk watching from his spot above them. Her arm felt limp; if she hadn't made the adjustment he might have wondered if she was listening to him at all. She didn't make a sound as he sank the needle into the skin, nor as he removed it, cleaned the tip with a cloth and placed it back on the trolley. Declan felt a desperate gloom descend on him, his shoulders weighty as he stepped backwards.

'Thank you, Doctor Harris. That will be all.' Doctor Malone had returned to his desk, was bent over notes, writing lines in thick blue ink. 'And I will see you again in a few days, Edith,' he said, not looking up. 'Your treatment is booked and I don't want to hear you've been difficult again.'

Edith said nothing, her head drooping further into her body.

Declan left the room before she had time to get out of her chair, not able to look at her as he made his way back down the corridor, his footsteps rapid on the stone floor.

Chapter 14

THEN

The flower garden made her feel calmer. Edith liked the feel of the soil under her fingernails, the heady clash of smells and the gentle hum of insects. There was space around and above her, not like in the building with its maze of rooms and corridors and shouts and people. There was no one here to hurt her, no Donna, no nurses; she didn't feel so much like the inside of her was wound like a cotton reel, tight, tight, tight.

And she'd told someone. She'd told Nurse Shaw. Edith was so tired, struggling to sleep in her room, imagining someone in the doorway, every noise the sound of someone on the stairs outside, wondering if it was a nurse doing the rounds, if it was someone else, someone with a key to her room . . . Nurse Shaw was nice: she'd listened. She'd find the key.

Edith looked across at Bernie working opposite her, head bent over what she was doing, pressing her thumb into the soil, marking out spots in neat lines ready for planting. Behind her the building lurked, a huge grey backdrop with its thousands of stones and windows casting long shadows on the lawn. Bernie glanced up in that moment and poked her tongue out at Edith. It made them both giggle, their hands shaking with the tiny sound.

An attendant watched them: Malcolm, nice, older than most; he'd been here since she was small. He used to give her toffees from a tin, to put in her laughing gear he said, when other people got visitors on Visitors' Day. Said it was a shame and ruffled her hair. She hadn't been as sad when she got the toffees; some of them would stick her teeth together. Malcolm wouldn't mind them giggling a little.

There was always an attendant watching them until the tools were handed back in. One time a fork went missing and they all had to line up and be checked. Martha had folded it into her cardigan. It was shaken out and landed next to her foot with a clump. No one had said anything, just stared at it. She didn't come out to work in the gang again and Edith felt better because, now she was always with Donna, Martha made things worse.

Bernie grinned up at her again; she'd seemed happier recently, talking about the new Doctor Harris who seemed to be helping her. Edith had seen him once; he had joined the orchestra and she had watched as he'd played his trumpet, some spittle landing on his shoe, the droplet staying there the whole rehearsal.

Malcolm was walking behind them as they worked, fanning himself with a newspaper. She couldn't make out all the letters in the headline, shwoosh, shwoosh, too fast. There was a picture of a building with half of its side missing, like someone had stamped on the edge and all the bricks had fallen off. She didn't like the picture so she looked away. Sometimes the staff talked about the war that was happening far away and she worried that it would come here too.

She went to fetch one of the smaller watering cans, stepping over the upturned shoes of the women in the gardening gang, keeping her eyes down as she walked past Franklin, the attendant with the half-smile on his face. The same expression all the time. He said something to her and laughed low and long. She didn't like Franklin. She'd seen him once, peering between the bars of the ward bedroom, a cigarette clamped between his teeth. Other patients whispered about him: he sold things he got them from outside.

She sped up, seizing the watering can, skirting round the patch they were working on so she didn't have to walk past him again. Some of the water sloshed out of the spout and she went to steady it. Bernie looked up at her as she passed behind, shielding her eyes with her hand. There was soil on her cheek. Edith was about to point it out.

'What are you doing, Edie?' Malcolm asked, standing in her spot.

Edith raised the watering can towards him.

'Come on, rattle your dags.'

She dropped to her knees, sprinkling some water on the patch of soil she'd put the bulbs in, gently pressing on the top as she'd been taught. They were growing amaryllis for the grounds; they'd be bright colours, although you couldn't tell that now. The bulbs were a dirty brown, wisps of roots spurting from the bottom, and they needed to grow. She thought that maybe flowers were like people: you had to uncover the soil on the top to really see them.

It had been warmer in the last week or so and she'd already forgotten the biting cold of the last few months, the wind whistling from the sea and straight into the grounds, down and around the corridors of the building, making her nose drip, her fingers numb. It had seemed like winter would never end. Now it was good to keep her hands moving, the ground still damp where she knelt. She could feel the weak sunshine and the attendants' gaze on the back of her neck as she worked.

Bernie finished digging and was dropping the bulbs into the new line of holes, covering them up and talking to them, as if she were coaxing them to grow, like babies. Bernie had a baby once, she'd told Edith, that was why she was put here in the building. She didn't any more. Misty was like Bernie's baby now, playing with the sleeve of her bed jacket and nuzzling into her neck.

Next to Edith's gang, through the hedge, the men worked in a vegetable garden. There was hammering as they banged nails into wood, and an almost constant squeaking as one man Edith didn't know went back and forth, back and forth with a wheelbarrow. She'd never worked in the vegetable garden but she knew Willie, who always wanted to hold the ribbon at Sports Day, spent most days digging up potatoes for the enormous saucepans in the kitchen.

A butterfly dipped in amongst the flowers behind Bernie, and Edith made a noise, wanting to point it out to her but not wanting to draw attention. Then it flew away just as a piercing cry went up, followed by shouting. The man holding the wheelbarrow was still now, staring dumbly at whoever was making the noises. All Edith could see was his head above the line of the hedge, as if it was stuck on the top of the leaves and not attached to his body at all.

One of the voices was raving, lots of words spilling on the top of other words.

'Take it back . . . I won't . . . I didn't . . . you don't know.'

He was angry, that much was clear; he was swearing and now the words were faster but didn't make any sense and he was being told to shut up and one man had started to laugh at him. Edith started to feel the swirl in her stomach, acid in her throat. The man should be quiet, she thought. He should stop being angry. He shouldn't say anything else.

'Come on, Tom, don't go off . . .'

The man got louder, screaming, and everyone was looking now. She could just make out the top of a wooden rake, sweeping in an arc; the man was waving it.

Tom. There were a lot of patients, some said over a thousand in the whole place, and she didn't know a Tom. She delivered the mail so she did know a lot of people, but not this man.

The other man was jeering and laughing, calling Tom a loony, fucking mad as a meat axe. His laugh was like a bark, making her jump. Malcolm stepped across, moved around the hedge. Edith could feel her heartbeat in her ears, bit her lip. She wanted to stop listening but it was too hard, they were so loud and all jumbled now. Tom needed to be quiet.

There were whispers amongst the other women as Franklin with the stupid half-smile turned away to have a gawk, his eyes all lit up like it was the most exciting thing he'd ever seen. He licked his lips, took a step forward, hovering as he watched. Some of the women stood up too, craning their necks to make out more over the hedge. Franklin didn't notice; didn't tell them to get back to work.

Then as soon as it began it settled. The voices went quiet and there were other murmurs, movement on the ground. Edith could make out a face pressed into the grass on the other side of the hedge, one hand holding his head down. Tom. He had ginger hair and a beard. For a brief second the eye, brown like a toffee, looked right at her and she started, one hand shooting back, leaving a mark in the soil.

Malcolm was back, straightening his shirt, talking to Franklin. 'He's being taken back to the building.'

Franklin smirked deeper than before as if he was sharing a great joke. Malcolm walked away from him, passed Edith still kneeling on the ground. Stopped: one hand on her shoulder. 'He'll be all right, Edith.'

She watched Tom being lifted up, a dark stain spreading in the centre of his trousers. He didn't look all right. She looked away, a memory of herself as a child feeling that awful warmth as it leaked out of her, or waking to find she had done it in her sleep. She clutched at her throat. Remembered standing, nightdress sticking to the tops of her legs, shivering on the floorboards as one of the nurses tutted and pulled back the sheets. The straw mattress that always smelt of piss. She would hang her head as the other women and girls walked past, leering at her, while she waited for the fresh sheets to be rolled back across. She hadn't wanted to do it. She didn't think Tom had either.

They had always made notes when she talked. Doctor Malone would look at her, big moustache quivering, and she would repeat the same facts over and over. He would pause sometimes in between writing, dip his fountain pen into the ink pot and ask something again, wanting something different, something the same? She had never been sure. She had told him about why she sometimes screamed in the night, why she woke all wet: that she dreamt she was back there, in the dark cave, with him.

She used to tell them what he had done to her but they would say they didn't believe her, that she was a liar. Then she would be taken through to the big white room and a nurse would hold her down, hands on the tops of her arms as she screamed because she knew they would put the pads on her and wheel the machine over. She would wake up in a different room and they would have tied her down so she couldn't turn her head. So she did start to lie sometimes, and she said he didn't do anything at all, that she couldn't remember any of that.

'All right there, Edie . . .' Malcolm was saying something to her, pointing at the soil in front of her.

'Looks like you're getting on well,' he said in a soft voice, as if the last few minutes hadn't happened and the flower garden was as still and as calm as it always was and the man the other side of the hedge wasn't being taken away in one of the straitjackets that squeezed your arms against your body so tightly that after a while you forgot you had arms at all.

He was shouting again as they dragged him away, about the treatment, and her hands started shaking as she thought about where he was headed. A tremor she often got. She held one hand over the other, clenched tightly, focused on the water in the can, a small fly, still, dead, resting on the surface. She focused on the darkened soil, the dips she'd made with her fingers, and Bernie opposite her already, humming slightly as she dropped her bulbs into the ground: quickly, quickly, quickly.

'Edith,' a voice called from behind her. Matron.

Nurse Shaw stood just behind, two pink spots high on her cheeks.

Edith wanted to smile at her; was it over? Had they found the key? Had Donna been moved off the ward?

But Nurse Shaw wasn't looking at her and Matron's face was serious.

Everyone was staring at Edith now.

'You'd better come with us.'

Chapter 15

NOW

The policeman was back. Both Martha and Edith had been summoned for second interviews and Declan was to sit in on them.

Rounding the corner he could see Doctor Malone, head bent to hear the chief superintendent, currently gesturing to the door of the interview room. They failed to notice Declan as he moved down the corridor towards them, the superintendent speaking in a low, urgent voice, Doctor Malone, an earnest expression on his face as he listened, nodding intermittently.

These days the superintendent was entirely caught up in the investigation of the fire, either down by the main gates answering questions from reporters or accompanying a variety of people across the grounds to inspect the buildings or instruct new work. One hand permanently cupped his neck, massaging the muscles.

There was always something to do in a place this size; small things could be missed. Every inspection seemed to highlight a new crack or faulty wire. Only last week a large chunk of plaster had fallen from the ceiling of the concert hall, just missing the male attendant mopping the floor.

The outbuilding that had caught had been made entirely of wood, its windows and doors locked from the outside; even the bell to raise the alarm had been under lock and key. Declan had heard rumours about meetings with Doctor Malone and other senior staff, a fear that the investigation might prove the fire could have been avoided. Would they would want an excuse that meant they weren't at fault?

'I understand,' Doctor Malone nodded as Declan approached.

Doctor Malone glanced up, choosing not to acknowledge him. The superintendent clamped his mouth shut. Declan loitered nearby, awaiting instructions, before the senior doctor looked up with an irritated twitch of his moustache.

'Go on in, Doctor Harris,' he said, ushering him quickly with one hand, a click of his tongue.

'You'll do what you can, then?' Declan heard the superintendent say as he moved inside.

'Absolutely, leave it with me,' Doctor Malone replied as the door clicked closed.

'Doctor,' the policeman said from his stool in the middle of the room, not bothering to get up to shake his hand. 'Matron's fetching the girls,' he added, thumbing through a pad in his lap, the material of his trousers stretched across meaty thighs.

Declan clocked the sneer on the policeman's face. What did he think had happened that night? What conclusion did the two men on the other side of the door want him to reach?

Footsteps, talking outside and Martha appeared in the doorway, Matron directly behind her, shooing her inside like an errant child.

Martha looked wan, shadows ringed beneath her eyes, limbs jutting under the thin material of her blouse. She didn't return Declan's sympathetic smile.

Matron moved across to sit in a chair against the wall, a crossword poking out of the clipboard on her lap.

Declan stayed perched against the countertop next to the medicine cabinet, watching as Martha sat on the stool in front of the policeman, pushing her hair behind her ears, flexing her ankle up, down, up, down.

'Well, Miss Anderson, thank you for coming to see me again.' The policeman bent forward, their knees almost touching.

Martha whispered a reply that Declan couldn't catch.

The policeman cupped a hand behind one ear and in a too-loud voice, practically winking at Declan, he said, 'Cat got your tongue. No matter.' He leaned as far back as he could go without toppling the small wooden stool, his stomach seeming to balloon in front of him. 'Well, Miss Anderson, Martha, you've now had time to collect yourself. I know you're being well looked after here by the doctors and nurses. We are all very sympathetic to what you've been through but it's been a good long while now, plenty of time to reflect . . .'

The policeman left the sentence in the air between them.

Martha shifted on her stool, scurf in the parting of her hair, dried skin on the backs of her hands.

'I wanted to ask you a few questions, nothing distressing mind, about that night. And we want some answers this time, eh, Martha?' The policeman's laugh was empty, forced. He went to place a hand on her knee before thinking better of it. Martha jerked backwards, watching the hand as he placed it back in his lap.

'So I'll begin, then,' he said, licking a fat finger and turning a page in his pad. 'I've been informed the nurses made regular checks on you all that evening, as they do every evening.'

There was a pause, the smell of disinfectant, the sounds of the room fading as Declan watched her, wondering whether she would sit in silence again. She nodded once. Perhaps she hoped if she answered the questions this time, the latest round of treatment would stop?

'That's a yes, is it? Could you possibly confirm things verbally – it really helps us,' the policeman added, giving a crooked smile.

'Yes,' Martha said, her voice catching on the syllable.

'And you told one of the doctors that although you didn't remember when the last check was, there had definitely been one that evening.'

Matron stopped what she was doing, her pencil hovering as she looked up. 'Because of the war we are a little stretched these days, but we still check, sir, we take the checks very seriously.'

The policeman's gaze flicked upwards, barely disguising his annoyance at being interrupted. 'Thank you, Nurse . . .'

Matron bristled in her seat.

'And is it true, Martha, that all the patients were in their beds by ten o'clock?'

Martha moved a hand to her throat, scratched at her skin. 'Yes, I think so.'

The policeman was leading her somewhere; Declan watched the man spin his web.

'You think so or you are certain? We have to be clear.'

'I'm certain. I didn't see anyone out of their bed.'

The policeman noted something on his pad. 'Were most of the patients sleeping?'

'I . . . it was quiet.'

'So you weren't asleep?'

Declan frowned as Martha's voice seemed to get louder, quicker. She tucked her hair behind her ears again. 'I woke up when there was all the smoke.'

'So you had been sleeping?'

'I . . . I . . . yes.' Martha's foot tapped more insistently on the floor.

'You've been reported as talking about the cause of the fire with one of the patients. Do you think you know what happened, Martha?' The policeman switched tack, the tone of his voice now low and urgent.

Martha looked across at Declan, who tried to set his face into a neutral expression. What had she said? Did she know something? Was it not the state of the building after all, but something more sinister?

'I didn't. That is' – Martha rubbed at the backs of her hand – 'everyone's talking and Doctor Malone asked me . . .'

'You had a theory,' the policeman said loudly, both eyebrows raised in encouragement, pad poised.

'Not a theory so much as a . . . a thought.' Martha glanced across at Matron, who had abandoned her crossword to listen, face pinched.

'A thought?'

'Yes,' Martha said, her fingers still rubbing at the same spot. 'Doctor Malone thought it was worth mentioning.'

'You knew how someone might have started the fire, was that it?' the policeman said, his gaze intense as he leaned towards her once more.

Declan couldn't remove his own eyes from the woman.

'No, I just said, we'd all seen the matches.' She licked her lips, swallowed. 'All of us, not just me . . .'

'Matches?'

'They were scattered on the floor of the dayroom. Anyone could have picked one up.'

'From what I've heard, patients can get hold of most things. You yourself smoke, do you not?'

This last question caused Martha to start, her head snapping up to meet his eyes.

'Oops, didn't know people knew? I've been told some of you are rather canny at what you can get hold of . . .' the man said, his chin tilting in a challenge.

Martha's mouth pinched together. 'Doctor Malone told me . . .' She faded away and Declan was left to wonder what that had been.

The policeman leant forward, slowly this time, his stomach bulging as he did so. 'How was it that you came to find yourself in Seacliff originally, Martha?'

'Me?' Martha licked at her dry lips, as if she hadn't been expecting the question, as if the conversation wasn't going how she had planned.

'Why were you committed?'

Matron was watching the exchange with a half-open mouth. Declan was straining to listen closely.

'They moved me here.'

'Moved you?' The policeman feigned innocence.

Martha cleared her throat. 'They moved me from the prison,' she said, her voice steady. She looked up at the policeman, a cold expression on her face, and he flinched a little under her gaze. Declan felt the room breathe in and out with them all. Matron's pencil fell to the floor with a light tinkle.

Declan remembered reading Martha's file, remembered the court records.

'And why had you been put in prison?'

'Is it not in my notes?' Her eyes met his, a hint of challenge in her voice.

'I'd like to hear it from you,' the policeman said, resting back again, legs spread wide.

Martha's body stilled, her voice low. 'I killed my husband.'

Declan knew Martha had been serving a sentence for murder, later reduced to an insanity charge; he hadn't read the reasons why.

'You burnt his body.'

The surprise of this last statement caused Declan's eyebrows to shoot higher.

Martha's mouth dropped open a fraction before she snapped it shut. 'I . . . that wasn't exactly . . .'

'You burnt the house down with him inside. You told the police he was dead: smothered. Was he still alive when the fire started, I wonder?' the policeman asked, the confidence returned to his voice, his gaze steady on her.

Martha's fingers pinched the flesh between her thumb and forefinger. 'He was dead.'

'How did you know what to use – to start the fire, that is?'

Declan couldn't help staring at Martha too, waiting for a reply. She stared resolutely over the shoulder of the policeman, her gaze fixed.

'Did you enjoy watching the flames?'

'Officer, I'm not sure that is an appropriate question . . .' Declan stepped forward, a hand up, his voice not as loud as he imagined in his mind.

The policeman ignored him.

Martha remained completely silent, her tongue darting out of her mouth, over her lips as the silence stretched on.

The policeman leant forward, moved close, his face invading the space in front of her. 'So you burnt your husband. Did you want to burn others? Was that what it was?'

Matron was completely still. Declan dithered, wondering what he should now do. He knew he should stop the interview but he found himself waiting for more.

'How was it that you got out of the building? Terribly lucky . . .' the policeman said, voice dripping with sarcasm. 'I was speaking to the chief superintendent and he tells me you have a little boy, I understand? He's allowed to visit you here, isn't he? Terrible shame if that were to end.'

Martha stirred on her stool, smoothing her skirt. She glanced quickly across at Matron.

'We need you to cooperate now, Martha . . .'

'I am,' she whispered. 'I just told you.'

Declan hadn't realised he'd been holding his breath.

'Enjoyed it the first time round, did you? Wanted to do it all again? All those women . . .' The policeman's voice goading.

Martha's expression changed, eyes panicked. 'No. I didn't. I couldn't . . .'

'It would be right to confess, wouldn't it, the moral thing to do . . .' the policeman said. He reached across the space between them and placed a fleshy hand on her thigh. 'If not, I might be forced to tell the doctors here those little visits from your boy should end . . .'

No one had time to stop her: she reacted almost immediately, pushing his hand away, launching herself at him.

It took all Declan's strength to haul her backwards; both wooden stools lying on their sides, the grunts of the policeman, a livid red scratch just below his right eye. Matron stood, seizing Martha's other arm as her chest heaved.

The policeman clutched at his face. 'Shame not to see your son again, Miss Anderson, wouldn't it?'

Martha started to scream expletives at him, straining in their grip. It was a few seconds before they all realised the door had opened and Doctor Malone had stepped inside. Everyone turned to stare at him.

Martha appealed to him. 'I told him, about the matches, Doctor, I told him . . .'

It was like she hadn't spoken. Doctor Malone stared at Matron, her grip tight on Martha's arm. 'Best get her back to the ward, Matron,' he said.

Martha sagged still in that second. Declan released her, watching as Matron hustled her outside.

'I hope she helped you with your enquiries,' Doctor Malone said to the policeman. 'Doctor Harris here will take a look at that scratch.'

The policeman lifted a hand to his face. 'Fucking nutcase,' he muttered, dabbing at it gently.

Doctor Malone left the room, the tiniest smile on his face.

Chapter 16

BEFORE

Mrs Clark brings through the meat for Father to slice, the vegetables in a big bowl, sits the gravy jug in front of me. I can see myself in its surface – I look all wonky and I laugh. Mother looks across at me, a finger to her lips.

I place my hands in my lap and look down. I don't eat with Father and Mother; normally I eat with Mrs Clark in the parlour, but I like being in this room with the big padded chairs that I have to be lifted on to reach. I sit on a cushion which is a bit scratchy but I don't wiggle and Mother tells me that I have to use the fork and knife like a proper lady. I want to get it right, I see Mother watching me.

Father stands at the head of the table and says grace. I close one eye but watch out of the other, the candles making his face glow orange; everything smells of herbs and the fire is popping in the corner. We say 'Amen' and I feel the bubbles in my tummy as he cuts into the meat.

'Mrs Clark always seems to cook chicken to perfection,' Mother says, sipping at her glass that has thick red liquid in it.

Father doesn't look up but smiles as he holds out her plate.

'We had chickens before,' I say, wanting him to smile at me too. 'It was my job to collect the eggs. They were warm.'

Mother's hand freezes, her eyes on me. Father frowns before Mother apologises and takes the plate from him.

'My favourite was called Silky.'

Both my parents are looking at me and something in Mother's face makes me stop. Is this like the other time, when I wasn't allowed to talk about before?

'Edith, your father doesn't want to hear your stories.'

'They're not.' I feel a stinging in my eyes. Mother knows they're not stories. She's asked me before. She asked me how I knew some of the big words, if an adult had told me, but I used to use them when I was the bigger girl.

'What is this about, Eileen?' Father isn't smiling now, the big sharp silver knife and fork in his hands. I can see the inside of the chicken.

'It's nothing, you know children, their imaginations can be . . .' The red liquid wobbles, makes red dots on the white tablecloth.

I don't understand why it matters that we used to have chickens.

'Silky was all white like a small cloud.' My voice is higher, faster; I'm not telling stories. 'And she would let me pick her up and I could always feel her heart through her feathers.' I had forgotten that until now, but suddenly I am back there, in the corner of the garden behind the wire that kept them in, holding Silky, my hands bigger than they are now. I had held her still for Mary to stroke. Mary had been frightened at first – she had been a lot younger than me.

'Edith, please . . .' Mother looks as if she might start crying; there is water along the bottom of her eyes.

Father's face changes; he lowers the big sharp knife on to the table. I want him to slice the chicken for me, I want a plate like Mother's.

'When was this, Edith?' Father asks, a sudden pop from the fire making Mother jump.

'It was when I was here before, Father, when I was a big girl.'

'She doesn't know what she's saying, Michael. I've told her not to . . .'

Father raises a hand and Mother stops talking immediately.

I feel as if the fire is in me now, all hot because I do know what I'm saying and Mother always tells me to shh and Father has asked me. 'It's true,' I say. 'When I was big, when I lived with my other mother, we had chickens. But then he hit me in the cave and I must have died, and then I came here.'

Father leans right forward across the table to me and it makes me stop. The only sound in the room is the cracking wood, and something in his eyes makes my skin go bumpy.

'What are you saying, child?'

I swallow, feeling my face scrunch up tight. Is he asking because he wants to know? 'He hit me in the cave. I died, but I'm here now.'

Father sits back, his cheeks getting redder. 'You will not talk like this,' he says.

'I'm sorry, maybe it's best if Edith eats elsewhere,' Mother says, scraping back her own chair.

I don't want to eat elsewhere, I like being here with the padded chairs and the candles and Father and Mother and I was just saying about the chickens. I can feel my body going up and down with my fast breaths and I want to make them understand and I'm not telling stories. It's not fair.

Father nods and Mother moves to my side and lifts me off the seat. I don't want to go and I kick my legs and my foot hits the table and I call out and Mrs Clark appears in the doorway and Mother makes her take me and I shout and I don't want to go and it's not fair.

'I'm sorry Michael, I'm sorry.' I can hear Mother all the way upstairs where Mrs Clark has taken me and I am left in my room and I can smell the chicken from here and I run to my bed and push my face on to the top and scream to let it out.

Chapter 17

NOW

'You suspect arson, then?' Declan said, lifting one of the wooden stools that had fallen on its side.

The policeman touched the scratch on his face, waving away Declan's attempt to inspect it. 'The superintendent wants us to be thorough.'

Although the patients weren't meant to have access to anything dangerous, Declan knew the rumours: Franklin the attendant, with his yellowed teeth and fingernails, always skulking around some of the patients, the smell of tobacco that accompanied those patients into Declan's consulting room. Arson wasn't impossible, but there was other gossip, too: rats chewing the cables, a small fire that had broken out a year ago, cause unknown, sparks from wires that had once shocked an attendant.

'But why?' Declan asked.

The policeman settled again on his stool, cricking his neck from side to side. 'You're the head doctor, it's not exactly a stretch of the imagination, is it?'

Declan knew he should correct him, explain some of the backgrounds, the cases he was working on. He knew he should try to point out that many of the patients had a diagnosis they could manage, that the hospital's aim was rehabilitation through work and exercise alongside medication and treatments. Many of the patients were not, to Declan's mind, incapable of rational thought.

Then there was the look that Martha had given the policeman, as if she wanted to kill him with her bare hands. Declan wasn't sure what to think.

Doctor Malone reappeared, escorting another patient into the room. All other thoughts disappeared as Declan realised it was Edith.

'I took the liberty of fetching Edith myself,' Doctor Malone said as he moved inside the room, Edith's eyes wide as she cowered beside him. 'And Edith here has assured me she will be no trouble.'

The policeman grunted once.

'Gentlemen.' Doctor Malone nodded and left the room.

'Sit down, Edith.' Declan motioned, standing behind her chair as if he were at a formal dinner.

Edith dithered for a moment, a quick glance at the policeman as if seeking permission, before she moved across the room, mouth lifting as she caught Declan's eye. She thanked him, sitting and tucking both feet on to the small wooden rung between the legs of the stool. Moving Matron's abandoned clipboard Declan went to sit, missing the seat by a few inches, one hand shooting out to get his balance. Edith didn't look over at him and he straightened and cleared his throat to cover his embarrassment.

'Miss Garrett,' the policeman launched in, the scratch under his eye moving up and down as he said her name. 'I'm hoping you will be able to help us in our investigation.'

Edith sneaked a glance up at him. 'I can try, Detective,' she said, her voice dignified.

'Good, good.' He was distracted, hadn't composed himself since the last interview, turning pages of his notepad. 'I was particularly hoping you might be able to shine a light on the movements of patients.'

Edith twitched her head to the side. 'Movements?' She glanced at Declan, who tried to reassure her with a nod. He thought of Martha, straining moments before in his arms.

'We have been informed that the checks that night were not necessarily performed on the hour; that due to shortages many are often neglected.'

Edith was looking down. Declan could see her scanning the floor, left to right, as if she was thinking of an answer.

'Were there hourly checks?'

'They shine a torch on us, check us.'

'Regularly?'

Edith pleated the material of her skirt in her hands. 'They do check,' she said, her words slow, quiet.

The policeman gave another grunt and Edith looked up, a hint of fear in her face now.

Declan found himself leaning forward. 'That's helpful, Edith, well done.' He felt gratified to see her shoulders lower, her forehead smooth again.

'And what about the patients. Were they all asleep when the fire started?'

Edith bit her lip.

'Miss Garrett.' The policeman leant forward.

'It was lights out,' she said, an uncertain waver in her voice.

'And you all just nod off then, do you?' The disbelieving tone was back.

'Well, it's lights out,' Edith said again.

He looked right at her now. 'What I'm asking, Edith, is whether you think someone could have got out of her bed. Whether someone could have started that fire?'

Edith's mouth opened and she turned in her chair to Declan. 'I didn't . . . no, I wouldn't . . .' Her eyes were wide, her throat moving up and down.

Declan held out a hand. 'Don't worry, Edith, it's only a question. Just say what you remember, nothing more.'

She nodded, clutching her two hands together as she stared at them. 'It was lights out. I was in my room. The dormitory is above me.'

The policeman seemed oblivious to the shifting atmosphere, to Edith's chest rising and falling. 'Did you see Martha Anderson? Was she out of bed?'

'Martha.' Edith's head snapped up.

Declan interjected, 'Edith was in her own room. Locked inside. She couldn't have seen anyone else.'

Edith looked at him then with such relief in her eyes, he felt a warmth in his stomach that he'd been a source of strength.

The policeman glared at him. 'She might have heard something, at least? Someone moving around?'

There was a beat.

'I . . . that is . . .' Edith was struggling with something, her face draining of colour. Declan's own eyebrows lifted. Had she heard something?

The policeman leant further forward, his piggy eyes eager. 'Yes, you can recall something?'

She tapped on her chest, once, twice. 'Martha,' she repeated again.

The policeman nodded once. 'Martha, yes, Miss Anderson, was she out of bed?'

Declan frowned as Edith looked at him briefly and then at the floor.

She swallowed then, colour returning to her cheeks. 'I was in my room. It was lights out.'

The policeman exhaled loudly, a quick glance to the ceiling.

Then, with little warning, Edith began to cry softly, her shoulders shaking, the policeman's face alarmed as she dissolved in front of him.

Declan got out of his chair, moving to crouch next to her.

'It's just so sad,' Edith said, the tears leaking out of her eyes and down her cheeks, making damp spots on her thin blouse.

Declan produced a handkerchief, lifted it up to her. Her hand brushed his as she took it from him with a watery thank you.

'I think we should end this interview here, sir,' Declan said, looking up at the policeman, a confidence in his voice.

The policeman shrugged. 'No matter,' he said, jotting something down in his pad and sitting upright on his stool, only Edith's sobs now audible.

Chapter 18

NOW

He steered her to his office. 'Shh, all is well, Edith, it's all right.'

The policeman hadn't put up a great protest, dismissing Edith's tears as another loony behaving unpredictably, no doubt, all his preconceptions about patients of Seacliff ringing true: an attack, a breakdown.

Edith snatched breaths between sobs, the handkerchief up to her face as she allowed Declan to guide her gently to his office where he pushed open the door and, awkwardly, as one arm was still around her shoulders, pulled a chair towards her. He lowered her into it.

He rubbed her back gently, feeling her spine beneath her blouse. 'You're all right. Let me pour you some water.'

He almost tripped as he reached for the jug and glass on a table in the corner, relieved as she took it from him, eyes red from the tears. A little slopped over the edge, leaving a dark mark on her blouse; he found himself staring as the stain spread.

What sounds and smells had she experienced that night? How had the fire affected her?

He waited, perched on the edge of his desk as if he were a teacher waiting for a class to finish their exercise.

She sipped at the water. Then, as if she was coming to, her eyes swivelled to him as she spoke. 'Please don't tell. If he finds out I'm emotional he'll . . .' Her face collapsed, the glass trembling in her hands. 'I just didn't want to say the wrong thing, to the policeman . . .'

Declan leaned forward, interrupting her, confused. 'If who finds out?'

She placed the glass on the floor, shook her head.

'Edith?'

She inhaled deeply. He could see her mind working, the worry etched on her forehead.

'If Doctor Malone finds out,' she said finally.

'Finds out what?'

Her voice sped up. 'Finds out I cried. He'll say I'm hysterical again, I'll have to go into the white room. Please, I know they're watching me, for the operation . . .'

Declan hadn't realised until this moment that she knew about the possibility of the leucotomy. 'It's fine, Edith, fine,' he soothed. 'I don't need to say anything.'

What else could he promise? He couldn't reassure her. He felt the worry steal over him: if they were watching her behaviour, she should be wary. Next time it might not be electric shock treatment, it might be the knife.

She slumped in the chair. 'Thank you,' she whispered, giving him a thin smile. 'I worried I would get it wrong, when the police-man asked me about Martha . . .'

He didn't deserve the smile, waved the thanks away with a hand. 'What did you worry you might say?' he asked, curious as to whether Edith did know something. How could she have, if she had been locked inside her room?

Edith didn't answer him at first, picking up the water and sipping at it once more.

'There's no need to be nervous, Edith, I'm here to listen.'

Edith's body stilled and she ran a finger over the rim of the glass. 'It was when he asked me about movements. The patients moving about . . .'

'Did you hear anyone?'

Edith paused, a small jerk of her head. 'I didn't hear anyone.' She took a breath, looked up at him, her brown eyes warm in the light from the window. 'But they had a key. Donna did. Martha and her could open some of the doors inside the ward; they could open mine,' she said quietly.

Declan's eyes rounded; he raked a hand through his hair. 'A key,' he repeated, straightening, pacing for a moment before spinning back to her. 'Did others know about this, Edith?'

'I . . . I told the nurses,' she said softly. 'But they didn't believe me. I don't want to be punished, Doctor, please, what if they don't believe me now . . .' She became distressed once more, her knuckles white as she squeezed the glass in her lap.

'I won't say anything,' Declan reassured her, his gaze steady, waiting for her to meet his eye. Her hands relaxed on the glass. 'It's not proof of anything, but perhaps it was best not to let on.' Declan thought back to the policeman, the song and dance he might have made of the information. 'I'm glad you trusted me enough to tell me though,' he added.

Edith looked at him with solemn eyes. 'I do, Doctor.' She reached to place the glass on the desk in front of her before sitting back down in her chair, tucking her hands under her legs as she looked around his office.

It was only then, looking over at her, that he realised she was finally here in his office, his mouth opening and shutting as the temptation to discuss the things in her file almost overwhelmed him.

He knew Doctor Malone would be furious with an impromptu session and Edith had only just recovered from her upset over the fire.

'Was it exciting?' she asked, her voice stronger, one finger up.

He was confused for a moment before he realised where her finger was pointing: to the photograph of his graduation propped up on his desk.

'I'd be terrified. All those people watching,' she said.

'A little,' he admitted. 'Do you not like being in the spotlight?' he asked, determined to steer her into talking about herself.

She shook her head vigorously from side to side. 'Once I was playing my flute in the music room and Nurse Shaw heard me and she asked me to play a solo in front of the whole dayroom and I just couldn't . . .'

He was pleased she seemed to have relaxed; the past few moments already separate from this new Edith who wanted to open up, to talk. He found himself settling on the edge of his desk to listen. There was already laughter in her voice, her cheeks flushed with colour.

'I wanted to race back up into my room. But you look, well' – she looked back at the photograph – 'you seem utterly unafraid.' She pointed to the expression on his face. Certainly, the photograph was flattering, Declan standing tall between his parents, beaming straight into the lens, his mortar board cocked at a slight angle.

'I think I was just very relieved, if I'm honest. There were times in the early days I wondered if I'd ever graduate.'

'Oh?'

'I didn't have an iron stomach, let's say. I'm much more comfortable in psychiatry.' He realised he was looking into her eyes, open in question, then shifted his gaze to the mole on her neck.

'They do operations here too,' she added softly; the brief bonhomie passed.

'Yes,' he said, feeling tongue-tied. He cleared his throat. 'Well, I'd better get back, see whether our friend is still waiting.' He took the coward's way out.

Edith looked down, nodded. 'I am sorry, about earlier, about crying.'

Declan went to kneel down next to her chair. 'That's fine, Edith, you went through a dreadful ordeal.'

She didn't meet his eye. 'Thank you, Doctor,' she said in a whisper, her body drooping, the energy gone.

Declan paused for a moment to see if she wanted to say anything else.

'I'm fine to return to the ward now, Doctor,' she said, her tone flat, and Declan felt his shoulders fall.

Chapter 19

THEN

Edith left the garden on trembling legs, her heart hammering as she followed in silence, Nurse Shaw still not looking at her.

Had they found the key? Where was Matron taking her?

The main building loomed ahead, the grey stone a castle about to swallow her whole. So many questions, but she kept them all inside.

'He's got some time and wants to see you,' Matron barked as Edith followed her through a wooden side door. She unlocked the corridor that led to the doctors' offices.

Who wanted to see her? Edith licked her lips. Flaking skin: she scraped at it as Matron knocked, it stung as she peeled.

Doctor Malone was behind his desk, dipping the nib into ink, looking up as she shuffled inside behind Matron.

'Edith for you, Doctor.'

Nurse Shaw waited in the corridor outside. Had she told Matron about the key? Had they found it? It wasn't her normal time to see Doctor Malone; why was she here?

'Good, thank you, Matron. Edith, take a seat. Matron, I'll let you know what needs to be done.'

Edith swallowed, watching Matron with wide eyes. What needed to be done? To whom?

'Doctor.' Matron nodded before leaving without a word; the last thing Edith saw as the door closed was Nurse Shaw staring back at her.

Doctor Malone leaned forward, searching her face. Edith remembered to blink.

'Matron reports you are experiencing paranoid episodes. Seeing things that aren't there and the like,' he stated, his eyes not leaving her face.

'I . . .' Paranoid episodes. That had been something he had talked to her about before, when she was younger and louder and in his office more. Paranoid episodes could be treated. 'No, Doctor, I . . .' A pen, an ink pot, sheets of paper, an opened telegram, a glass paperweight; her eyes scanned his desk. No key.

'You told a nurse, did you not, that you thought one of the other patients was planning to get you – those were your words?' Doctor Malone huffed, his pen now poised over a fresh sheet of paper.

'I . . . it wasn't . . . I . . .' What could she say to stop this? She had just told Nurse Shaw about the key, she hadn't meant . . . She could feel herself getting hot, damp under the arms, under her hair. 'I didn't mean . . . I thought Donna had a key . . .'

'A key.' He looked up at her sharply and for a strange second she thought it might all be all right. She had been right to tell Nurse Shaw. They would find it; they would summon Donna here.

'Are you suffering with delusions?' His eyes narrowed.

'Delusions?' she whispered, the hopes disappearing in smoke as he lifted his chin, continued to assess her.

This wasn't like their normal monthly session. Then he barely asked questions, often not lifting his eyes from his desk as he announced no new adjustments to her medication; was she suffering side-effects, was she benefitting from the fresh air, the work? Nod, yes, nod, no Doctor, thank you Doctor: that will be all. He would sign his name, send her on her way within a few minutes. She was quiet, quick to respond: no fuss.

'Are these similar to the imaginings you had when you arrived? That you are being tampered with?'

She didn't talk about those imaginings any more; she hadn't thought about them for years. This wasn't the same. The thoughts were crammed inside her head; she rubbed at her nose. 'I . . .'

'It is a concern, of course, if those thoughts are reoccurring. I would recommend a course of treatment if so, to ensure . . .'

'No, Doctor.' A small lurch in her seat, his moustache twitching in response. 'No, I haven't seen anything. Please, Doctor, you must believe—'

'Don't become agitated.' The words spoken with a wave of the hand.

She snapped her mouth shut, tried desperately to keep her voice level, respectful, her eyes cast down. She wasn't a hysteric, she wasn't taking fright; she wasn't anything. The voices were loud in her head and she tried to silence them as she scrabbled to concentrate.

'Please, Doctor.' She tried to force a small smile, felt her face move. 'I was mistaken. I haven't imagined anything. It's all been a terrible mistake.'

She held her breath as he paused, couldn't help staring at the nib of the pen, the ink that could write down the words she dreaded, that hadn't been written for years. His signature that sent her to the white room.

'Please, Doctor,' she whispered, licking her lips, feeling the sting of her pink flesh. 'I didn't mean to be any trouble.'

He set his pen down. He stared at her over his strange half-glasses; he stroked at one side of the hair beneath his nostrils. He didn't sign his name.

Today Edith was sitting on one of the red vinyl-covered chairs in the dayroom. Normally she liked the dayroom second best after the flower garden. There were people around so it was safe and it could be calm, just the noise of the rubber soles in the corridors as nurses approached, or the quiet wheeling of the tea trolley, the slight rattle of a cup in a saucer.

Her eyes were raw, a headache just behind them. She had spent much of the night awake, going over the day before: her visit to Doctor Malone, Nurse Shaw's eyes not meeting hers, the pen hovering over the sheet imagining the blue ink, the trolley that would collect her.

She was sure she'd heard someone on the stairs in the night. The rooms were all locked from the outside; it shouldn't have been possible, they hadn't found a key. It had been in her head, Doctor Malone had made her agree. She'd taken two more red pills. Good girl.

The noise again.

Maybe it was a nurse? But the hourly round had only just happened and they often didn't come back for hours any more, not like before the war when you could almost count the exact moment they would open the door to check with their torch. She sat up on her elbows, her neck muscles tight, staring and staring at the door, imagined she saw shadowed feet in the crack at the bottom, heard a scratch. Another scratch. She hadn't slept at all after that. Had she seen a key?

She mustn't let the nurses know she wasn't sleeping well; she kept her eyes open as she sat on the chair. When she told the nurses before they made her take another pill, a small, white, round pill that made her whole body heavy, made her sleep in the winged chair in the dayroom in the day, wake with saliva on her chin and cardigan. She didn't want that. She kept her eyes wide, looked around the room for someone to talk to.

Bernie had a cold so she wasn't allowed in the dayroom; she had to stay in the dormitory on the ward, an enamel bowl by her side, a cup of water next to her. She'd been sleeping when Edith had gone to see her, Misty curled up at the foot of the bed.

There was only Joyce who slapped the walls and Julia who was always glum. Shirley was there too, sitting over in the armchair winding wool into strands before snipping them into lengths. An attendant stood next to her waiting to take the scissors back.

Martha and Donna weren't around, though, so Shirley didn't seem as menacing, her legs wide apart in the chair, bandages on the ankles that merged into the feet, her rolls of flesh filling the seat so you couldn't see the cushion under her bottom. Her chin crushed into her chest as she bent over her work. Edith liked making things with wool but wouldn't go over to her. Instead she set up the table to play patience, the cards laid out in rows in front of her.

She'd hoped Patricia might have been there, lining up the chairs, making sure they were straight or trying to make her play a game, calling her Fred or crying. She hadn't been there for a while and Edith wondered if she had a cold, too. Even though her changing moods sometimes unsettled her she could make Edith laugh, imitating the nurses and doing silly dances and accents. Last month, before they made her move wards, she'd stood on one leg for half an hour because Edith told her she couldn't. When Deputy Matron called for her to stop she'd refused, and started to hop away when one of the attendants came towards her. Edith wondered if she thought it had been worth it even after she was dragged out.

Nurse Ritchie was on duty now; Edith could see her through the glass window into the office where they sat looking out at them. Nurse Ritchie had small, barely-there eyes and called them loonies and laughed when things weren't funny and she was always cruel to Bernie, calling her 'midget' and 'squit'. The attendant Franklin was fetching something from a cupboard in the office and Edith watched him turn and ask something, his big ugly mouth open. He reminded her of the fish she'd gutted when on a kitchen gang, all rubbery lips. She remembered sinking the tip of the knife in and slicing along, then pulling all the guts out. They were slippery and cold, like jelly. As if Franklin felt her watching he turned and caught her eye, then he gave her a wink, but it wasn't like the winks Malcolm gave her; it made her mouth fill with a sour taste. It did something nasty to her insides.

Sometimes at night she pictured his face and she remembered once when she had the treatment, she thought he'd been there in the room. She shouted out but then someone put their hand over her mouth and the hand smelt like cigarettes but then she'd fallen back asleep and it might have been dreams because you don't remember really. That was the treatment when she woke and there were purple marks at the top of her legs and she'd cried out and told Nurse Ritchie it ached and ached. Nurse Ritchie called her a bloody hysteric and slapped her for insolence.

She hadn't been looking at the door, hadn't seen which patients had filed in. It was only when they both passed right by her that she realised.

She forgot which cards she was hoping for: the jack of diamonds, the ten of clubs. Or was it the jack of clubs?

Nurse Ritchie was peering through the glass.

There was a shift in the room but Edith was one of the last to look over at what people were staring at, too busy watching Donna and Martha stop next to Shirley. Finally Edith dragged her eyes away. At first she thought it was a new patient: a woman with lank, red hair, a slow, shuffled walk, too-pale skin. She looked familiar, though, and Edith frowned, feeling her nose wrinkling as she watched the woman glance up before returning her eyes to the floor.

Edith's mouth dropped open. She didn't notice anything else: no nurses' station, no Donna, no sounds of the heating pipes, the squeak of passers-by, the coughs and mutterings of the room. It all disappeared in that moment and it was just the girl she was following with her eyes. It was Patricia, but not Patricia.

Patricia was always frantic, Edith couldn't remember her ever sitting still. Even after treatment she would be exhausting to watch: reshuffling furniture, shouting out games she wanted to play, food she wanted to eat, snapping her hairband between her fingers again and again. Donna used to tell her to shut up all the time. It became a game; she'd seek her out. She'd make her get angry, slap, kick, hit, until she was dragged away. And then she was dragged away for the last time, to a different ward.

This Patricia looked like Patricia: the same stubbed nose, blue eyes, her hair a little duller. Patricia had been radiant, though, Patricia had . . . Edith couldn't make it out. What had happened? As if Patricia had a twin, a subdued mirror image. She was frightened to go over, to talk to this woman who wasn't Patricia. She stayed watching, cards forgotten, as the woman edged around the wall, one palm flat against it, head still turned away.

There were twins in one of the men's wards; Edith hadn't known until she'd seen them standing side by side when she'd been delivering post. She really hadn't been able to tell them apart. She thought her eyes were playing tricks on her and it frightened her to think that there could be more than one of the same person. She wondered then if Patricia had a twin who had come here. She caught Martha and Shirley looking at her too, then at the wool dangling limply from Shirley's hand; Martha brushing at her eyes, blinking and looking away. Donna, however, was staring straight at Patricia, following every footstep, her mouth a smirk. Was it triumph in her eyes? Edith couldn't focus on the cards in front of her, all the red diamonds and hearts swimming, the faces of the kings and queens blurring in and out.

She didn't want to look at Patricia, to see that dead-eyed expression, knowing for certain in that moment that Patricia had had the new treatment. They called it a leucotomy and Edith had heard Doctor Malone say it was a groundbreaking cure. He was in the nurses' station too now, watching Patricia-who-wasn't-Patricia through the glass, a pen to his lips, a small smile on his face.

When Donna spoke, Edith startled in her chair. 'Poor Patricia,' she said, leaning down over one shoulder, the foul odour of cigarettes. 'Not so pretty any more,' Donna whispered, one eye open, shut, a flicker.

Edith froze, wanting to get up, move away, aware of Doctor Malone a short distance away, needing to stay absolutely still: no trouble. Patricia was edging along the wall towards the table. Martha was watching her now, her arms crossed as if protecting herself from the sight.

'You told them to search my room,' Donna said, reaching over her, her breast brushing Edith's shoulder as she picked up one of the cards, examining it in her hands, a smile on her face as if she was saying something nice. She placed it back down in the wrong place. 'You better be careful what they find in yours next time, princess.'

Edith couldn't swallow, mouth dried up, her whole body clenched. Doctor Malone was still on the other side of the glass; a glance her way. She tried to smile.

'Such a shame,' Donna said, looking across as Patricia approached them, as Patricia looked straight at them and just kept moving by.

Chapter 20

NOW

Doctor Malone left a message with the staff. He had a private matter to attend to in Wellington and would be gone for a short time. Instructions were issued and Doctor Harris was to temporarily take over all cases.

Declan swung into action the moment he heard, heading to Nurse Ritchie in the nurses' station, her lemony expression unchanged as he arranged to meet with Edith Garrett first thing the next day.

He fetched her notes, staying up through the night until he knew them inside and out, pillow propped against the wall, papers fanned out on the bedspread and floorboards, the bare bulb of the lamp giving off a weak glow as he squinted at the handwriting, made more detailed notes about her admission, her original diagnosis, her recent regression and prepared his first questions for her.

She had left his office with such little hope the last time, he was determined to see what he could do for her. A niggling doubt tugged at him: the portrait of the young Edith not matching the woman he had encountered.

She was waiting outside his office before their set time, unable to stand still, about to slip away.

'Edith,' he said, drawing himself up, feeling her eyes on him as he juggled her folder, unlocked and held open the door for her. 'Come in, take a seat.'

She stepped past him into the room. For a second he imagined he smelt citrus, sweetening the smell of carbolic soap from the corridor. She took a seat opposite his own, both her hands tucked underneath her legs. Closing the door he took a small breath, her eyes expectant as he sat down, coughed and adjusted the position of his chair.

'Edith, I'm glad we now have a session together,' he said, the palm of his hand resting on her folder.

He tried to sound confident, hopeful he might glean enough information to help her, to appeal her case to the senior doctor. He was the recent graduate, he reminded himself: well versed in some of the more modern methods. If Doctor Malone could be persuaded they might work in this case, then perhaps Declan could save Edith from her fate. He opened her folder and drew out the admission notes.

'I'd like to determine a couple of things in the time I have with you . . .' He began, counting on his fingers. 'One, that your original diagnosis is correct, and two, that you are following a sensible course of treatment.'

Edith removed her hands from under her legs, loosening a little. 'Do you mean,' she said, the words coming slowly, 'that there's a chance I am not what they say I am?'

'What do they say you are?'

He saw her face flush. 'A–a . . . schizophrenic.' She stumbled on the professional term.

'The struggles with the mind are not always as easy to diagnose as a broken leg. But,' Declan added, not wanting to raise her hopes, allow her to see the doubt he had over her label, 'let's start at the beginning and see where we get, Edith.'

'Can you make me better?' She asked it quickly.

It seemed so simple put like that: make her better. Could Declan make her better? What was it that made any of them this way?

'Perhaps we will see improvements.' He adjusted the sentence. 'No, Edith, I *hope* we will see improvements.' He outlined a little about the course he had undertaken at university; he could see her listening, did his best to explain. 'Our unconscious mind can trigger behaviours; that is to say, I think the mind is a powerful thing and we can heal by discovering what is troubling us.'

She sat taller, her face hopeful. 'Will I stop having treatment now?'

'Certainly there will be no need for electric shock therapy under my care at this time,' Declan said, his voice firm.

'And you won't be watching me, watching if I need the operation?' she ventured, chewing her lip.

Declan swallowed, shuffling the notes in front of him. 'We're getting ahead of ourselves now.' He tried to smile, to put her at ease.

Edith drooped a fraction.

What more could he promise? He couldn't be sure Doctor Malone would even listen. The thought made him more determined to seek some doubt over the diagnosis, seek evidence to support his opinions.

'I know it might be bothersome, but I would like to go back and explore some of the things that meant you were first committed as a child. Would that be acceptable to you?'

Edith nodded, tapping her teeth with two fingers.

Declan felt his shoulders relax a little, heard his voice grow in strength. 'Excellent. Well, there is a large gap, but I've read some recent notes and the original file on your admission; I believe you were five?'

She nodded again, thumbnail in her mouth.

'Can you tell me in your own words how it was that you came to be at Seacliff?'

There was a pause as Edith worried at the nail in her mouth.

'Edith?' Declan leant forward in his chair and prompted her gently.

Her mouth stilled, her hand dropping back to her lap.

'I don't want to tell you the wrong thing,' she said slowly.

Declan tipped his head to the side. 'Edith, nothing you tell me can be wrong; if that is what you think or feel then it is right. Please feel that you can be completely honest with me.'

She scratched at her neck, her fingers brushing her throat over and over.

'Nothing will happen to you, I promise you that.'

She lowered her hand, nodded slowly as if convincing herself. She paused, inhaled quickly, as if building to the story. 'My parents put me here,' she said finally. 'They told me I was going to see the doctor, but then they left me here.'

Declan pictured Edith, aged five, her tiny feet padding along the flagstone floor behind the grown-ups. 'Why did they put you here?'

Her eyes darted to his. 'I said things that made Father unhappy.'

'What things?'

She looked down at her lap. 'Bad things.'

Declan coughed, wanting to push a little further but sensing he needed to tread carefully. 'What do you remember about that time?'

'I remember meeting Matron because I had never seen anyone wearing a hat like that, not even in church, and I remember seeing the rows of beds on the ward and I remember realising I wouldn't be going home because I saw Mrs Periwinkle in Mother's carpet bag on one of them.'

'I'm sorry.' Declan stopped her with an apologetic look. 'Who was Mrs Periwinkle?'

Edith's mouth lifted. 'She was my most beloved toy: a doll. She was always with me. We would have tea parties together.'

'How about before all of that? Before you came here, when you were with your parents, and Mrs Periwinkle?' He added the last part with a smile, trying to get Edith to relax, get her comfortable so that the memories would flow more easily.

'I lived with my parents.' Edith's voice was quiet as she began, peering at Declan as if checking she should continue.

Declan sat back in his chair, wanting her to feel that he was really listening.

'We lived in a white house with a porch with a swing seat on it and honey pear trees in the garden.' She was looking off into the distance behind him.

Declan nodded encouragement. 'Go on.'

'I liked the pear tree part of the garden but I didn't want to look out on the gravestones on the other side. That was where the dead people went.'

Declan frowned slightly at this, casting an eye down at the admission notes in front of him.

Edith continued, lost now in her past, 'You could hear the town clock from the house and it was loud because we were right in the centre.'

'You lived in the centre of town?' Declan turned the page, casting an eye over the first file. Edith's descriptions of her home when she was five years old didn't give that impression. 'I believed the house to be by the sea?'

Edith shook her head. 'No. Although,' she added, in a voice designed to please, 'I saw a photograph of the sea once, at Mrs

Boone's house before she died. But our house was next to the church in town. Mother liked living in the town; she would take me shopping and buy me ribbons.'

Declan turned the page of notes again, deciding to change topic. Children could confuse things. 'Tell me about your siblings.'

Edith's face looked pained. 'I had a brother. A baby brother, Peter. Things got worse when he was born; they didn't want me to . . .'

'A younger brother?' Declan turned over the statement in front of him.

'A baby brother, yes. He slept in a big basket in the room next to mine and I wore my new shoes with the blue buckle when we went to church with him in a long white dress.'

Declan felt the frustration bubble within him, the written notes in front of him and Edith's statements not making sense. 'But when you arrived at Seacliff I have a statement you made talking about your older brother.'

Edith looked up sharply, her eyes widening in panic. 'No. Peter was a baby,' she repeated, her words quickening. 'I used to hold him when he was first born. Mother didn't mind at first, but then Father told me I wasn't allowed in case I hurt him. But I would never have hurt him, Doctor. I never saw him again after I came here,' she added, her voice dropping to a whisper.

Declan traced a sentence with his finger, trying to get Edith back on familiar ground, glad she had raised the topic of her father. 'You told Doctor Malone something happened to you as a child. That you were hit.' Declan softened his voice. 'Was that your father? Did he ever hit you?'

Edith's face screwed up. 'No, Father would never hit me. He could get angry but he wouldn't hit. He often quoted from the Bible.'

121

Declan remembered reading the fact he was a pastor on the first page of Edith's file, had suspected that all the talk of possession had stemmed from her father's religious beliefs. In fact, it strengthened his own belief that Edith had been misdiagnosed in those early days.

'But you did tell Doctor Malone someone hit you as a child.' Declan looked up from the notes, the sentence in black and white, his voice a little harsher than he had meant.

'Not my father. He never hit me. I was hit but that wasn't when I was with my parents from Dunedin. That was when I was here before.'

Declan slumped a little as she spoke. 'What do you mean, "before"?'

Two furrows appeared in the middle of Edith's forehead. 'I . . . I don't know . . . I, please, forget I said anything. I don't remember now anyway. I started to forget it all years ago, I told them that and it was the truth . . .' She was appealing to Declan, palms up, an urgency in her voice.

'Please, Edith, don't become excited, I want to know what you have to say.' Declan tried to reassure her, felt he was on the cusp of something that might make all this make more sense. 'It's all very helpful.'

Edith sat back, her eyes darting from the notes in front of him to Declan, her mouth parting slightly. 'Will you punish me if I talk about before?'

'Edith, I would never punish you. Whatever we discuss here is private, between you and me.'

She leant forward, her brown eyes intense. 'Do you promise?'

Declan nodded. 'I promise.'

'If I spoke about before when I was young, they got angry, they said I was lying, then they said I had something evil inside me, another me . . . The old man and Father tried to take it out.'

She started to scratch at her chest and Declan flinched, watching her grow more uneasy.

'Edith.' He tried to inject a soothing tone in his voice. 'Please, you don't need to explain, you are free to talk about anything you remember. We are just talking.'

She squeezed her hands together again, clearly still unsure whether she should continue. 'The doctors didn't believe me either. I . . . a lot of it has faded now. I don't remember much,' she added.

'Tell me what you do remember,' Declan said, leaning forward, searching her face.

Edith inhaled slowly. 'It wasn't my father that hit me, it was my stepbrother, when I was the other girl.'

'The other girl?' Declan felt his eyebrows knit together. Another person? His confidence in her misdiagnosis started to crumble. Had Doctor Malone been right all along and Declan had just wanted to see something else?

'Yes, in the house by the sea. In Oamaru. I was a big girl.' Edith's hand tapped at her teeth again. 'I died. Then I came back.'

Declan tried to clear his head, to follow her thought process. If Edith believed herself to be two people this would suggest she was someone who believed herself to have multiple personalities; he had read about a few cases like that. He felt a heavy weight in his stomach: schizophrenia started to make some sense.

He held up a hand. 'What do you mean, you died?'

Edith swallowed. 'I lived in a house in Oamaru, called Kara . . . Kara something, when I was the other girl. My mother, Nina, had me and Mary. My stepbrother lived with us. He . . . he did things. One day he hit me and I died.'

'Do you mean,' Declan said, his forehead creased, 'there is another girl somewhere inside you?'

'No, I *was* her, when I was here before.' Edith's voice moved up a register as she tried to explain herself. 'I told them. They didn't believe me.' The words were louder now, her face flushed. 'They said I was lying but I wasn't. I wasn't lying.' Her arms flew out, big and expressive. 'I told them, Doctor Harris, I told them everything and they didn't believe me and so I had to stay here.'

Declan's hopes faded as she continued to talk to him in half-sentences. She was indeed mentally unwell. He let her continue, trying to keep his face neutral as she spoke. 'They punished me, they took me to the white room . . . It's not as clear now. I used to wake at night remembering what he did – he did bad things, Doctor, and I told them it all, and I told them where he left me when I was the other girl . . . when I was Primrose.'

Declan tried to nod in encouragement but found his body unwilling, felt his face fall, disappointment etched on it.

'He left me there in the dark.' She looked up at him, eyes rounded, and then stopped suddenly. 'You don't believe me,' she said in a tiny voice.

'I . . .' Declan cast about for something to say, not wanting to encourage her delusions but not wanting to destroy the confidence they had built together.

Tears now filmed her eyes; her bottom lip quivered. He watched a teardrop make an unsteady path down her cheek.

'Edith.' He didn't want to lie to her. It was impossible; what she was saying was impossible. 'Edith,' he repeated, 'it's not that I don't believe you. I do believe you *think* these things happened.' He was careful, his words slow. 'But,' he added gently, 'what you're saying. Well, it is impossible. You know that, don't you?'

He had engaged in lucid conversations with her; she had intelligence. She had to realise what she was saying simply didn't make sense. He had been so sure, *so* sure Doctor Malone had got it wrong. She couldn't really think these things?

She gave him a sad smile. 'I understand, Doctor.' She scraped back her chair. 'I think I'd better go now.' She straightened, brushed at her face. 'I thought maybe, maybe you would believe me, but no matter.' Her voice was light, as if they were discussing something inconsequential.

Declan found himself rooted to his seat, unable to take control, to say anything.

She didn't give him more time to react. She turned and walked across to the door, a half-wave as she looked back. 'Thank you for talking with me.'

He muttered a reply, his head clogged with the information she had given him, his thoughts jumbled. By the time he stood to call her back she had left his office.

The file was still open in front of him, the notes and her words all clashing and merging in his head. He looked back at the door; it had shut with a gentle click. He sat, picked up the first page, reread it, looking desperately at it for another angle. Then a shot of anger fired through him and he threw his pen down on the desk, ink spattering over the top page.

Chapter 21

BEFORE

Mother always dresses differently when we go to this part of town: her lips and cheeks paler, a house dress that has a tear at the collar that she's darned. We are visiting the street near the mill, the big chimney puffing, puffing, making everything seem fuzzy and grey.

We always take bread baked by Mrs Clark and knock on the doors of the houses all squeezed tight together, no hedges or gates, doors so close to the pavement you can take one giant step into the road. My neck prickles as I recall flashes of another house with smeared windows, a roof patchy with red.

We visit a mother of three young children who has a gap where a tooth should be, right at the front. Mother has told me not to stare at it. The woman is wearing the same torn singlet as last time, her hair thin and stuck to her forehead. The youngest child is only a baby, all angry round mouth, tiny fists beating the air. Mother doesn't like holding the baby, I can tell. Mary had screamed in the same way when she'd been hungry.

We haven't been inside long when I need to go. I tug on Mother's skirt, crossing my legs. Mother apologises as the woman shows me where the dunny is outside, not inside like our house. I don't want to go to the dunny in the garden, there was a dunny in the garden of the other house.

Mother shoos me and I step outside. The grass tickles my ankles as I step towards the crooked wooden building, a twisted iron bed propped up in front of it, curled brown weeds twisting around the frame. I look back at the house, see the shape of Mother in the kitchen window talking to the woman. She lifts a hand, pats her hair. She always keeps her gloves on when she's there.

I gulp as I tug at the wooden door, see a cracked seat, a dirty jug of water on the floor. I can't go in. But I really do need to go; I bob from one foot to the other before taking a step inside.

The memory hits me the moment the stench is in my nose.

I'd only been wearing a vest that day, stretched tight now that I had grown lumps like Mother had. Mother had been washing my tunic and I'd been drawing things in the dust behind the tin bath.

He'd called to me from the bottom of the wooden steps and I'd stood, the wood scratchy under my bare feet.

'Primrose' – his voice was different now, lower since he'd grown so tall – 'I've got something to show you.'

I hadn't wanted to go. I could hear Mother talking to his father in the kitchen; I wanted to go to them.

'Come on, you'll like it,' he said, nodding to the washhouse. 'Or I suppose I could show Mary.'

I'd scrabbled after him then.

He'd disappeared inside and I'd followed him.

The darkness had been immediate and I'd fallen against the wall with a sharp, high cry as the lock slid shut.

Spinning, I felt my palms scrape against the wood as I'd tried to steady myself. I was so close to the dumpy hole I could hear the flies and the stink all around me, in my nose and hair; something scuttled across my neck in a whisper.

It was a moment before I realised he was saying my name.

'Primrose,' he sang, so that I span round in the darkness, stomach rolling at the smell.

'Pack it in,' I said, trying to sound bolder than I felt. He was two years older, but in that instant it felt like more.

'Want to be let out, Primrose?'

Where was his voice coming from? It seemed as if it was all around me.

I nodded, not able to make out shapes, rooted in the tiny space.

'What's that?' he laughed, enjoying my fear. He'd liked it when he'd crept up on me the week before in my bedroom, pushing me down on the bed, arms pinning me. He'd liked it when he'd followed me to the creek, springing up from a rock so that I'd toppled in with surprise, when he'd stepped towards me in the cave . . .

'I'll let you out, but I've got something I want you to do for me,' he said, his voice close, my skin suddenly bumpy through the thin layer of my vest.

His hand grabbed at me and I moaned as he pushed me up against the wood, damp, cold. His body was pressed against me, his mouth suddenly on my neck as his fingers pulled at the vest, as they climbed up my stomach. Cigarettes and shit.

I have fallen in the doorway, my knees scratched and sore, my chest rising and falling. I twist and push against the wood, land on my hands on the soft mud outside with a cry. The daylight is shocking and I blink over and over, back outside the wooden outhouse.

The smell fades; the smoke of the mill curls in the sky. Mother is still in the kitchen with the lady with the missing tooth.

I am not back there; I am not with him; I am safe.

Chapter 22

NOW

Declan stamped along the sand, feeling the wind behind him, nudging him gently on. He had been wrong. The Edith he thought existed seemed to be a fabrication of his own hopes. He had read the statement of five-year-old Edith in Doctor Malone's scrawled handwriting: hard to follow, a collection of claims about being hit, about living by the sea, about being left alone. He had dismissed them as the ramblings of a frightened child, not evidence of something medically relevant.

It did seem plausible that perhaps a traumatised child would break away part of herself to survive, become someone else, this other girl who knew swear words and smoked cigarettes and was the rebel that the young Edith wished she could be.

The things she said now, though – that this other girl had existed, not been part of her: that was impossible.

He stopped, turning towards the slate-coloured sea, looking out to the horizon, watching a carrier move across the water. The war in the Pacific seemed a distant thing at that moment, lost as he was in the battle going on inside himself. What could he do to help her? The mind was complex and Declan knew there were things they still couldn't explain; the consequences of undergoing a devastating trauma.

There was something in Edith's manner that seemed so innocent, so guileless. She carried herself with a quiet dignity. He had been fooled into believing she might be sane. There was no other word for it. He had felt her mind connect with his in the times when they had spoken. He imagined her in another setting, a tea shop perhaps, licking her finger as she turned the page of a book, her curls tied back, an appraising gaze as he approached, a quiet confidence. He'd thought Edith had slipped through the cracks, tarred with an old, inaccurate diagnosis. He'd desperately wanted to prove Doctor Malone wrong, prove she did not need more treatment.

He kicked at the shingle underfoot, his shoes now soaked through. He needed to head back. All her talk of before and being another person were ravings he hadn't expected. Perhaps she believed herself to have been that other girl; perhaps she really did believe herself to be more than one person. He paused on the shore as he realised she would likely spend the rest of her life at Seacliff. He recalled his first week working there, a nurse talking about Julia, a widow who never spoke, found lying dead in her bed. He imagined Edith the same age: hair thinned, white over time, lines deep on her face and neck, liver spots on her hand. She would know nothing apart from the experiences within the building. He shivered and wrapped his arms around himself.

He turned to leave the beach, trying to leave all thoughts of his meeting with her out on the sand, to be swept away on the breeze, broken up by the wind.

Some of what she said niggled at him as he walked all the way up through the fields to the driveway of Seacliff. Such specific details. Some would be easy to check, he thought, as he stamped his sandy feet on the steps outside, wiped his shoes along the boot scraper. If he could dismiss them completely as ravings, perhaps that would help him make peace with it all; he could be satisfied it was over.

There was barely a change in temperature as he moved quickly down the dark stone corridors, his steps quick as he thought of his destination. He arrived, nodded at a nurse he didn't know who was sitting at a table, thick glasses, nose-deep in a book. Two patients browsed shelves behind her; one was sitting on a window seat. The nurse noticed him then, flushing pink, placing her book down, spine up, as he moved across the room.

He nodded at her and she tentatively reached for her book again. Moving across to the small corner section of the patients' library, he scanned the shelves of the dusty geography bookcase, reaching for the atlas with both hands. It was enormous and impossibly heavy. He laid it down on a nearby table on its front, turning over the back cover to look at the index. Drawing a finger down to the correct letter he picked out the name, noting the page number and grid reference. Muttering them to himself he carefully flicked back until he reached the right spot.

Tracing his finger down the correct page he followed the line where land met sea and then he stopped. There it was. A district in Oamaru. The town itself was about a hundred kilometres north of Seacliff. The district Edith had mentioned all those years ago did exist. Yet her family had lived in Dunedin.

So how had she known? Had she heard the name somewhere? Did they have family there? He was about to close the atlas when he noticed a symbol, just off the coast near the place Edith had named. He looked up the symbol in the key at the front. He frowned, a small curiosity lit. He remembered a memory written in Edith's admission statement about this landmark.

Impossible.

It was a coincidence. It had to be. He closed the book with a small thud and lifted it to place back on the shelf. A lucky guess, he thought, as he slid it into position, or something she had picked up from another patient? He couldn't be fooled any more; he had been wrong about her.

He walked back across the library and down the corridor into his office. Her notes were still laid out on the desk in front of him and he stood over the scattered sheets for a moment. Then, with a decisive sigh, he piled them all back into the folder and stepped across to the filing cabinet to return them.

Chapter 23

NOW

Edith looked less tired today, arriving in his office with a small smile, her curly hair pinned back, her cheeks flushed from being outside.

She pulled out a small white flower from her cardigan pocket and held it up. 'Isn't it lovely?' She thrust it towards him and he found himself leaning towards her, half-closing his eyes to sniff at the petals before she pressed it to her own nose.

'Very pretty.' He righted himself, wondering whether it was her unpredictability that had first piqued his interest in her. He moved behind his desk and sat down as she perched on the chair opposite him, ready to talk. He was determined to start this session afresh, gauge how he could help her moving forward.

'I love the warmer weather,' she said, her voice light, conversational as she tucked the small flower back in her pocket. 'The flower garden always looks best in the sunlight.'

He found himself struggling to reply. This was a different Edith from the raving, nervous Edith of the day before: relaxed, confident, sane; the Edith that made him wonder whether Doctor Malone had got it completely wrong.

'You enjoy your work in the gardening gang?' he asked.

Her face darkened, as if the sun outside had ducked behind a cloud. She half whispered the next words. 'I did. I am now in the kitchen gang, since what happened.'

'I'm sorry, I hadn't realised,' Declan said. He thought back to the notes on Edith's recent behaviour. There had been an episode in her dormitory, a violent attack on another woman – a woman called Donna whom he'd never known but who had perished in the fire. The electric shock treatment had started again after that day, and various privileges had been removed.

He quickly moved the subject on. 'What other things do you like to do?'

'I like my flute,' she said, 'and I like being part of the orchestra. Music can just carry you off and out of things, can't it?'

He found he was nodding, enjoying her reflections, remembering how she had sat, her instrument resting in her lap. He stopped, tugged on his tie before hastily jotting down a few notes.

'And I love being part of something bigger, making something together. Do you like being part of the orchestra, Doctor Harris?'

He stopped writing and looked up, a little startled, not used to patients turning the tables on him. 'Oh, yes.' He cleared his throat. 'I do.'

'The trumpet wouldn't suit me at all, far too bold,' she said. 'I would hate for everyone to hear my wrong notes.'

Declan laughed at that. 'Oh dear, is it that obvious?'

She looked horrified, a hand flying to her chest. 'Oh no, Doctor, I wasn't meaning you. I just meant, how loud it is and . . .'

He stopped her with a smile. 'Don't worry, Edith, I'm not offended. I was teasing.'

'Oh.' She let out a relieved exclamation and laughed. A soft sound, quick and light.

Declan wanted to keep her talking; he wanted her to laugh again. 'Tell me about some of your best times, Edith. What makes you feel happy?'

Edith bit her lip and then, as if he'd granted her permission, she began to talk quickly. She told him about Patricia, about the fun they'd had when they were little, creeping into the kitchens, sneaking tit-bits from Clive, who always saved them buns with extra raisins.

'And we'd have to hide them or Matron would be told, so Patricia would stuff them in her shirtsleeves. She could be so naughty, but so fun.'

She told him about the dances they made up down in the pavilion in summer, and Malcolm finding them dissolved in giggles on the lawn. She told him about their outings down to the village to the pictures. She loved the smooth-faced movie stars, the flickering black-and-white show.

She was quiet again for a time and Declan watched her face change, her eyes become dull as she looked to the side, not meeting his eye. 'Going to the pictures was always Bernie's favourite thing. Apart from playing with Misty.'

'Who was Misty?' Declan encouraged.

Edith worried at her sleeve, her eyes fixed over his shoulder. 'Bernie's cat.'

Declan assumed the slightly strange reaction was down to Edith remembering her friend.

'Bernie loved Misty,' Edith added.

'Bernadette,' Declan added softly. 'Yes, she spoke about her once. She was a patient of mine, before . . .'

'I know.' Edith looked back at him now. 'She loved meeting with you, Doctor, she would tell me that.'

Declan cupped a hand round his neck, rubbing. 'That is very nice to hear.'

'She knew you would be able to help her. And you did, Doctor. She said you were different from the other doctors. I understand now.' Edith looked at him with such an open face he found himself growing hot with delighted embarrassment.

'And what' – Declan cleared his throat again – 'what do you most miss about Bernie?'

Edith pursed her mouth together, her eyes unfocused. 'I miss lots of things. She would ask me to do her hair. She told me I was like an older sister.'

He watched her face closely, her expression softening as she spoke, her lips parted as she paused. He found he was staring at them, waiting for more words.

'You sound like you were very close,' he commented.

Edith opened her mouth to say something else, and then closed it again. Tears swam in her eyes and Declan found himself pushing back his chair, moving around his desk to offer her a handkerchief. As he leaned towards her he smelt her familiar fragrance – citrus, reminding him of sunshine, freshly cut grass. He found his head swimming in it; Edith's words, when they emerged, blurred as he was brought back to the room.

'I miss her holding me. You never touch anyone here.'

Declan felt his proximity to her, swallowing as he struggled for something to say. He could feel her breath on his neck and he straightened quickly.

He felt a small relief when he heard distant whistles, footsteps slapping on stone, a door slammed hard. Declan wondered if another patient had escaped.

Edith fell quiet, seeming to listen to the noises too.

'It's always loud, isn't it?' she said. 'There's always something happening.'

He nodded, thinking of the whispers that morning at breakfast amongst the staff. He didn't tell Edith about the discovery in the toilet block next to the boiler house. That one of the male patients had hanged himself with a towel. The whistles again, manic laughter: she was right, there was always something happening.

Declan walked over to the window, wanting to move on from his own dark thoughts. 'Where would you go, Edith, if you wanted to be calm?' he asked, looking across the lawn and down towards the sea. The grass had been mown, stripes in different shades of green. He turned to see Edith, head tipped to one side, face bathed in sunshine. The light from the window was turning strands of her hair a warm chestnut.

'To the summerhouse, I think. I like it down there. Or the orchard, the trees filled with different fruit. When I am allowed to walk around the grounds again, that's where I'll go.'

'What about outside Seacliff?' Declan asked, moving round to sit behind his desk.

'Outside?' She repeated the word as if it were an impossible thing.

'If you could travel somewhere,' he asked.

He didn't think she was going to answer him. Then she looked up, her eyes sparkling. 'I'd want to sit by a lake surrounded by mountains. I saw a picture once in an encyclopedia, of Lake Tekapo . . .'

'I've been there,' Declan said excitedly, forgetting for a moment where he was. 'We pitched a tent next to the water. I saw so many shooting stars from there, it was extraordinary.'

Edith was looking at him with rounded eyes as he imagined a child might look at a magician. 'Shooting stars,' she breathed.

'Have you ever seen one?'

Edith shook her head and Declan cursed himself for his stupidity. Edith slept in a room with locked shutters; the high windows in the dormitories were often barred. There was no chance of them star-gazing from there.

'I'm sorry, Edith, that was crass of me.'

She smiled at him, shrugging a shoulder. 'That's quite all right, Doctor, I like to hear your stories. They sound exciting.'

'You might be the first person to ever call me that.' He laughed. She shared his mirth and in that moment he knew he must help her. Although Edith was most likely sick, he did know that she was not a volatile, violent patient: of that he was certain. He must persuade Doctor Malone that Edith did not warrant an operation.

He hadn't heard the knock or noticed the door opening, and suddenly Nurse Shaw appeared in the space. The noise they were making must have drowned it out and he found himself straightening in his chair, rearranging his expression. Edith was still giggling as the nurse announced herself.

'I'm sorry – I'm obviously interrupting, Doctor.'

'Oh,' Edith said, looking round. 'Nurse Shaw, Doctor Harris has been making me feel so much better. Did you know he's been to Lake Tekapo?'

Declan felt a swell of pride flood through him, gratified to hear the lift in Edith's voice.

Nurse Shaw raised a neatly pencilled eyebrow. 'That sounds very nice, Edith,' she said in a tone that Declan hadn't heard her use before, as if she were talking to a dog or child. 'Now, shall we get along back to the ward? You'll be wanting to join your kitchen gang to prepare dinner, won't you? Doctor Harris is a very busy man, so we must let him get on.'

Edith stood up, her previous confidence already slipping as she walked over to the doorway, meek in the face of authority. 'Of course. Thank you, Doctor Harris,' she said, facing away from him, the words mumbled.

Declan felt a flash of annoyance at the nurse. He had made progress with Edith in this short session, and now it all seemed to be ebbing away. He stood up behind his desk. 'Not at all, Edith, it was very good to talk you today, and we'll continue in our next session.'

Edith turned then, looking directly at him. 'I'd like that,' she said, her voice strong.

Nurse Shaw took her elbow. 'Let's get along now.' She turned to Declan. 'Doctor,' she said, nodding.

Declan tried to smile at her as she walked Edith out of his office, a hand still on the young woman's arm as they moved into the corridor.

He sat down slowly at his desk, tapping a pencil on the blotting pad in front of him. He looked down to see he had etched a large, cursive 'E' on to the top page of his notes, and quickly scrunched up the paper in his fist.

Chapter 24

THEN

They had unlocked the doors but Edith just lay there. It was one of those days when she wanted to stay in her small, square room, on her bed, stare at the marks on the bare ceiling, the damp streaks, the too-familiar patterns in the grain. The room was stuffy; she imagined the building surrounded by the heavy sea fogs that could settle over the place, turn the horizon into a milky soup. She could hear shouts coming down through the wooden floorboards from the dormitory, feet pounding: sometimes she imagined hell was above her.

Her lids wanted to close; she craved sleep but she couldn't relax, wondering all the time if this was when they were going to get her, searching her room for things they might have left there. She checked every drawer, wondering if her comb had been left at that angle, if her flute had been taken out of its case, if the wooden chair in the corner was a little nearer the bed than before.

Donna and Martha had been back last night. She had heard noises on the stairs, the smell of cigarettes like a vapour, and their voices, softly, softly. 'Not long now,' they whispered, before a note was pushed under her door, a crude pencil drawing of her naked that had made her retch into her chamber pot. They would use the key to her room. It was only a matter of time. She knew she couldn't tell anyone again, could only make things worse for herself. The days and the nights were muddling now, and she'd had the dream again last night when she had finally fallen asleep. She hadn't had it for years, not since she had first arrived at the building.

Her room was filling up with sea water, more lapping through the door. She had stepped out of bed, shocked at the cold, scooping pointlessly with her chamber pot as the water just kept coming. She was screaming, pounding the walls, the shutters, rattling the door until her fists bled, calling out. The water kept coming. She couldn't stop it. It inched its way towards her, soaked her feet, made her gasp in shock as it slowly climbed her legs, submerged her bed, her whole body shivering as she thrashed across the room in it, her nightclothes sticking to her body.

She couldn't swim; she was going to drown.

She felt the water cover her chest, lifted her head, tried to keep her face out of it, tasted salt on her lips. She screamed again and again, felt her whole body lift, the floor leave her, legs moving in water, not able to stand, her body pushed against the wall, the water choking her, running into her mouth, nose, eyes. She had woken then and hadn't been able to sleep since. She felt like she did after the treatment, not quite there in the room, groggy and slow. She wasn't sure she could get up if she wanted to. And if she did, what would be the point?

A sound outside the door and Edith struggled up on to two elbows: wide awake, tense.

'Edie,' Bernie said as she appeared in the door, pink back in her cheeks now she'd finally shaken off her cold, her eyes sparkling with news, her mouth spilling out words so quickly Edith struggled to keep up, collapsing back down with the effort.

'It's Visitors' Day. Everyone's getting ready. Do you think they'll come?' Bernie asked, not stopping for a reply, moving across to sit at the foot of the bed. 'They must this time, it's been ages and I've been so much better. I told them what Doctor Harris said, that he thinks I am making excellent progress . . .'

Bernie often talked about the new doctor; she saw him almost every week, and when she told him things he just listened and talked back and didn't send her anywhere for treatment. 'When I'm in there I feel like I'll get better,' she'd told her. Edith had felt herself freeze when Bernie had said it, knowing if Bernie got better she would leave her at Seacliff alone, but then she realised that was a good thing for Bernie, so she smiled back.

Edith still saw Doctor Malone once a month; he told her to keep taking the red pills and she tried not to talk at all.

'. . . in their letters they promised they'd come.' Bernie had never stopped writing letters to her parents, sitting at the table in the dayroom, leaning over the page. Edith didn't know what she put in them; even if she could write like Bernie she didn't know what she would say. She knew she would have to be careful not to write anything much; someone was always listening and probably reading, too, and then you'd get treatment if you wrote the wrong thing. Edith didn't get letters anyway. When she'd first started delivering the mail, she'd needed help with some of the names on the envelopes and telegrams, but the letters never turned into her own name.

'I hope they bring me my treasure box. They know I miss it and I keep asking. It's my birthday soon, so maybe they'll bring me a present too.' Bernie hugged herself as she spoke and Edith sat up slowly, moved her mouth into a smile. Of course she wanted her to have visitors, wanted her parents to come.

'They were at a wedding last time so they couldn't come, and the time before that Father wasn't well and couldn't face the

142

train journey. And I won't talk about the baby like last time. So maybe . . .' Bernie tailed off, pulling a comb from her pocket and holding it out to Edith. 'Will you make me look pretty for them, Edith? Pretty like you.'

Edith licked her dry lips and croaked a reply, reaching for her comb. 'Of course,' she said, beckoning Bernie to sit.

The visitors came in a rush, a few in motorcars, trucks, many more walking up from the train station below in a large clump. Edith could see them if she peeked through the window of her room where the latch had broken and she could push it out just an inch. She could see all the tops of their heads; hats, shoulders, hands clutching handbags, heads bowed towards each other as if they were talking, moving in the same direction like the birds she sometimes saw in the sky. It seemed like that now, no one breaking away, all disappearing around the corner, heading for the heavy door to the main building.

Normally she stayed in her room on Visitors' Day, knowing no one would come for her. She knew what had happened to her parents; Doctor Malone had told her more than ten years ago.

She'd been eight years old. Bernie hadn't been there then, or Shirley, Martha and Donna. Patricia and Edith would play together. Patricia had a teddy bear that she let Edith hold and they would take the bear everywhere with them; Teddy was his name and they made Teddy dinners and gave him treatment and made him better, although he was still a loony like them.

They'd been sitting on the stone bench out in the garden when one of the nurses came to get her. The nurse, she couldn't remember her name now, had worn tortoiseshell clips in her hair, the edges peeking out below her hat, and had so many lines on her face. That nurse left years ago after a special tea in the dayroom where Matron made a speech and they all clapped because she was going to retire

143

to a house in the village, and they all ate rock cakes. She came and got Edith that day and she took her to the superintendent's office.

Edith felt goosebumps spring up on her arms as she followed, the questions already banging around inside her head. Why was she going to the superintendent's office? What had she done now? What had she said? She hadn't mentioned being the other girl.

They stopped outside the office and Edith felt popping and bubbling inside her stomach. The nurse reached for her hand; it had been all dry, and Edith remembered she'd called her dearie and kissed her hair before leaving her there. Edith touched her head where she had felt the kiss.

The kiss filled her with hope: a memory of being touched. She remembered praying she'd see her mother on the other side of the door; that she'd be allowed to go home again, that she was better, and she wouldn't have to have treatment and could go to a proper school. She opened the door quickly, rearranging her face for her mother, and then wondered why the room was empty apart from Doctor Malone, who was standing next to a bookshelf filled with leather books on her right, and a man sitting behind the most enormous dark-brown wooden desk.

Her eyes had immediately shot to Doctor Malone, who'd been wearing his jacket with the brown corduroy collar and the silver thing that he listened to your heart with round his neck. She remembered her chest leaping, her body getting all hot, as she didn't want more treatment. She hadn't mentioned being her for an age. She hadn't said anything about her stepbrother who'd attacked her. Why would they choose now? She thought back to what she'd said last time, but it didn't make any sense. It wasn't fair.

She stood in the open doorway until Doctor Malone summoned her forward. She waited in front of the big desk and watched the superintendent stand up. She couldn't see his face; it was mostly in shadow, a large window behind him, but as she looked up she

144

could make out a pair of spectacles on the end of his nose that he removed when he spoke.

The man put out an arm and pointed to a stiff leather chair. She hadn't understood until Doctor Malone told her to sit in it. Then she had struggled to get up on to it, the cushion squeaking as she moved. It had curved wooden arms and she hadn't sat in a chair like that before. Then the man offered her a large round biscuit from a little china plate on the desk and she nodded and thanked him as she took the biscuit, and a lot of what he said at the start she couldn't remember because the food there wasn't very nice and she wasn't given biscuits.

The superintendent moved to the side of the desk and wasn't looking at her as he spoke. He was talking about Hawke's Bay in the North Island. Edith had cousins there; her mother's brother lived there. She wondered if her mother's brother was visiting her. But then why was she in the superintendent's office?

'You know there's been an earthquake, Edith,' he said as he tapped his glasses against the palm of his other hand.

She nodded her head up and down. The nurses had been talking about it and they had felt something a few days before in the morning in the dayroom, as if something had made the earth tremble. She didn't really know what an earthquake was but heard that the roads split and lots of buildings fell down. She'd heard one of the attendants say heavy stone things had dropped on people.

'I'm afraid your parents and younger brother were victims. It's been confirmed this morning.'

She didn't say anything. She imagined her parents and her baby brother Peter, who wouldn't be a baby any more, he'd be a little boy, and a heavy stone falling on all of them. She blinked quickly, didn't want to think about stone and buildings and earthquakes. The biscuit was sticking to the roof of her mouth.

'Do you understand, Edith? They're dead.'

She nodded again, quickly. She didn't want to be in the super-intendent's office any more, and she didn't want to be in the stupid chair. She looked over at Doctor Malone who had been watching her, his eyes smaller, his hands frozen in front of him as if he was about to catch something. When she looked at him he didn't lower his hands; he stepped forward as if about to grab her. 'Edith, do you understand what the superintendent is telling you?'

'They've died.'

As she said the words, she realised she did know what he'd told her. Her parents and her little brother were dead because of the earthquake, because they'd fallen down in a split in the road, down, down, down, or been squashed by a building. They were gone. She moved on the leather, the backs of her legs sticking to the seat.

'I'm afraid so,' the superintendent said. 'We'll let you know when the funeral is, although of course you won't be able to go.'

She'd looked up then. 'Go?' She imagined leaving Seacliff, walking down the long driveway, past the neat borders, flowers in every colour, past the gates and the man who sat in the little hut by them, down to the train station and away on the train, the steam billowing in a cloud as the whistle blew loud and so clear she could hear it from her bed on the ward.

'To the funeral,' the superintendent confirmed. 'Right now, I'm going to be getting on with some work, so, Doctor, if you could escort Miss Garrett back to the dayroom, that will be all.'

She allowed Doctor Malone to help her off the leather seat, walked back along the corridor with him, his shiny shoes enormous next to her feet; she stared at those shoes as they walked in silence, just the sound of his heavy soles, on stone, on wood and then stop-ping outside the dayroom. Everything felt different, as if she and Doctor Malone were the only people left. He put a hand on her shoulder and she felt her body automatically lean away, imagining that hand securing the pads on the sides of her head. He removed it, muttering something under his breath; his moustache, browner then, only flecked with grey, moving. She stared at him, not hearing the words, and was then ushered inside to a waiting nurse.

Her parents were her only visitors. They had come three times, on her birthdays, and now she didn't know when her birthday was. After the earthquake no one came. She did think of her parents sometimes. She could remember her mother most clearly; she had flushed cheeks and a voice that always sounded slightly out of breath. She had made her hot milk before bed and had brushed her curly hair every morning in long strokes till it shone. Her father had talked about God a lot; he spoke at the front of the church under the big wooden cross and Mother and her would watch him from the front pew. At home he would always carry a Bible around with him but he never opened it when he quoted from it; he knew it from in his head.

Bernie was desperate to look her best, was wiping at her face, licking her thumb and scrubbing at her skin, wanting to get rid of any marks. She had got like this before, got Edith to comb her hair, pin it back, smooth it until she stood, shoulders back, chin lifted, asking her to say something, to tell her she looked perfect. Last time Edith had waited with her outside on the stone bench as the visitors trooped past. They'd stayed there until the hubbub of voices returned, after a short time, away from the dayroom; parcels handed over, promises made, they swarmed back past in a group, pace quick until they got far enough away down the drive and felt they could slow up. Bernie hadn't wanted to move from that bench, just in case.

Now that was all forgotten and she grinned at Edith, eyes flashing. 'Will you come?' she asked, and Edith found herself nodding in agreement, the heavy weight inside her lightening a fraction.

'Of course, if you like.'

'I'm nervous.' Bernie laughed, holding her stomach with two hands as she watched Edith slip on her shoes.

She went ahead and Edith followed, looking back once at the small room.

They sat on one of the benches that had been pushed back against the wall of the dayroom, like when they had dances sometimes and you had to wait there to be asked. One time, Franklin the attendant who smirked and smiled at her with rubbery lips asked her. She'd been the only one on the bench and she hadn't wanted to dance with him and his hands were all slippy and hot but she'd had to.

They were waiting now and the dayroom started to fill up. Edith saw Martha sitting on the edge of one of the red, vinyl-covered chairs. A small, older woman with dark-brown hair with strands of grey sat opposite and a boy, probably about five or six, squirmed in a chair next to her. He was holding a wooden train carriage in one hand and running the wheels up and down one table leg. Martha's face was transformed; Edith thought she looked almost pretty as she leaned over to talk to the boy, reaching to stroke his cheek.

Donna was some way off on the other side of the room, leaning, one foot up against the wall, staring at Martha and the boy; looking for all the world as if she was hungry, as if she wanted to gobble them both up.

Shirley crossed the room, sat down opposite an older couple, spilling out over her chair as she started to cry almost immediately, head down in her thick arms, getting louder. Nurse Shaw came in, talked to the group quietly and Shirley got even louder until most of the room were watching. The woman inclined her head back, blinking at the ceiling as if to stem tears; the man went to stand as the nurse tried to quieten Shirley, one hand circling her back.

There was no Patricia today. Edith wondered whether she would still run into her mother's arms, whether the new Patricia knew she had a mother at all. She would have hated to see the dayroom all messed up. But then she remembered new Patricia wouldn't notice anything different about the chairs and she felt the same mood descend on her that she'd woken with that morning, as if the grey sky outside was inside her head, heavy and fat with unshed tears.

There was Julia with the same glum look; she wasn't reacting to the man sitting opposite her keeping up a one-sided conversation, looking at the clock on the wall and going on and on. He could have been the same age as her, had the same-shaped nose, the same narrow face.

The voices were low with the occasional muffled sob or weary sigh. Martha was still talking to the little boy, leaning across the table. Edith looked around and caught Donna's glare. Even in a room of people it made her breath catch in her throat, her hands cold. Donna pushed herself off the wall and stepped across the room to the door. Edith's eyes didn't leave her. It was only when she stepped outside that she felt the air rush back into her body, her muscles unclench. She tried not to think of the night before, the certainty that Donna had been there. Would she ever be able to close her eyes, feel safe again?

Bernie hadn't noticed; she was still jerking her head over to the door, the window and back as if her parents were about to rush in, apologise for their lateness, take a seat at one of the square tables.

The hands of the clock dragged round and they watched as the first visitor scraped back his chair, his wife in her Sunday best following, square handbag held out in front of her like a shield. This seemed to be the signal to other visitors, and gradually the room emptied until it was just in-patients and nurses scattered around the room. Bernie was silent.

'I'm sure they'll come next time,' Edith reassured her, a second too late.

Bernie paused for a moment and then gave her a watery smile. 'You're right.' She nodded. 'They'll be planning to come for my birthday.' She snuck her hand into Edith's and squeezed.

Edith smiled back at her. 'Of course. That's it.'

Chapter 25

NOW

Declan didn't know why he was going there. It was his day off; he barely had one a month. He tried to convince himself he was an explorer, heading north for the sheer joy of the coastal road and the freedom of release for a whole day. The Bedford truck belonged to the hospital. He stood watching the man fill the tank with the rationed amount, the copper bristles of his beard bright in the weak sunshine, chewing on something, a bored faraway look, one hand held out for the money.

Back on the road he had the window down, his elbow up, shirtsleeves rolled over his forearms. In the mirror he watched the turrets and towers of Seacliff disappear in the distance and, as the breeze entered the truck, whipping at his face and hair, he had a sudden urge to holler, to cry out, smacking his hand on the steering wheel instead. He was free. He glanced for a second at the empty passenger seat, imagining for a moment someone else sitting there. A corkscrew head of curls appeared in his consciousness and he shook his head as if trying to shake off the image.

It wasn't long before the buildings were clustered closer together and he was driving into the centre of Oamaru, passing hand-painted signs to the harbour, crude line drawings, a faded poster for boat trips, sightings of blue penguins promised.

He parked the truck, taking an age to do it, unused to such a big vehicle, back and forward inch by inch, feeling heat in his face as he finally switched the engine off. Stepping out and stretching he looked up to see fat clouds butting up against each other, the sky a blend of different shades of grey, the sun all but hidden. He wrapped his coat around himself, picked up the notepad from the passenger seat and put on his hat.

He checked the rough sketch he had made that morning, reread some of the details from Edith's admission statement: vague, childish sentences. The 'house with the red roof', 'the house with the dunny out back', the 'house by the sea'. He felt a small wave of hopelessness wash over him as he looked across the road at large stone buildings, people moving past on the pavements, shops, barbers, tobacconists; overwhelmed with where to begin.

A woman with a basket in one hand and a harried expression on her face was approaching. Too young, he thought, as he cleared his throat, rehearsing already how best to engage a stranger. He skirted round her, feeling more and more foolish with each step. He could be drinking coffee in Dunedin, reading the papers; not here, wandering streets that were alien to him, pursuing a niggling, impossible thought.

An elderly man in a cloth cap was sitting on a bench outside the tobacconist's, his two hands resting on his thighs as if waiting for something to happen. Declan stepped into the road and headed towards him.

The man looked up as he approached.

Declan indicated the bench. 'Do you mind?'

The man neither nodded nor shook his head.

Declan sat, his body angled towards the man. 'It might rain,' he began, cursing his lack of originality as the elderly man agreed with a look at the sky and a curt nod.

He needed to dive in, he thought. He needed to ask him. It wasn't strange. He didn't need to explain why. He could be anyone looking for a distant relative.

'I'm looking for someone – a family who lived in this area, or live here still,' he added, knowing the words were coming out too quickly.

The man turned towards him a little, nodding his head towards a row of shops. 'The wife's in buying a hat. She has so many hats. I told her there's a war on but . . .' He shrugged, leaving Declan to guess at the rest of the sentence.

Declan nodded, trying to convey sympathy.

'So, go on,' the elderly man continued, as if Declan was simple.

'There was a woman, Nina. She lived in Oamaru in the 1920s. In a house with a red roof,' he added, feeling his tongue thick in his mouth. 'A house near the sea.'

Even as he heard the words leave his mouth, he knew it was hopeless. The elderly man had already pursed his lips together, was slowly shaking his head from side to side. 'Don't know a Nina.'

'And the um . . . the red roof?' Declan added in a less confident voice.

The man screwed up his face, his skin weathered as if he was often outside. 'Lots of them.'

Declan was already making to leave.

The man shifted on the bench. 'You could ask her.' He indicated a woman emerging from a shop door.

She had already started talking as she made her way across the road. 'They are getting new stock in on Tuesday so he says I should see him then. They've got some things being delivered from

Auckland . . .' She didn't acknowledge Declan, who had stood and was awkwardly turning the rim of his hat around in his hands.

The elderly man cut her off with a raised hand. 'Bronwyn, this young man is looking for a family.'

Bronwyn stopped short, her amber eyes turned on Declan, one of the pupils a little off-centre so he wasn't absolutely sure where he should look. He found himself flustered, forgetting the details, fumbling for the notepad. 'Thank you, sir, madam. Yes, I was wondering if you've ever known a woman named Nina?'

'I have.' The woman said it slowly, as if nervous about revealing as much, but then, as if she couldn't resist, she blurted, 'I know two, in fact . . .'

Declan felt something inside him lift. He licked his lips.

'Although one died; must have been three years ago now because we were living in Brooker Street. Was that three years ago?'

The man shrugged. 'All merges together now. I still think we're in our forties and I could last a full game of rugby.'

The woman ignored him and looked Declan up and down as if assessing whether to continue to help him. 'Are you a relation?' One eyebrow arched as she asked the question.

'A . . . a friend of mine is,' he said, slowly. 'Distantly,' he added, hoping the lie didn't show. He was a dreadful liar. He tried to look at the woman, but the eye had thrown him off balance again and he knew he was looking nervous. He cleared his throat.

'Well, Nina Jones lived here all her life . . .'

'How old was Mrs Jones?'

'Miss. She never married. Rumours were that she had a sweetheart once, but nothing came of it . . .'

Declan tried to look interested, doubting this was the right woman, if she had never married.

'She must have been born in the 1870s sometime; her brother was the editor of the *Oamaru Mail*. They printed one of your letters, dear, do you remember?'

Her husband didn't have time to react before she continued, 'She was tiny and she lived in one of the houses on Willow Road. She used to run a committee on the preservation of the precinc—'

Declan tried to cut her off, but it seemed she was now determined to share every detail of this deceased woman's life. Finally, after another few facts, Declan was able to say, 'She isn't the right age. The woman I'm looking for would now be in her fifties or thereabouts, and she would have had children.'

The woman opened, then closed her mouth again. 'Fifties.'

Declan nodded. 'She lived in a house with a red roof and was possibly a seamstress. She would make clothes.'

'A lot of us make our own clothes,' the woman said with another arch of the eyebrow.

Declan was getting nowhere fast. 'Do you remember much about the other Nina?'

The woman raised her voice a fraction, not hiding her annoyance at Declan's interruption. 'She was here a few years, married, but then he left and she lived with a man, Rowland – you remember' – she turned to look at her husband – 'quite the scandal, although we didn't move in those circles; they weren't the right sort, if you understand me. She did do some mending for people I knew.'

Declan felt the breath suspended in his body for a moment. This woman sounded like a possible match. 'What age was she?'

'Oh, she'd be late forties or so now, I'd think.'

Her doubt threw Declan off his stride. 'How do you mean, you think?'

'She hasn't lived here in years. They moved away after the war ended, that I'm sure, a long time ago now.'

'Away, where?'

'Well, I don't know. It's not my way to get into other people's business.'

Her husband made the smallest cough and Declan glanced at him, a thin smile already fading.

'So they no longer live here.' Declan felt his body slump as he said the words, his excitement draining away. He didn't want to hear the answer.

What else could he ask? It had all seemed tantalisingly close. For a few seconds he'd imagined the woman directing him to a house with a red roof and a washhouse in the garden, chickens pecking at the dirt, a woman with an apron tied around her waist greeting him from an open door. It was all over. They had moved away. There was no one to find. Of course there was no one to find; what had he been thinking? And yet for a second, the details of Edith's imaginings had seemed real, had seemed like something she really had experienced. He was about to make his exit.

'Wild family in many ways,' the woman said suddenly, as if aware she was losing her audience. 'The girl left.'

'Left?' Declan stopped, turning back. 'Left with the family?' He was confused now.

'There was a girl. Nina had a daughter with her first husband, I forget her name. She ran away a little time before they upped and moved. The woman collapsed in the grocery aisle once – my friend told me she had to summon the doctor.'

'Ran away where?' Declan asked.

The woman gave him the look that told him she thought he was a simpleton. 'That's rather the point of running away, isn't it?'

'But was she ever found?'

'Well, I'm not sure now. I don't think so, but perhaps. I didn't know them myself.'

'Why was she running away?'

The woman raised both eyebrows. 'Blow me down if I know. Young people – could be anything. She had a name that was a flower. Unusual.'

Declan felt unease swirl within him.

The woman paused for a moment, looking to the sky, her lips moving. Then, just when Declan was about to give up waiting, she looked back at him, one eye slower to focus than the other. 'Oh, I remember now. Primrose. Her name was Primrose.'

The first of the rain fell around him in big, fat drops.

Chapter 26

BEFORE

Mrs Boone has died and Father wants Mother and me to join him to 'pay our respects'. I've never seen someone who has died before and I wonder if Mrs Boone is still covered in the rug she wore by the fire.

The pavement is wet from the rain and my button-up shoes are darker on the toe where the water is getting in. Mother and I are under a big, black umbrella but sometimes little drops get me and cling to my dress.

We crunch, crunch over the stones to the big front door and the man who doesn't speak opens it when Father pulls on the rope that makes the bell ring. I want to pull on the rope but I don't ask because Father doesn't look as if he will say yes, and he has told me I have to be on my 'best behaviour'.

The man shows us into a different room this time, down the hallway to the right, past the bottom of the big staircase with the shiny balls on top of the posts. The room is darker because the curtains have been pulled half closed. It's funny walking into it: my eyes have to blink twice. It isn't a big room, not like the other room with the fire and the sofas; there isn't a lot of furniture in it, just a grandfather clock and a table pushed up against a wall, and on the table is a long wooden box which Mrs Boone is in.

The room smells of spices and I don't want to look in the box and I can hear the ticking of the clock, which seems very loud in the small room. Father has taken off his hat and he moves over to one end of the box and Mother puts her hand on my back and that makes me jump a little and I don't want to move my feet forward, but she is moving and I don't want her to move away from me so I hold on to her skirt and hide behind her leg to see what Father is doing. I can only see a bit of Mrs Boone's nose over the edge and I am glad I'm not taller like Mother who would be able to see inside the whole box.

Father says a prayer and Mother holds my hand when we say the Amen. There are flowers on the table. They're already wilting. It seems sad that the flowers are dying too. I stare at the flowers and not at Mrs Boone's nose, and then Father tells us we can leave.

When we are back in the hallway I pull on Mother's skirt. 'Mother used to put aspirin in the water to make the flowers last longer.'

Mother stops by the bannisters and looks over her shoulder quickly at Father who is talking to the man who doesn't say anything. 'Shh,' she says, pushing me in the back towards the front door.

'It would mean they would last longer. She told me.'

'Edith, please.' Mother is standing too close to me.

I want her to know about the flowers, though. 'My other mother said it was the best thing for them.'

Mother grips my hand tightly, so tight that I make a noise because it hurts. Father looks over at us from next to the shiny balls at the bottom of the stairs and I am worried because his mouth moves into a thin line and his moustache twitches as he stares.

'Everything all right?' he says, walking towards us.

'The flowers, Father . . .'

'It's nothing,' Mother says, as the man who doesn't speak shakes out our umbrella in the porch.

'I want to tell him about the flowe—'

'Don't, Edith,' Mother says.

'Don't make a scene, Edith,' Father adds, his voice extra quiet.

I'm not making a scene, I think, but I don't say anything because I know that wouldn't be being on my best behaviour. Sometimes I hate being little and want to be big again because when my stepfather Roland told me off I would tell him to bugger off and run to the plannies and smoke the cigarettes I stole from the pocket of Mother's house dress.

The man who doesn't speak hands Mother the umbrella and we leave over the crunchy stones.

Mother and Father don't talk at all when we walk, and the rain is harder now, bouncing off the ground, and my button-up shoes are wet through. I almost miss the lace-up shoes I had when I was the other girl; the heavy soles stopped my feet getting wet. I remember I'd always wanted pretty button-up shoes then. How silly.

I'm glad we've left the house and the box with Mrs Boone lying in it. She is going to have a funeral; Father is going to speak at that too and then she will go to heaven. This thought makes me stop still in the street. Mother keeps walking and I am out in the rain feeling the fat drops hit my head and drip from my plaits.

'What happens when you're not found?' I ask.

'What do you mean?' Father says.

'Edith.' Mother bites her lip. 'You're soaked through.'

'What happens?'

I wasn't found and put in a box. I was left there; even if I probably wouldn't have wanted to be put in a box, I was still left there. And now I'm here and my head is hurting again and I feel the ache that I feel more and more now when I think of my old home and what happened.

'Will she find me?'

'Will who find you?'

'Will my other mother find me?'

'Edith . . .'

Father is gripping the handle of his umbrella and telling us to get home now. He is angry; I know he is angry, even though his voice is so quiet I can hardly hear him over the rain. Someone on the other side of the road stops, looks over – a man in a round hat, his collar up. Father turns away, his cheeks two bright spots of pink like Mrs Periwinkle's.

'Get that girl home.'

Mother tugs on my arm and pulls me under the umbrella next to her.

I know I was never found; he left me there. He wouldn't have told them where I was; he had always lied to them – ever since he had appeared with his father to live with us. He'd lied when Mother asked him about the yellowed bruises on my thighs. She'd believed him: that they were nothing to do with him. His dad had asked what she was suggesting. He'd lied that it wouldn't hurt when he'd followed me down to the plannies, pushed aside my singlet. He'd lied when he told me he didn't follow me: I used to see him in the creek watching me in my swimsuit.

He wouldn't have told them. And only he would have known where I was.

My skin has little bumps on it now and my teeth have started to chatter but it isn't just from the rain.

What happens if no one finds you?

I feel like the water is inside me, too. Inside the other me. The one still left in the cave. I walk all the way home feeling full of it, my head swimming with it.

And that is when the dreams started.

Chapter 27

NOW

Her name was Primrose.

He realised he had never planned anything much, imagining a hopeless day in Oamaru and returning to Seacliff satisfied he had truly tried everything.

Her name was Primrose.

It was an unusual name. How had Edith known it? He sank deeper into his jacket, a cold stealing over him as he tried to explain it away. He barely registered the waiter removing his cup, the liquid stone-cold. It was all impossible.

He knew he couldn't drive back now. What did all this mean? If one detail was correct, what else might be true? He shook his head from side to side, feeling dizzy with it.

He got up quickly, leaving a tip, reaching for his hat and pushing outside. The woman hadn't been sure, but had directed him up to a few streets that ran along the clifftop. The rain had eased and there were drying spots of water pockmarking the pavement.

He walked for a while, past the harbour and up on to a road that wound itself back along the coast. There were road names he didn't recognise, a telephone exchange, a post office, a dusty poster, peeling in one corner, appealing for army recruits. He wondered how many men from the town were over in Europe or fighting in the Pacific, felt the familiar squeeze of guilt that he had stayed at home. Pushing the thought back, he felt a renewed focus. If he was here, he needed to be useful.

His breaths shortened and his legs ached as the incline became steeper. Then there was a fork in the road; a cluster of houses sat behind a newer row of homes that looked out over the sea.

With only a handful of vague details to go on, he seemed to spend hours searching the nearby houses for a red roof, disturbing a man who had moved in with his daughter a few years ago, an elderly woman in the middle of cleaning, hair tied up in a scarf, a harassed look on her face as he apologised for wasting her time.

He was hungry now, and the weather had picked up; the wind was stronger, making his ears ache as he kept searching. He reached the end of a row of two-storey houses, some with manicured patches of lawn in front of them, tended flower beds, others with rusting trucks on the driveway, rotting benches beneath peeling windows.

At the end of the row was a small house, the tin roof rusted, burnt orange in places, and something in him stirred. He moved across, eyes not leaving the building, which looked as if it might collapse in the next storm. It was derelict: boarded-up windows on the ground floor, a shattered pane of glass on the first floor. He tried to peer through the cracks in the wood, his hands avoiding the nail sticking out, see inside the house, but it was impossible; the glass was smeared or the curtains closed and he only saw darkness.

He moved around to the back of the house, down a pathway overgrown with weeds and plants that caught on his trouser legs. He emerged into a garden and found a porch, a few steps leading to a back door that was locked shut. He stood looking out over overgrown grass, an area at the bottom that might once have been a vegetable patch, a washhouse on his right, the roof now collapsed in. He felt his hands prickle, the truth edging closer, the beat of his heart a little quicker.

He approached the washhouse door, which had rotted, swinging back on its hinges as he pushed at it. Scratching somewhere in the darkness; he felt his skin itch. The smell was musty and damp, the air heavy in the small, dark space; a whisper of cobwebs brushed his cheek and he jerked backwards, swiping at his face. He made out a hole in the floor, a stained ring of wood around it; on the shelf above it a stub of grubby candle. He stared at it a moment, wondering when it had last been lit.

Backing out of the rancid outbuilding he breathed in deeply, the air sharp and fresh, his lungs full of it. He looked up at the house. The windows at the top were intact and he could make out the white-plastered ceiling of a room, felt a spark of excitement. Perhaps he could get up there, peer inside? He felt another stirring within him, that perhaps this could be the place Edith had described. He shook his head: impossible.

He couldn't stop himself moving, though, looking for something to try and climb up; he roamed the garden, the long grass soaking through his shoes and socks, his feet damp as he returned triumphantly with a ladder that had seen better days. Propping it up on the side of the house he placed one foot on the lower rung, his shoes slipping, a hand shooting out to clutch at the flaking wood. He stepped up slowly, feeling his heart beat faster as he moved higher, trying not to think of the crunch of bones if he fell, that he could lie there for days, weeks, without being found.

Ivy crept up and over the windowsill as he placed both hands on it, the leaves tickling the palms of his hand. The glass was dirty, spattered with rain marks and dead insects, a large cobweb across the top left pane. He stepped up on to the top rung, shifted his hands, trying to feel more secure, and stared inside. It was a small bedroom. On a single shelf on the wall opposite he could make out

164

an old tin; a book, thick and leather-bound; a comb; what might have been postcards or letters; and a doll with one eye missing. He stared at the doll as if it were staring straight back at him through the glass, remembering another half-sentence from five-year-old Edith, something she had said about her old doll: she hadn't been smart like Mrs Periwinkle – she'd only had one eye. He felt his left foot slip and cursed under his breath as he gripped the windowsill tighter.

For a moment he thought he saw a flash of something through the half-open doorway: a movement. The room was making him feel edgy; he felt sweat bead on his hairline despite the cold. He looked down and saw a single bed underneath the window, a worn blanket on top of a filthy mattress, straw poking out in tufts. Above it was a lopsided picture of boats bobbing on a blue sea set in a cheap wooden frame; next to the bed, a small table, another stub of candle and a small, square sepia photograph. He squinted at the image, of what looked to be a teenage girl; a thin, worried face, staring up at the ceiling. He was too far away to make out any details but he felt his muscles tighten. Primrose? His eyes swept across the rest of the room, resting on the marks on the bare wooden floorboards that could be footprints.

A gust of wind nudged at him and he clung on, eyes closed, before descending the ladder slowly, wanting to be back down on solid ground. The doll was the last thing he saw as he lowered himself, its one eye watching him. He pictured it suddenly whispering a goodbye, and shivered. He slipped on the second-to-last rung and felt himself twist as he landed in the grass, breaking his fall with an arm, feeling a muscle pull in his shoulder.

Lying there breathless he slowly pushed himself into a sitting position. Rotating his shoulder he stood up, taking a last look at the window. Lowering the ladder, he left it propped against the side of the house. As he did so he noticed faded lettering on the back door, near the top. He craned his neck to peer closer, making out the hand-painted letters, many worn with age. A word, 'Karanga', made him jerk backwards.

He wondered about it all: the name 'Kara something', the doll, the girl in the photograph, the feel of the place, as he made his way back down the pathway, as he brushed the debris and mud off his clothes, as he moved back down the road. He turned down the winding coastal path, the wind buffeting his coat, making it billow out behind him. If it was the same house, what did that mean?

He didn't know why he did it; he felt a tug in his consciousness, something forcing his head to turn. The house had been empty. He'd been sure. He pictured the dust, the boarded-up windows, the single shelf, the doll, the air of neglect. He only glimpsed it for a moment: a silhouette in the side window of the house, a woman looking out in his direction. The girl from the sepia photograph, trapped in the small, square window. He blinked and the image left him, the window now empty, a grey rectangle, blank, but something still unsettled him as he finally walked away.

Chapter 28

NOW

As he pulled into the driveway of Seacliff he came to, looking up at the imposing institution; no memory of the drive back, the landscape slipping past, the sun sinking. His neck craned to see higher and higher, the silhouette of the turrets and towers against the moonlit night sky, the dark windows striped with iron bars, locked shutters. The place appeared like a great grey sleeping giant, swallowing up everyone within it. One narrow window at the top of a nearby turret glowed orange. For a moment he imagined Edith up there, sleeping peacefully in a circular room, waiting like a medieval princess for a kiss to awaken her from her endless nightmare. He shook his head, shifting in his seat as he circled the driveway and moved through the narrow stone drive into a courtyard behind the kitchens.

Turning off the engine he sat for a moment, not wanting to get out of the vehicle; instead he imagined Oamaru again, the things that matched the notes he'd read, the snippets Edith had mentioned. He caught his eye in the driving mirror, clouded with what he had discovered. His rational mind was perplexed, two thin lines appearing between his brows. How was it possible? He thought back to an article he had read at university, something he had dismissed out of hand: a child in India who had purportedly known facts about a woman who had died a few years before in a different village to her own; she had been able to pick out relatives, and recalled details of her death a few days after childbirth. He'd skimmed and scoffed and now he was desperate to find it again.

The doll, one eye staring.

The name on the back door; the feeling he'd had when he'd seen the house.

He returned the keys to the porter's lodge, stumbling on the stone steps outside as if he were full of drink, fumbling with the enormous bunch of keys at every door. None of it made any sense. And if it did, what did that mean for Edith? How long had she been here? Years.

That room: the girl in the photograph.

Primrose.

He didn't see her until she was right in front of him, her mouth opening and closing as she spoke to him, the words delayed.

'. . . tor . . . verything all right . . . em out of sorts . . .'

He looked up, still on top of that ladder in Oamaru; something he had seen in the corner of his eye. Movement? The face in the window.

'Doctor . . . shall I get someone . . . sit down . . .'

Nurse Shaw was right in front of him, her face filled with questions, eyes flooded with concern. One hand wavered over his arm as if she was about to touch him.

He stared at the hand, the clean, clipped nails, blinked once as it dropped back at her side. He had an overwhelming urge, a need, then, to share what he had seen, to speak about all the things that had been crowding inside his head, building up over that day, in the drive back to Seacliff.

'Nurse, would you mind if I asked you, that is to say . . .'

Where to begin?

He looked again at her face, the neat arch of one eyebrow lifting as she waited.

'To ask . . .' She repeated his words slowly, a look he hadn't seen before passing across her face.

'I have a, well, I was wondering if . . .'

She made a series of slow nods, her expression encouraging. He recalled a teacher at his school, waiting as he spat out the words, not interrupting, willing him to succeed. He licked his lips. How could he put the things he'd been thinking into words? How did he even know what he had seen? What he had started to imagine?

Somewhere nearby other voices, shouts, interrupted his thoughts: a whistle for attention. Nurse Shaw looked over her shoulder, wavered, looked back at him. He couldn't face her leaving. He didn't want to be alone with these thoughts any more. He reached out, a hand firmly around her wrist, ignoring the startled intake of breath as he steered her to the nearby open door, the men's billiard room. It was empty, three tables in a line, a sea of green felt, the balls and cues kept in a locked cupboard in the corner; everything always locked up and away from them.

He turned to look at her. 'My apologies, Nurse, I . . .' He looked over his shoulder, imagined ears everywhere. Nurse Shaw's eyebrows lifted in question. The room was ghostly dark, bluish white rectangles on the table from the high, narrow windows.

'Doctor . . .' Something about the way in which she addressed him brought him to; he could hear surprise in her voice. And something else he didn't recognise.

'I'm sorry, I just, I didn't want others to hear . . . to think . . .'

Her eyes rounded a fraction. She seemed a little breathless, one hand on her chest. 'It's quite all right, Doctor, please, do go on . . .'

He was grateful to her, swallowing, taking care to form the right sentences. If he said things aloud it would make them more real. 'It's a little . . . delicate . . .'

Did he imagine it, or did she suck in a little breath?

He started again. 'I know you're terribly busy, I'm sorry, I won't keep you, I just . . .'

She took a step forward, bolder now, her voice steady as she looked at him. 'Not at all, Doctor. Please.' She nodded quickly then, that same expression, coaxing, a half-smile on her face.

He felt the tension in his shoulders ease as he nodded back. 'Right, well, you see, I was wondering whether . . .' This was it. He could say it now. He could ask her outright. Was it really such an impossible question?

Another step forward and the nurse was very close; he could see a tiny spot on her white lapel. Yellow, small. A patient's vomit? Spittle? Lunch? The spot was mesmerising as the words jumped and merged in his mind.

The doll.

The name of the house.

Primrose. Her face in the photograph. Her serious expression. Edith. Her memories.

He cleared his throat, 'Would you say, that is, I mean, have you ever wondered perhaps whether it might be possible . . .'

She was inches away now; he felt his neck crane back a fraction, his back almost flush against the cool stone. Half her face was in shadow, one side warmed by the glow of a nearby lamp.

'. . . whether there are things that perhaps we can't explain with science. With reason even?'

'I'd lov— I . . .' It was her turn, it seemed, to fall over her words. She straightened then, took a step back, one hand up to adjust the hat on her head; her words were slow when they came. 'I'm not sure I understand your meaning.'

'Do you think people can experience things we can't explain? That is to say, might it be possible that if an answer looks to be logical, it follows that it *is* logical, that there is truth there?'

There was colour in her cheeks as she replied, 'I believe we can't explain everything, Doctor. Love, for instance.'

'Love.' Declan felt himself flush, wrong-footed. What did the nurse mean by that? He thought back to the image he had conjured earlier: a sleeping Edith in the turret, waiting, lips slightly parted. He felt his cheeks grow hot. He didn't mean his next words to be so loud. 'No, I mean, if a patient is repeatedly telling you something you know can't be true, but it then proves to be true, well, what would you think to that?'

Did he imagine her shoulders falling? Her mouth pinched tight as she answered, 'A patient . . .'

She seemed lost. He hadn't phrased it correctly. He wasn't sure what he was asking. Didn't dare speak aloud his swirling thoughts. If someone had lived before, how could someone living now, who had never known them, know the details of their life? He almost laughed aloud at the absurdity of it. Of course he couldn't say the words aloud.

'A patient, yes. She has lived here much of her life. She didn't seem to demonstrate many of the traits I'd expect to see in someone with her diagnosis, so I dug a little deeper. I thought perhaps there was something else, some other way to explain things.'

He imagined Edith suddenly in the room with them, leaning over the billiards table, wild curls falling in front of her face, a bold laugh as she missed the ball she'd been aiming for, a kindly remark as he took his turn. He was smiling as he continued, 'I wonder if a terrible injustice has been done; she can be so lucid, a musician, gentle . . .'

The nurse took a step back. 'It's Edie,' she whispered.

Declan licked his lips, worried now he had said too much. Nurse Shaw had a different expression on her face. 'Yes, yes, the patient is Edith.'

Her mouth opened and closed, then she gave a curt nod of her head. 'Well, if anyone can help, I'm sure you can, Doctor. She's lucky to have you. Although . . .' Her eyes dulled as she went on, 'Matron did tell me Doctor Malone had placed her on his most recent list.'

'List?' Declan repeated, distracted by the thought of a returning Doctor Malone. If he came back now it would be too late; he wouldn't be able to see Edith any more. And if he couldn't see her, how could he find the proof he might need?

Nurse Shaw looked over her shoulder as another whistle went. 'Malone's list,' she said, watching him closely, 'of patients.'

He felt his head cloud as the nurse finished, steel in her voice. 'Edith has been selected for the new procedure.'

He missed the expression on the nurse's face as his jaw fell open and the words bounced around the inside of his head over and over. The new procedure.

It was confirmed. Edith would have a leucotomy.

For a second he was stunned, the room, the nurse, the whistles and sounds all melting away so it was just him standing in the semi-darkness. Then he snapped out of the daze, almost knocking the nurse over as he pushed past to the open doorway. 'I must go.'

The whistling had got worse; there were footsteps somewhere nearby, and shouts, but Declan clattered down the corridor in the other direction.

Nurse Shaw's words repeated over and over in his head as he made his way to the library, up on the next floor, taking two steps at a time. A leucotomy. The list.

If anyone can help, I am sure you can, Doctor.

Chapter 29

THEN

Every night waiting for noises, sleeping in snatches, waking with frightened breaths. This morning she'd seen something half-stuffed through the crack under her door. Pulling on the fabric she had darted backwards, realising they were panties: dirtied and stiff. Someone had left them there in the night. She had thrown them across the room, pressed herself against the wall.

Deputy Matron had heard her crying, unlocked her door, peered down at her crouched in the corner.

'Someone left them there,' she'd cried out before she remembered not to say anything, the balled-up panties hidden somewhere under her bed. 'They were there. I saw them.'

Deputy Matron had stared around the room, seen nothing.

'Breakfast. Now. I'm writing this up,' she'd said before leaving, and those words had made Edith's heart rate quicken, her palms damp.

She felt things shift, time dissolve as if she were back when she had first arrived at the hospital. She had seen Doctor Malone every week then. He was the most terrifying person she'd ever known: tall and impossible to please. Even more frightening than Father when he'd told her to 'stop' in that low voice of his when she'd said the things that made him angry.

He had asked her things then. She'd wanted to get the answers right. She wasn't a liar. She wasn't possessed by the devil like her father said. She was Edith, just normal Edith, and she didn't want to be there in that hospital with the loonies. Then more time would pass and she would wake in a room with her lips cracked and dry and she would be wheeled through to the dayroom and lifted into a chair. She'd be given a soft rabbit with worn fur, one arm dangling on loose threads. She would stay there all day; tiny in the big winged armchair, curled up tight so that she could fool herself she wasn't there at all.

She received letters from her parents but she hadn't been able to decipher them. She would ask the nurses to read them to her but sometimes they wouldn't: no time, the handwriting was too small. Sometimes she would tear them up before anyone looked at them, not wanting to hear their words. She couldn't write back and ask to go home. She was too afraid to ask any of the nurses to help her, not knowing if they would laugh or shout or send her to Doctor Malone. She would stay in the chair and curl tighter and tighter, not speak to anyone: attendants, nurses, doctors, until they took her through to the white room and placed the pads on her head again and then she wouldn't remember after that.

She hadn't known how long she would live there. She'd always thought it would be a week, a month. Then she started attending classes, learning the alphabet and numbers as if it were a real school. Forming the shapes on a small chalk board. She was one of the smallest. She often didn't understand. And some days she couldn't go to classes, or couldn't remember what day it was and whether she had done that class before. Some weeks would seem to repeat the same day over and over.

174

She learnt that the more she shouted and repeated the same story, telling the doctors the things that had made her father angry, about when she'd been Primrose, the more she would go into the white room. She stopped telling them about Oamaru, her old mother, the house with the red roof, how he'd touched her in the outhouse, the stench of the dunny, watching the penguins, the sea; she even stopped telling them what he'd done to her in the cave. Her other mother would never know. She started to be quieter, answer their questions only inside her head, tell them something different out loud. She didn't go to the white room as much. For a while she hardly went there at all.

Years passed, her parents died, she watched some patients come and go. Others stayed. She delivered the mail, took the red pills three times a day, ate, played cards, talked to Patricia, got called 'pet' by the woman who always sat in the flowered winged chair by the nurses' station, who died there but no one noticed until one of the nurses shouted at her to get up.

She went to bed and grew taller and nurses changed and left but Matron was always there, and Doctor Malone. For a while she didn't have the treatment and kept things all tied up in her head so they wouldn't get out and they wouldn't send her to the white room. And then she realised she had forgotten the things she'd said anyway, and would look at Doctor Malone as he asked about them; her memories became all of the building, the bad fairy castle and the patients in it and the weekly menu and the people who lived at Seacliff.

She bled every month and she was moved to one of the women's wards. Patricia joined her. It had been home. Then Donna had arrived, Donna followed everywhere by fat Shirley. Edith never knew where they would be; jabbing her in the chest, pushing her when the nurses weren't looking, whispering things into her ear that made her want to cover them both with her hands.

Although it was bad, it was ten times worse for Patricia. Donna found ways to get her into trouble at every turn, knew just what to say or do to get Patricia screaming at her, tugging on her hair until whistles rang out and Patricia was dragged away.

Edith tried to stay out of their way as much as she could. She tried to stay close to the nurses, spent more time with Bernie, too: never alone. Then Martha arrived. Martha fought and scratched at the nurses and attendants for weeks, in and out of the straitjackets that deadened your arms so that they hung hopelessly by your sides. Edith watched her spit and kick at Nurse Ritchie, watched her face be pushed into the floor, her cheek pressed to the vinyl as Franklin grabbed at her, smirking as he lifted her up and away, his yellowed fingers gripping her arms.

She wore bandages on her wrists and Edith saw dried blood once. She had a son. She'd killed her husband. Donna was always watching Martha, but one day Martha stood over Edith, asked to play cards with her. Martha had smiled, two faint dimples in a face hollowed like she had scoops out of her cheeks, dark-grey shadows under her eyes, and Edith had smiled back. They played that day and the next and Edith got used to looking for her, a warmth as they sat in silence, just the gentle rustle of the cards. Donna watched them.

Then, Edith didn't know how, but suddenly Martha was with Donna, everywhere with Donna, and Shirley, both women now glued to her side. Martha would sneer and laugh as she picked on them, as she taunted Patricia every day, until the day when Patricia had leapt on Donna, slapping at her face, calling her a whore, bit Nurse Ritchie. That was when they took Patricia away from the ward. Martha had laughed as they'd removed her drooping body.

Then it was just her and Bernie, and Bernie couldn't protect Edith; no one could help. Edith wondered if it might stay that way forever.

Bernie, her friend. About to turn sixteen. It gave her an idea.

She'd mentioned the date weeks ago and Edith repeated it to herself for three days until it really sank in. Then she asked Nurse Shaw to tell her when the date was one week away. And then, when Edith was just listening to the things in her head and looking out at the lawn, at the rain drizzling down the panes of glass, Nurse Shaw leant over her chair, smelling of toothpaste, and reminded her.

'One week, Edie, it's now one week until the sixth.'

Everything inside her head died down as she focused on the words, as the realisation sank in that she had seven days to get things ready. She hugged herself tight with the secret, glad Bernie wasn't there or she feared she would blurt it out to her in a bubbly gush and that would ruin the surprise.

She'd been told about surprise parties by Patricia when she first arrived. Patricia's parents had arranged one for her before she came to the building and Patricia told Edith it had been the best day, as they'd all eaten cake until they could burst, and danced and sang. Edith promised herself there would be all those things for Bernie.

She was too shy to play her flute, but Rosa from the orchestra would play her violin and Nurse Shaw told her she would help keep the party a secret from Bernie and tell all the women on the ward when the time was right so they could be part of the big surprise. Nurse Shaw was going to bring out bunting and tie it all round the dayroom. Nurse Shaw had often been kind to her, even if she hadn't believed her about the key. She asked her if she could go to the kitchen. Nurse Shaw said yes and that Edith could go on her own, as it was only outside the nurses' station and she could see her from there. She got up right away.

Edith stood outside the kitchen door, peering through the steamed glass, wanting to see Clive who always gave her extra cheese scones. There were a lot of heads, white hats and movement. She stood on her tiptoes searching for Clive, his wide shoulders, the curl of grey hair at the nape of his neck, always busy. What if he said no? She saw one of the chefs turn, large knife held up as he shouted across the kitchen, bringing it down on a board. Another carried a large tray covered in a tea towel; one was sinking pans into a large butler's sink in the corner; two men, wearing a slightly different uniform, sat peeling potatoes between an enormous hessian sack: in-patients on the kitchen gang. Then there was Clive, reaching up to a shelf and bringing down a large saucepan. She felt the air inside her puff out in one quick go and found herself lifting a hand, trying to catch his eye.

The man with the knife looked up, his eyebrows lifted. He'd joined the kitchen a while ago, had big hairy arms, a scar on his chin. He stepped towards the door, the big silver knife still in his hand. Edith couldn't stop staring at it, at the way it flashed under the strip lights. He pulled at the door with his other hand.

The noise of the kitchen: the clatter, the voices, the hiss and bubble of the food almost blocked out his words: 'What are you wanting then?'

'Clive,' she whispered, finding herself unable to look up at him, focusing only on the hand holding the knife. The black hairs were even on the backs of his hands.

'What's that?'

She swallowed. 'Clive, please, I want to talk to Clive.'

'The old man, eh? Got a thing for an older guy?' He laughed at his own words and turned back to shout across the room, 'Hey, Clive, one of your girlfriends is visiting.'

She felt her cheeks get hot, only just realising what he meant by the words. Wanting to tell him she wasn't Clive's girlfriend. She'd never been anyone's girlfriend.

Clive shuffled towards the door, his thick eyebrows knitted together as he came outside into the corridor. 'Edith.' The lines on his face seemed even deeper when he smiled. 'You here looking for treats?'

She shook her head, feeling better now Clive was standing in front of her; she didn't mind looking up at him.

'Well, then, what is it?'

The words spilled out of her in a rush. 'It's Bernie's birthday in seven days, one week, and I want her to have a cake. Would you make a cake?' She stopped, panting slightly.

He lifted his eyebrows, like hairy grey caterpillars. 'A cake?'

He sounded unsure; she felt her heart pitter-patter. It wouldn't be the same without a cake, with candles Bernie could blow out.

'With candles, sixteen candles,' she whispered, holding herself tightly. He had to agree. She had it all planned.

'Candles, too.' Clive chuckled at that, a low sound that bounced round the corridor. The noise made her frown. Was he laughing at her? Was that good or bad? Clive had always been kind to her, sneaking an extra sausage roll because she'd told him they were her favourite, waving at her when she passed by the kitchen garden.

'Even with a war on, eh?'

She wasn't sure what that meant; felt her face fall.

Clive smiled. 'I'm joking, love. 'Course I can. Do you want to help me make it, Edith?'

'I'd love to make it,' she said, picturing an enormous sponge cake coated with jam, sprinkled with icing sugar.

'Well, I can get all the things we need. How about you come along and make it on the Tuesday so it's nice and fresh for her birthday. How does that sound?'

She was nodding as he spoke, grinning now, feeling her mouth stretch across her face.

Clive was laughing again. 'Never seen someone so happy about a cake. That's made my day, that has. You're a good girl, Edith.'

She felt lighter on her feet as she left, remembering to spin round and thank him halfway down the corridor.

'I'll see you Tuesday, Edith, in your breaktime. Three o'clock, yes?'

'Three o'clock,' she called back. 'Tuesday, three o'clock, Tuesday, three o'clock,' she said again as she turned back.

She'd get Nurse Shaw to remind her, too. Tuesday, three o'clock.

After that she made sure to keep things extra quiet, felt the secret glowing inside her every time she looked across at Bernie.

'What is it?' Bernie asked. 'Why are you smiling at me like that?'

'I'm not smiling,' Edith said, pushing the smile down. Of course she was smiling. Bernie would have her birthday party, a surprise. There would be a cake with sixteen candles.

She could barely sleep the day before. They'd made a big cake. Clive took it out of the oven, golden and perfect, and she'd been allowed to spoon the jam on. He'd coated it in a thick cream topping and produced sixteen candles which he let her place all over the top of the icing. She pictured Bernie leaning over the tiny flames and blowing them out.

On the morning of her birthday Edith tried not to fidget with the excitement in her chest. Bernie was combing her hair on the edge of the bed, a long, dark-brown curtain. Edith wanted to say 'Happy Birthday', but knew she had to pretend it wasn't a special day for the surprise to work. They took their medication and went out to work in the flower garden.

Afterwards Bernie went to see the new doctor, the one who had joined the orchestra. Edith didn't think he had noticed her; he never looked her way. Pushing open the door to the dayroom all other thoughts were forgotten as she gasped. Nurse Shaw had kept her promise: the room was lined with bunting, faded cotton flags in different colours on ribbons all around the walls, the cake perched on a china cake stand in the centre of a table.

Nurse Ritchie bent over it, huffing and muttering as she burnt her finger on a match. 'What next?' she'd said, picking up the box and drawing out another one.

Donna stood nearby, her back resting against the wall, watching everyone, her left eye fluttering at intermittent moments. She lit on Edith and today Edith tried to lift her chin, tried to return her gaze. Shirley and Martha moved across to stand either side of Donna. Martha looked skittish, eyes darting to Donna and then the table. They seemed to be waiting for something, too. Edith didn't want to think about them now, tried to focus on what she had to do. She looked at the clock, mouthing the numbers, remembering where the hands should be. Bernie would be here very soon.

Nurse Shaw appeared in the doorway, more women filing past her to get inside, and Edith sucked in her breath as Nurse Shaw nodded at her: the signal. Moving across to the table, the sixteen candles glowing orange, Edith lifted up the cake stand ready to do what she had planned.

There was a shout from somewhere, a scuffle, and Nurse Ritchie wheeled round, the box of matches left on the tray as she moved to see who was making a fuss.

'Ready, ladies?' Nurse Shaw called out from the doorway in the same moment. 'Edie?' She nodded at Edith who nodded quickly back, feeling a flush of warmth. The excitement she had woken up with that morning took over, nerves pushed aside, Donna and her gang forgotten as she moved over to the table to lift the cake.

Then Bernie was there, back from seeing Doctor Harris, not picking up on the nervous energy in the room.

The cake was heavier than Edith expected and she was careful. The crowds parted and Edith could see Bernie surrounded now by women wishing her a happy birthday. Nurse Shaw opened her mouth ready to start the singing and Edith knew she had to join in and then the rest of the room would too. She had only taken two steps forward when it happened, so quickly. She stumbled on something, felt a hand in her back as she tripped and then she was falling forward, the world tipping slowly sideways as the cake left her hands, a pain in her left arm, her head hitting the floor, the top of the cake, icing in her curls, the sponge broken into bits, the clink as a hundred matches scattered on the floor.

She lay there, aching, watching Donna melt behind Shirley on her right, a smirk on her face as she slipped round her; Martha, a quick nod as she straightened up, reaching for something on the floor.

A hand on her back, or a foot that had tripped her. There had been too many people milling around; no one had seen. She felt a hand now on her shoulder, Nurse Shaw's voice in her ear. 'Edie, are you hurt?'

She didn't speak, couldn't, felt her face pressed to the floor, seeing the cake in pieces in front of her, the matches scattered across the floor. Someone, Donna, had started to sing 'Happy Birthday' in a sugary voice. Two other voices joined in. Edith moved her head: Bernie stood looking down at her, her face white. Edith's arm throbbed, her face and hair covered in crumbly stickiness. She could feel it all stuck to her cheek. Bernie hadn't even seen the cake, would never know what it had looked like.

She didn't know why she started laughing.

182

Chapter 30
NOW

Declan hadn't slept that night. Instead he spent it rereading her bare notes, searching for articles or references in books to things he barely dared think were possible. He frowned at them, scattered now in a large ring around him, his legs cramping from kneeling amongst them for so long. He was frustrated by the large gap in Edith's notes, knowing he was missing information from her first few months in the asylum.

He needed proof. Something that could support the things she had detailed as a child.

He needed to ask Edith. He wanted to describe the house to her, try to summon up some of the memories she had spoken about all those years ago. He wanted to know if they were truly faded or gone. He wanted to help her remember, see what more she might say.

He must see her immediately.

He dressed quickly, pulling on his socks and shoes, straightening his tie, redoing the buttons on his shirt, fumbling with them as he looked around for a different pair of trousers. Flattening his hair with one hand he cleaned his teeth with the other, feeling his stomach whirling like the water moving down the plughole.

Winding down the stairs from his room he almost missed the scene below. In-patients were moving back and forward, clearing the site of the charred ward. Edith's old ward. It seemed the investigation had changed pace, or they had their answers, as twisted metal, damp lumps were wheelbarrowed away. A small crowd stood a little way off, staring at the site, a place most people turned away from as they moved past, not wanting to remember that thirty-seven women had lost their lives, packed so tightly together. Declan held a hand up to the narrow window, grateful again that Edith had got out. Now he needed to help her even more.

He could barely eat and felt a sense of purpose as he strode along the corridor, nodding with authority at Nurse Ritchie who gave him a small, surprised frown in return. He moved into his office, placing Edith's folder on the desk.

A sound behind him made him turn. It was Nurse Shaw tapping lightly, a small tray in one hand.

'I brought you a coffee, Doctor.' She lowered the tray on to the desk, removing the cup.

Declan thanked her distractedly.

She didn't meet his eye. 'Just avoiding changing the bed pans.'

'A nurse's life, eh?' For a moment he wondered where this new confidence had come from, to tease as if he really were the man that filled this white coat.

He went to sip the coffee as she stood, the tray at her side. 'About last night – I shouldn't have said anything, about Edith, I mean,' she blurted.

He lowered the cup. 'Oh no, on the contrary.' He swallowed down the brief swell of panic as he thought of Edith's name on that list. 'I am grateful that you did.'

He noticed her face relax, a tiny lift of her mouth. 'I'd better be going. I'm sure you're busy too, and Doctor Malone will no doubt be wanting me shortly.'

Declan burnt his tongue on the liquid, the cup sloshing slightly as he pulled it away from his mouth. 'Doctor Malone? I thought he was away in Wellington?'

'He got back this morning, Doctor, just before dawn – gave the night nurse quite the fright apparently, thought he was a ghost.' She leaned towards him a fraction. 'I think she might have been dozing.'

Declan failed to pick up on her jovial remark, didn't react, his mind whirring. Doctor Malone was back. Already. What would this mean for him? He thought of the file on his desk, a file he now must return; the questions he had intended to ask Edith that morning. He placed the cup on the desk unseeing. Nurse Shaw was still talking but he couldn't concentrate at all. He felt the weight of the news push him hopelessly into his chair, his earlier confidence seeping away.

'Doctor Harris . . . Doctor, is everything satisfactory?' Nurse Shaw hurried around the side of the desk to hover beside his chair, just as a sharp knock sounded and a wave of pipe smoke entered the room.

'Harris,' came Doctor Malone's voice.

Nurse Shaw leapt back as if she'd been scalded, eyes wide as she spun to face the door.

'I . . . oh.' Doctor Malone stopped, mouth open as he took in the nurse standing so close to Declan. 'Sorry to break up the tête-à-tête. Nurse, do you not have somewhere you need to be?'

'Yes, of course, Doctor Malone,' she replied, her head lowered as she passed him and exited into the corridor.

Declan remained in his chair as Doctor Malone stepped over to his desk.

'Thank you for holding the fort, so to speak,' Doctor Malone said, striding over to the filing cabinet and opening it up. 'Busy day getting back on track. I trust you've made thorough notes.' He looked at Declan over half-moon glasses as he piled up a few folders in his arms. 'We'll return to life as usual, then, Doctor.'

Declan didn't know how to react, watching Doctor Malone push back the filing cabinet, turn with the armful of files.

'Sir . . . if you need more time . . .' Declan waved a hand, trying to conjure up something on the spot.

'You'd best get on, Doctor, first patient will be due any moment,' Doctor Malone said, staring pointedly at the clock on the wall above the door before he left the room.

Declan leaned back in his chair, resting his head against the leather. He shut his eyes, mind racing as he tried to think what to do.

He needed to talk to Edith. Pushing his chair back, ignoring the time, he hurried out of the room.

The dayroom was quiet, a group of patients bent over a jigsaw puzzle that had barely been started, some milling around the table where drinks were laid out waiting for them. For a second he thought she wasn't there; then he saw her, sitting in the chair by the window, staring out over the lawn. He felt his heart lurch. Hurrying across to her, he realised he didn't actually know what he was planning to say, just that he needed to seize an opportunity to speak with her.

She seemed smaller, younger, lost in that chair. He bent down beside her and it was a moment before she turned and noticed someone was there.

'Doctor.' She smiled suddenly, as if she had been far, far away.

'Edith, good morning, I'm glad I caught you . . .' His breaths were short, heart hammering.

Edith was looking over his shoulder, a small frown forming on her face.

And then he understood why: Matron was calling out his name. As he started, he caught the eye of Nurse Shaw in the doorway. She was standing stock-still, a tray of small paper cups in her hands, looking at him and Edith. He felt himself fidget, as if she had somehow caught him doing something he shouldn't.

Matron marched over. 'Doctor Harris. Tom Barton has seemed very troubled over the last day or so – his temper is worse; I was hoping Doctor Malone could see him but he is under pressure to catch up with everything and I was wondering if you would agree to . . .'

Matron's words faded as Declan watched Doctor Malone appear in the doorway. Behind him, Martha squeezed past him into the dayroom, her eyes bright, an excitable expression on her face. Declan watched her as she scooted quickly into a chair nearby and started playing with a pack of cards, laying them out in rows, her eyes down as Doctor Malone called out, 'Edith Garrett!'

Martha bit her lip, looked across at Edith.

What was going on?

Edith looked towards the door, the small smile already faltering. She didn't move.

'Edith,' Nurse Shaw repeated, 'the doctor is waiting.'

The smile disappeared completely from Edith's face, her gaze resting on the imposing figure of Doctor Malone in the doorway. His mouth was set in a grim line and Declan felt a stone of fear rest in his stomach.

It seemed that Doctor Malone was restless, his fingers rubbing together as he watched Edith cross the room. He turned, a man used to being followed, and Edith made little quick steps to catch him up, looking worriedly back at Declan who was left standing, helplessly rooted to the spot. It was only when he followed them

187

both out into the corridor that he noticed the policeman standing a little way off. What were the police doing back here?

Declan itched to follow but Matron chased him into the corridor to talk to him again about Tom Barton. He agreed to see him, his mouth moving with the words as he watched Edith, Doctor Malone and the policeman disappear around the corner.

He tried to concentrate but for the rest of the morning he couldn't sit still, couldn't focus on the patients in front of him, almost prescribing the wrong medication for one, mixing up the notes on another. He kept thinking of Edith, sandwiched between the two men, alone as she faced them. What did they want? Why had they been clearing the scene? What conclusion had they reached?

The dining room was full of it at lunch; patients and staff huddled over trays exchanging looks and whispers. Martha sat surrounded by in-patients, appearing to hold court as she spoke to the gathering masses, one kneeling on the bench, others leaning across to catch every word. Declan frowned as he slid his tray down on the table, interrupting two nurses sitting side by side, who immediately clammed up when he sat down opposite them.

He could hear indistinct words. He thought he heard Edith's name, moving in a whisper around him, and then wondered if it was simply because she was still on his mind. He felt guilty then, knowing he was thinking too much about her, not focusing on others in the same way. Then he thought of the list. Imagined her lying on a trolley, waiting to be put under. How long did he have? He went to cut a piece of the pie on his plate, his knife hovering over it.

Nurse Shaw was moving towards him, skirting round empty chairs. She stood at his table, leant towards him. 'Have you heard? It seems Martha remembered something.'

Declan looked at her keenly. 'Remembered what?'

'A patient, with a match – she told the police it was Edith.'

Declan stopped chewing, swallowing the meat and pastry, its bulk almost lodging in his throat. 'Edith,' he repeated.

Nurse Shaw's expression changed again, reminding him of the previous evening. 'Martha didn't want to say anything but she was told she had to, if people were at risk.'

'But surely no one would believe it?' Declan scoffed, wanting it to be a joke.

Nurse Shaw crossed her arms. 'No one really knows what to believe.'

Declan looked around, at the whispered talk at the tables, imagining them all sharing this piece of news. 'You don't believe it, surely?'

He remembered her soft expression as she'd talked about Edith, someone she had wanted to protect. Her Edie. What had changed? A look passed across her face then, a hardening, and Declan knew Edith had lost this ally.

'Edith slept on the floor below her,' Declan continued, his voice rising, some people at a nearby table looking round. 'How could Martha possibly have seen her do anything?'

Nurse Shaw raised an eyebrow and Declan felt a momentary flash of embarrassment that he seemed to know so much about where Edith had slept.

Her next words were slow. 'It does seem odd. They were all locked in their rooms, but Martha was insistent.'

Declan recalled what Edith had told him about a key. That patients had moved around the ward. He had promised her he wouldn't tell anyone. He searched for anything else to say, not wanting to make things worse. 'There've been fires before, the foundations have moved, rats could have bitten through the wires: any number of things.'

Nurse Shaw was chewing her lip as he went on. He tried to lower his voice; others at a nearby table were peering round, watching their exchange. More whispers would follow, he was sure.

'Well, I'm just passing on what I heard,' Nurse Shaw said, going to move away. 'You should be happy, Doctor. Martha's getting out. Doctor Malone has said she can go home; she'll raise her son.'

Martha was going home.

As Nurse Shaw walked off Declan threw down his knife, a loud clatter as it landed on the table.

'Twenty-one, twenty-two, twenty-three . . .'

Voices from behind him. They were counting the cutlery back in, Deputy Matron ticking off every knife and fork as they did after every meal. Twenty-four, twenty-five, twenty-six. The numbers always a reminder of where they all were. What the dangers were.

Declan left the dining room, heading down the stairs, fumbling to find the right key to open one of the many doors. He was in a familiar corridor heading back to the ward, past the nurses' station and around the corner towards his office.

In the distance he could hear a raised female voice, and his walk sped up. He recognised that voice. Rounding the corner he saw an attendant pushing a patient lying restrained on a trolley, as if his imaginings were coming to life right in front of him. Was this it? Was it too late? He felt sweat bead his hairline, his hands clammy. Edith was shouting, please and no, begging, all the muscles in her neck popping, her fingers grabbing at the air.

He wanted to call out but instead he followed the trolley, watching as she was wheeled around the corner, watching her back buck, her curly hair mussed, mouth wide, the words bouncing off the walls and making him flinch. He wanted to run over the flagstones, unbuckle the straps, release her wrists, carry her away from there. The door ahead was already open and the attendant pushed the trolley through; one wheel stuck for a moment, so he swore as he bruised his hip on the steel. Then they were moving again and Declan was wondering if he should stop him, fabricate an excuse, distract the attendant. But then what? What could he possibly do next?

He thought back to her sitting in the chair under the window, her expression calm, the slow smile as she turned and caught him kneeling next to her. That moment seemed a lifetime ago. What might have happened if he'd been able to see her for another day?

How could they wonder at her agitation if they had accused her of things she would never have done? She wasn't violent or volatile. In fact, after what he'd discovered, he knew with an absolute clarity that she wasn't any of the things they had accused her of being. A sour taste rose in his mouth as he thought then of everything she'd been put through, and what was waiting for her now. The trolley turned at an angle, about to push through to the treatment room.

Doctor Malone appeared in the doorway, looking back down the corridor towards Declan. He disappeared briefly as the attendant pushed the trolley inside. And then, once the attendant had left, walking away in the opposite direction, he looked straight back at Declan, tipped his head slightly, before slamming the door to the treatment room behind him.

Chapter 31

BEFORE

The dreams come almost every night now.

I was there in the darkness, in the cold and the damp and no one knew where to find me. The sound of the sea nearby, the tide coming in, was getting louder and soon it would cover me and no one would be able to get in. The heavy weight wasn't just on top of me but was all around; I was trapped from the sides. I couldn't move my arms or legs and he was putting more weight on me. My head hurt, I knew it was bad and I knew I needed to get Mother, to tell her what he'd done and get her to help me. But she wouldn't come: she didn't know where I was. No one would come. Ever.

I wake in the dark, my skin sticky, hair stuck to my face, my mouth a large 'O', screaming. I'm not by the water, I'm in the big soft bed I now sleep in, Mrs Periwinkle at the end watching me, my slippers laid next to the stool of my dressing table, the pink lampshade on top. I'm in my bedroom and my mother is here now, asking me what's wrong as I cry out.

'I have to get out . . . he hit me, he's gone now, I have to . . .'

Father appears in the doorway in his dressing gown, a lamp in his hand, showing up the netting over his moustache. 'What's she saying?'

Mother sits on my bed, stroking my hair back, holding me to her; I feel the hard bump of her stomach with the baby inside. 'Nothing, it's just a bad dream, she isn't saying anything.'

I can't help it, though. I'm crying and I want my mother and I want to go home and tell her where I am and that she needs to find me.

'I want Mother.'

'I'm here.'

The big sobs make my chest go up and down, tears falling on my nightdress. 'I want Mother. I need to go to her.'

'I'm here, I'm here . . .'

'No,' I say, shaking my head left to right, left to right. 'Not you. I want my other mother. She won't be able to find me. She won't know where I am. She'll think I've gone.'

'You're here, you're here with me, Edith.'

I push her arm away, feel my fingers in my hair. 'He hit me. He hit me on the head.'

'Edith,' Mother repeats.

Father takes a step into the room, his voice like a hiss through his teeth. 'She can't keep saying these things, Eileen. People will talk.'

The lamp jerks as the words come and Mother's hand stops on my forehead. 'Edith, please,' she says in a low voice. 'Please stop.'

I can't stop, the dream is too real to stop. 'He hit me, he hit me hard, it hurt. She doesn't know where I am, she won't be able to find me . . .'

'Edith.'

'I'm not Edith.' I push her hand away. 'I don't want to stay there, it's dark and it's wet, I don't want to stay . . .'

'I know you don't,' Mother says, stroking my head as she pulls me to her, then twisting so that she is looking at Father. 'It's just a dream, she doesn't know what she's saying.'

'It hurts, it hurts, I don't want to stay here, it's dark . . .' The tears leak out of me, water falling.

Father's voice somewhere. 'This can't carry on. I can't have her saying these things.'

Mother is whispering quickly, 'I know, I know.'

I'm wild, a new thought entering. 'He might touch Mary,' I gasp. 'I can't let him touch Mary.'

'Eileen.'

I think Mother has started to cry, too.

'Don't you . . . Eileen, come away from her . . .'

When I hear that I reach out, suddenly needing to feel her. 'Don't go.'

Mother rises from the bed as my hand swipes at her.

'Don't leave me, please, please . . . they won't find me . . .'

'Edith, I'm sorry, I can't . . . your father. It's just a dream, a dream . . .'

'Eileen.'

Mother stands, chewing her lip as our eyes meet. 'Yes, I'm . . .'

'Don't leave me,' I whisper.

'Eileen.' The lamp flickers. 'We have to do something. This can't carry on.'

Chapter 32

NOW

Declan spent the rest of the afternoon staring out on to the grounds. The site of the fire was almost clear now; he could no longer see the ruined edge of the old building. Men were raking the ground and Declan wondered what they would do in the space: could anyone truly forget?

He saw deliveries arrive and leave, light rain spatter the windowpanes. He couldn't concentrate on the notes in front of him, ink droplets falling on to the blotting pad as he stared into the distance. He got up, finding excuses to move around the corridors, found his way back to the treatment rooms: he needed gloves, he was looking for a medical pad, he thought he had left his stethoscope somewhere. The door remained closed and when he did see it open it was clear Edith was still unconscious, a grey-haired nurse he didn't recognise moving inside to check on her. Could he ask what had happened to Edith? Would she wake not knowing her own name?

He shivered, heading quickly to his office, bile in his throat. He knew he needed to pull himself together, was seeing Tom Barton next whose notes stated he could be volatile at the best of times; he had a history of exposing himself to women. Reason for committal: 'masturbation'. He needed to concentrate – a new patient always meant Declan needed to build up trust, and yet his mind couldn't help returning to that tiny room with the inert woman inside. He had failed her.

He paused outside the dayroom, hearing the usual hubbub from inside. He pushed open the door, a woman in a dressing gown turning towards the sound before looking away. Declan's eyes roved the room until he found the armchair Edith had been sitting in, the seat cushion flattened, empty now. His gaze lingered before he pulled his eyes away, making a show of getting a biscuit from the tray, as if that was what had pulled him there.

As he leant over the tin he noticed Martha sitting at a round table beyond, beneath the portrait of King George VI. She was still surrounded by people, as if she were a planet and the other patients her moons, circling her, moving closer to hear more. She was talking to them, small gestures at their wide-eyed faces. Then, as if she could feel his eyes on her, she looked up at him, saw him searching her face. Her expression morphed into something else; a flash of guilt, he imagined, and then her eyes narrowed and she gave a defiant tilt of her chin. He felt the biscuit sticking in his throat. Martha was going home to her son. Edith was going nowhere.

He had to do something. Was he too late?

◆ ◆ ◆

He found his way back to her at the end of the day. No marks on her; no sign of the new operation. He hadn't realised he had been clenching every muscle until he almost collapsed on to the stool beside her bed. She didn't wake. Declan should have been back in his room by now; it was long past his shift, but he found he couldn't leave her in there alone.

Nurse Ritchie appeared, her thin mouth set in a line when she saw him sitting there, one hand resting on the sheet next to Edith's hand, so close he could have stretched out his fingers and touched her.

Declan snatched his hand away, stood up quickly, disorientated in the windowless room, wondering how much time had passed.

Nurse Ritchie stepped forward, indicating the bed. 'I was going to take her back to the ward now.'

'I was . . .'

Nurse Ritchie raised an eyebrow. 'Doctor Malone told me to wake her if she wasn't awake by 7 p.m.' She pulled the small clock from a chain pinned to her dress and looked at it. 'And it's 7 p.m.' She was nothing if not a stickler for timings.

Their voices caused Edith to stir. She moaned softly, her arm automatically lifting before the leather restraints forced it back down.

Declan felt a thrumming in his chest. He coughed. 'I would just like to check that she has come around all right after the insulin we gave her.' He wracked his brains for something that might take her a while. 'Could you fetch her a tray of food?'

Nurse Ritchie opened her mouth. 'I'm not sure the . . .'

'I'm sure you can rustle up something. I think it is important she eats,' he said, cutting across her, hoping he sounded as authoritative as he needed to be.

'We normally bring them a tray on the ward,' she started again. Then, perhaps noting Declan's determined expression, she continued, 'But I can go and see if Chef has some soup and bread.'

Declan nodded curtly, pulling on his stethoscope as if he was about to examine Edith. Nurse Ritchie left, and Declan felt his body droop with temporary relief. He sat back on the stool, leaning over the bed slightly.

'Edith,' he whispered.

She had closed her eyes again. He hoped she hadn't lost consciousness. He had seen some patients drift in and out, barely lucid after the treatments, their memories affected, everything sluggish and distorted.

'Edith,' he repeated.

She opened her eyes slowly, turning her head slightly, clearly struggling to focus on him.

'You've had treatment,' he began. 'Can you remember anything?'

Tears sprang into Edith's eyes. 'I don't . . . I can't remem . . . It hurts,' she said finally, trying to lift a hand but again finding herself restrained. She lowered her eyes down her body, jerking both hands at the same time. Then she dropped back on the pillow, staring up at the ceiling with a resigned expression.

Declan lingered, knowing he didn't have long until Nurse Ritchie returned with her lemony expression, smell of bleach and tray of food. He had so many questions for her, but in that moment he didn't know what to say. She looked so tiny in the iron bed, drained against the white sheets.

'I thought . . . I thought it was all over,' she whispered. 'That this wouldn't happen any more . . .'

Declan felt an ache for this woman who had lived here all these years, had to undergo these treatments. There was a faint smell of burnt hair, as if she had been singed in the process.

Edith suddenly angled her head towards him. 'But Martha told them. Told them I did it. And now I have to have more treatment.' She licked her dry lips. 'You have to get me out, Doctor. I want to leave.'

'You're going to get some food; you'll be going back to the ward.'

She started shaking her head quickly from side to side. He could see marks where the pads had been placed on her head, red and swollen slightly. 'No, no, no.' Her voice grew louder.

'Edith, Edith.' Declan leaned over her, a hand out on her forehead, trying to calm her.

'No, no. Seacliff. I need to leave Seacliff. I need to leave this place. No more of this.'

Declan paused, not wanting to respond straight away, not knowing what he could promise. She was still shaking her head, muttering no, softly, over and over. He could feel her move below his hand and he removed it and stood feeling foolish by the side of the bed.

Her eyes were drooping again as she tried to keep talking to him. 'I thought it was over. Now I have to leave. I was always telling the truth, but I got treatment. Now when I lie I get treatment . . . and Martha told them I did it . . .' The words were confused, sentences running into each other, Declan struggling to keep up with her meaning.

She shook her head again, getting herself worked up, as if trying to rouse herself, to fight against the desire to drop off again. 'No, no, leave . . . I have . . . Doctor . . . please.'

'Edith, Edith.' He tried to get her to stop. His voice was gentle, coaxing. He thought he heard footsteps outside. 'Edith I can try, I can . . .'

She stopped, closed her eyes, and was listening to him.

'I'm going to see what I can do,' he said, not wanting to embellish more. Did she know what he knew? Did she know about the list?

'Do you promise?' she whispered at last.

'I . . .' He couldn't say the words, remembered all the times he had tried and failed since the fire. He swallowed. 'I promise.'

She opened both eyes then, the smallest flicker as if she was trying to smile. 'Thank you, Doctor. Thank you.'

Nurse Ritchie pushed inside, her bottom on the door, bustling backwards, carrying a tray with a bowl of thin soup and a chunk of bread, a glass of water. Edith closed her eyes again, seeming to be asleep, and Declan ushered the nurse outside, her huffing as he gently closed the door behind them both.

Chapter 33

NOW

Nurse Shaw was standing outside his office as he approached. He barely saw her, completely lost in the past hour.

She coughed slightly when he was a little way off, still turning over the promise he had made, wondering how he could help her best. If he could prove she didn't start the fire, that her diagnosis was wrong, they would have to listen to him . . .

He dragged his eyes up. Nurse Shaw was standing in front of his office door.

'Hello there,' she said with a small laugh.

'Oh, hello again.'

'You look rather glum,' she said, her voice light.

Declan rubbed at his eyes. 'Do I? I–I've just seen a patient, she's . . . well, it's no matter. How can I help you, Nurse?'

He watched a flicker of confusion cross her face. 'A patient?' She looked down the corridor the way he had come; the doors to the treatment rooms were at the other end. 'Edith,' she repeated, the name dull.

'Can I help?' he repeated, wanting to be in his office or in his room; wanting to be alone.

'I'm off out, can't you tell?' she asked, both arms flung out at her sides as if she was about to spin on the spot.

He only noticed it then. She looked different: a slick of lipstick on her mouth, her hair pinned up, no sign of the large white hat they all wore.

'You look lovely,' he said, a beat too late.

Her arms dropped to her sides and she fiddled with the pocket of her cardigan. 'I was wondering, well . . .' She swallowed.

It dawned on him slowly: her standing so close to him the evening before, her expression as he pulled her into the billiard room. She was about to ask him out.

'I wondered if you would like an evening away from this place? From the loonies?' she said it with a laugh, but the word sounded harsh anyway.

Declan couldn't stop the frown forming.

'You know, well, not . . .' She was stuttering a little over the words now.

He knew he should probably make it better, but he was bored of others bandying the term around, remembering some of the patients: polite, amenable; they didn't deserve it.

'I didn't mean . . .' It was like she had read his mind, two spots of pink now deep on her cheeks.

He lifted a hand, a heavy sigh escaping. 'I won't tonight. It's been a long day and I'd be no company.'

'Lots of time for your patients, none for yourself, Doctor.' She pursed her mouth together as if to stop herself saying anything else, and gave a quick nod of her head. 'Good evening.'

He watched her go, thought for a moment perhaps he should follow her – an evening out of the institution, a chance to stop the constant prattle in his head; the past few days were weighing him down. She was nearing the end of the corridor; he saw her lift a hand to brush at her face, wondered at the action, but then she turned the corner and the moment to change his mind had passed.

Chapter 34

THEN

The day started early, Edith delivering mail around the building. Malcolm came with her, unlocking the doors with his big bunch of keys and telling her about his wife who was having problems with her eyes.

'I'm sorry,' Edith said, staring at each envelope, her eyes stinging with tiredness. She had heard voices outside her room in the night, scratching on the wood, had dragged her mattress on to the floor, pressed it up in front of the door, leant her back against it.

'She had to go to hospital . . .'

Edith handed Joyce her envelope. Did she feel comforted by the thick sheets of paper? Or did the words want to make her smack the walls harder? Did Audrey feel better after she'd received hers? Maybe whoever wrote hadn't minded that she'd been found in the bath with her wrists open. Audrey's eyes welled up as she took it, but sometimes you couldn't tell if that was people being happy or sad.

'. . . they say she'll be blind by next Christmas.'

Malcolm stopped in the corridor and she turned to him, catching the last of what he was saying.

'That's very sad,' she said, knowing Malcolm loved his wife. He mentioned her often. She loved their garden; Malcolm once described her as green-fingered and Edith had been worried until he had explained.

She reached out for Malcolm's hand and held it briefly. His eyes darted down before his face relaxed. 'If we'd ever had a daughter, Edie, I'd hope she'd be just like you.'

She didn't know what to say to that. Malcolm would have been a good father, she thought, but she'd had a good father, everyone had told her that; he was a holy man, and she'd still ended up here.

She thought of Father that evening as she filed into the bathroom later, the big gable-lined window casting rectangular shadows across the wooden floorboards, the five baths in a row, opposite five other baths, chairs in between them for the nurses to sit on. She knew she should be used to it by now: the lavatories with no doors, the sideways looks from some of the attendants, someone else always there.

She felt her insides tighten when she saw Donna sitting in one of the baths opposite, her fringe damp and sticking to her forehead, Martha stepping into the bath next to her, her back just a series of bony lumps against pale skin. Nurse Ritchie sat in the chair between them. Edith was aware of their eyes watching her as she undressed in front of them, their mutters making them laugh, the nurse too, as she covered her breasts and stepped into the tepid water, her skin breaking immediately into goosebumps.

She sank into the water, trying to cover her body, bending over and washing herself as best she could. She remembered Father talking about sins of the flesh and it felt sinful, all of them naked in the same room.

She had refused her bath on that first day, bitten the nurse who had held her down, tried to remove her blouse. She'd been sent for treatment, so small the leather shackles hadn't been able to buckle tightly and her skinny arms were able to thrash and flail until Doctor Malone had sunk a needle in her arm and she didn't remember anything else.

She only had a few memories from that first year at Seacliff, a loop of the same: the white room, the needles, crying for her mother, the towering figure of Doctor Malone, wishing someone would hold her. She replayed the day they'd arrived together: her parents sitting either side of her on a sofa, her legs dangling from it, not able to touch the floor, as they spoke to the doctor about the things she said about her other house, her other mother, her other brother.

One time, Mother had asked her to tell her more. She'd held Edith's face in her hands and looked her in the eyes and asked questions. Edith knew some of the answers. Mother never asked questions in front of Father, but once Edith heard her beg him to listen to her before they went in the motorcar to Seacliff.

Then her mother had sat on that sofa with her and Edith had felt her body shaking softly, watched a tear drip from her chin until Father stood and beckoned her to leave. Edith had got down off the sofa to follow them but the doctor had stopped her, a hand on her shoulder. She hadn't understood when he'd told her she would be staying there. She didn't want to stay, wanted to go with her parents. She wanted to go back to their house and her bedroom where she had the window that looked out over the honey pear trees and the vegetable patch where she'd helped Mother dig out the potatoes last summer. And Mrs Periwinkle hadn't come with her in the motorcar, so she couldn't stay because she never left Mrs Periwinkle anywhere.

The doctor repeated the same words and Edith started crying, frightened now, as she had never been alone without her parents and she was hoping that they would come back, appear like they used to when she was very little and Mother would pretend to be hiding and then she'd come back and say, 'Ta da!' and it would all be a game and she would giggle and giggle. This didn't feel like a game, though, and a giant woman appeared in the doorway wearing a stiff, white hat and a dark-grey dress and Edith was to go with her.

Matron was taking her to a ward, she said, and Edith wasn't sure what a ward was. They didn't have a ward at home. Edith wondered if her parents were at the ward already and whether the doctor had been wrong.

They passed more rooms, so many rooms, and Matron opened door after door with different keys and every time she locked them again Edith wondered if Father and Mother would be able to remember the way.

Matron turned a corner and then looked down at her. 'We're here,' she said.

She walked into the ward, which was a large room with rows of beds down one side, wooden floorboards and a high, barred window at the end. Matron walked down the middle, stopping in front of one of the beds. Sheets were fitted tightly across it and there was a small carpet bag at the foot of it which looked like the one that lived on the top of Mother and Father's wardrobe at home, and when the nurse opened it Edith saw Mrs Periwinkle and that was when she cried and cried for her mother and she promised she wouldn't talk about the other girl any more. She just wanted to go home.

'Have you ever seen a fatter behind?' Donna cackled, making her own friend flush beetroot red as Shirley stepped into the bath opposite, her veined breasts enormous, rolls of stomach hanging down, her bandaged legs now naked, pale, mottled.

Edith looked away as she heard Nurse Ritchie's low chuckle.

'Nancy, have you ever seen this? It's like she's eaten three of you. There'll be no water left.'

Edith glanced over at Nurse Shaw on the other side of the room, sitting on a chair next to Rosa. Rosa was giggling and splashing water as if she was a child, and Nurse Shaw was staring ahead as if she was pretending not to hear Nurse Ritchie. Shirley finally lowered herself into the water; some sloshed over the edge on to the floor with a splat.

'Oh, she's beached.'

'Donna,' Martha said. Something in her voice made Edith look up again; she caught Martha's eye, surprised by her admonishment. They studied each other. Did Martha wish she was far away, too? Leaning over a tin bath pouring water over the small boy from the visitors' room? The moment passed so briefly Edith thought she'd imagined it.

Donna moved in the water, and Edith felt panic bloom: Donna didn't like it when people spoke to her like that; Patricia had spoken to her like that. Edith tried to sink underneath the water, bunching her legs up and resting back against the smooth metal, wanting to disappear from view. The water wasn't deep and she felt a chill on her breasts and stomach.

'Not like Edith over there, who's just skin and bones . . . nothing of her . . . pretty little Edith . . .' Donna's voice was loud in the echoing room.

'Pretty little Edith,' Martha sang out next to her, as if the moment between them hadn't happened at all, as if she knew she needed to fix something. Shirley tried to join in.

Then, without warning, Donna rose out of the water and it seemed the whole room sucked in a breath.

Edith glanced quickly again at Nurse Shaw. Would she say something? Tell her to sit back down? Nurse Shaw didn't meet her eye, staring hard at Rosa, still splashing.

Donna stepped out of the bath, not bothering with a towel, everyone watching as she crossed the room, watery footprints on the floor.

Edith pressed herself back against the cold metal as she stopped next to her, wiry pubic hair at eye level, staring down at Edith's body.

Her father's voice again: sins of the flesh.

'Have you ever seen a body like it?' Donna said slowly, her eye: open, shut, droplets clinging to her skin.

No one said a word as Donna bent down, so close Edith saw the separate strands of hair stuck to her forehead.

As Donna's hand reached down Edith made a noise, staring at the thin fingers now in the water, yellowed nails making the surface ripple: so close.

'If only she didn't sleep all alone in that little room of hers . . .'
Edith kept watching the fingers.

'If only one of the nurses would give me the right key . . .'
Edith's eyes darted across the room to where Nurse Ritchie shifted in her seat. Had she heard? Had she given Donna a key?

Donna's hand reached up and Edith looked down at her chest in horror as her fingers stroked her nipple.

Edith couldn't think; couldn't breathe, a tremor in her hands.

A cough from across the way. Nurse Shaw's bright voice as if this was a normal bath time: 'Come on, Rosa, out you get.'

Edith still immobile.

'Back to the ward,' Nurse Ritchie called out.

Donna stayed where she was as water drained, as the others reached for towels. Nurse Ritchie walked past the bath, looked right at Edith, said nothing. As if she couldn't see the naked patient's hand on her flesh.

She was Donna's new plaything. The nurses didn't care, the doctors didn't believe her and she would never be free.

Donna squeezed her nipple, Edith gasped as she bent closer, her damp hair brushing her cheek as she whispered, 'See you later, princess. I'm looking forward to it.'

Chapter 35

NOW

He looked for Edith every day. She had been returned to her room but Declan couldn't think of a reason to visit her there. He lingered at meal times in the dining room, pushing the food around his plate, hoping to catch a glimpse of her. He fabricated reasons to drop in on the dayroom, glancing quickly at the various patients. He was late for appointments, barely present, spending his evenings in the library searching through books for stories about the impossible, children who had made fantastical claims. There was nothing.

He lay awake in the darkness wondering how she was, twisting in his bed, trying to get comfortable. Sweaty dreams would shock him into waking: Edith unconscious, Malone performing the leucotomy, the trephine boring into her temple, a thin trickle of blood running down her cheek, spooling in her ear as he worked.

Was it over?

He fastened his belt another notch, pulled at his loose clothes.

Yesterday he had paused in front of Matron, her starched uniform impossibly white, dazzling him into more mumbling. He wanted to ask her about Edith, ask how she was, but he found himself biting down the questions.

She had looked at him, crossing her arms as he stopped her in the corridor. 'Yes, Doctor.'

He found himself enquiring after her health.

'Very good, Doctor,' she replied with a raised eyebrow before moving around him, her walk brisk as she moved away.

'Good,' he whispered, staying there in the corridor, only moving when an attendant started towards him pushing a male patient in a wheelchair.

He woke to a hubbub a day later. The whole place was full of excited babble for the first time in weeks. Since the fire, Seacliff had been permeated with a gloom, like a stubborn sea fog, but this morning faces were animated and patients and staff were making plans for the day ahead.

A pod of whales had washed up on the sands of Karitane beach, a short way away, and it had been decided that this might be a stimulating day out for some of the patients. Declan would normally have been swept along in the tide of feeling too, curious to catch a glimpse of the mammals that desperate locals were attempting to keep alive, but he found his energy sapped, his thoughts straying to the body in the bed.

The attendants were instructed to fetch buckets; patients were told to bring waterproofs, wear boots. The sky was filled with fat, white clouds that promised to spill before the day was out. Sandwiches were cut up and flasks of water were prepared in the kitchen, the staff there muttering about the extra work, about spoiling them.

Declan was herded along with a group of patients on to the idling bus, which took them along the winding road that clung to the coast, above the long grass and the white sand and the ocean. He stared out of the window, the vast expanse of water sitting heavy under the sky, as brooding as his own thoughts.

212

He hadn't anticipated the desperation that washed over him as they looked out over the beach. The enormous creatures were lying flat on the sand as locals moved amongst them, digging trenches around their bodies that ran back to the sea, filling them with water, throwing tin pails of water over the stranded whales. There were four: three larger ones, one smaller than the rest. You could see their bodies rise and fall as they struggled, helpless.

He moved over the uneven sand towards them, frowning at Tom Barton who was whooping and circling them, overexcited at the sight. Others were already racing backwards and forwards to the sea clutching buckets slopping with water, throwing it over the bodies before returning to the shoreline, concentration on their faces as they worked. Martha was a little way off, pouring water into one of the trenches around the largest whale. She was dressed in a lightweight coat that swamped her. He could feel his eyes narrow. When she looked up at him, she flinched at his expression before averting her gaze.

He scanned the beach, fooling himself into thinking he was simply taking in the scene. Surely she hadn't been allowed out of Seacliff? Then he spotted her. He felt his body lurch and he stumbled on the sand. She was crouched next to the smallest whale: still. One hand was resting on the area above its eye, patting it softly; she was whispering, a tender expression on her face. Declan felt a pain in his chest as he saw how pale she looked, her curly hair cut shorter, patchy, her arms bonier. She wasn't wearing her coat, had bundled it up beneath her like a makeshift cushion. Declan hoped she wouldn't catch cold.

There was a commotion in the corner of his eye and he turned to see Tom had managed to clamber up one of the larger whales and was being summoned down by a furious-looking Matron, whose hair was escaping her hat as she clamped a hand to it.

'Doctor Harris!' She called over to Declan to help get the man down.

Some locals had formed a small group and were staring in disgust at the sight of the man moving along the whale's body, out of everyone's control.

Declan raised a hand, wavering as he made his decision before heading over to Matron, still trying to keep Edith in his sights. He heard the harsh tones, the mutterings, and willed Tom down. They couldn't make him; he sat straddling the whale, patting him as if he were a horse he were riding. Matron fetched an attendant and they both circled the man and creature, other patients frozen, their buckets empty at their side as they stared up at Tom.

Ignoring the pleas, Tom remained there, getting up again when he was ready. He moved back along the whale, slipping as he moved down its tail. Tumbling on to the sand. Matron rushed towards him, already admonishing him as he looked up at her, grains of sand stuck to one side of his face, in his hair, all over his hands.

Edith had gone by the time he turned back to the smaller whale, a tiny figure beyond now standing looking out over the still sea, her arms folded across her chest, her cardigan stretched across her back so Declan could make out jutting shoulder blades. He found his feet moving in her direction before he had time to think.

Stopping halfway he noticed two people talking together on a patch of long grass that marked the edge of the sand. The smaller figure, a nurse, Nurse Shaw, was pointing in his direction, her sandy hair blowing sideways in the breeze as she spoke to the larger figure of Doctor Malone. His face, disgruntled, as he followed her finger. It stopped Declan in his tracks. What was she telling him? Why did he feel uneasy, dithering on the sand between the shore and the whales? He took a breath, all the questions he had bubbling beneath the surface. Edith so close. He wondered when his next chance would come.

He found himself changing direction, heading back to the whales and picking up a tin pail from a nearby pile. He spent the next hour moving between the sea and the whales, splashing water over their bodies, head down, not looking at the lonely figure getting her feet wet in the sand as the tide rolled in, just working purposefully, trying to let the task block out his thoughts.

Please don't fade away, he prayed silently, the water dripping into the trenches beneath the whale. *Please don't give up.*

Three of the whales died, including the smallest one. The tide was in now, nudging at their bodies, too late to help them, and Declan felt a desperate sadness tug at him as he returned his pail to the pile, nodding at some of the locals he'd been working alongside. There'd been talk that the local iwi would be following the Maori custom of removing the jaws of the whales. Thankfully, the patients would be gone by then.

He hadn't seen Doctor Malone since he'd spotted him in the long grass looking his way, but he had stayed away from Edith all afternoon, feeling eyes on him. Something in him knew he was right to be wary; he couldn't shake off the expression on Doctor Malone's face. He was still thinking about it as he made his way back to the bus, his boots damp and covered in a layer of sand. A firm hand placed on his shoulder made him jump.

'Doctor Malone,' Declan said, his voice higher than usual.

'Harris.'

They walked in that strange arrangement over the sand, Declan stumbling on the rutted surface, his boots sinking deeper at times, pebbles spitting out under his feet. He was waiting, aware of Malone's hand still on him, as if it were red-hot, burning through his clothes.

'I hear you've been getting on familiar terms with some of our female patients.'

Declan licked his lips, tasting salt. 'No, sir, not at all. I . . .' He felt his skin crawl.

Doctor Malone's grip tightened. 'You're a young man, of course; I understand you have urges, but the patients are off limits, Harris. We all know that.'

How could Doctor Malone ever imagine he would take advantage of anyone vulnerable in his care? 'Sir, I would never . . .'

'Rules are rules and we always need to behave with professionalism. I would hate to have to tell your father . . .'

Declan's mind was one step behind the words, listening to them as if there were a few seconds' delay. Edith's face flashed before him. Had he become over-familiar? The last part of the sentence overlapped that thought. His father. What would Doctor Malone tell his father? He felt an old fear drip down his back as if the seawater had sneaked under the collar of his shirt.

'And a woman like that. Her recent behaviour has been erratic; I hoped perhaps her prognosis was good, but there was an incident before the fire and now these rumours, a possible arsonist in our midst . . .'

Declan stopped on the sand. 'You can't really believe that she is capable of that?'

Doctor Malone hadn't noticed the pause, was one step ahead, turning awkwardly on the shifting sands, his eyes narrowed.

'There are other reasons, surely, for the fire. It hasn't been the first incident of its type – I understand before I arrived there had been other fires, and parts of the building do seem to suggest the foundations . . .'

Doctor Malone took a step forward, forcing Declan to look up at him; he was always taller, but on this incline Declan felt as if he were ten years old again. His voice was low but direct. 'You will stop this talk this instant. We have a witness at the scene who has been clear in what she saw . . .'

'Martha Anderson,' Declan burst out. 'She wants to see her son; she'd say anything. How do you know it wasn't her that began the fire in the first place . . .?' His arms were wide. 'She had a key! Did you know that?' Declan's voice was loud. 'Edith told me, told me Martha and that other woman, Donna, that they'd got into her room.'

'A key?' Doctor Malone flicked at something on his cuff.

'Edith told me.'

Doctor Malone looked over his shoulder at curious passers-by. 'Doctor Harris, I will not say it again. You will stay away from Edith Garrett. Or you will be leaving Seacliff. Do I make myself clear? She is not stable, Doctor Harris, although that will change soon, of course.'

Declan felt his whole body go cold. 'It's true, then,' he said, his words careful, desperate to not display the emotion that was building inside him like a tidal wave. 'Edith, sir – you're considering a leucotomy.'

'She will have the operation, yes.'

'But surely now that you know about the key, the fact you can't be certain others aren't being honest, that could change things?'

'That changes nothing,' Malone said, cutting right across his pleading. Declan felt as if he'd been punched in the gut. 'Nothing. You should know not to trust the patients; they're wily, Doctor Harris . . .'

Declan threw up his hands. 'And yet you don't hesitate to trust Martha Anderson when she . . .'

The older doctor's eyes bulged. 'Do not speak to me in this manner. We cannot take any risks, must be seen to be doing something. The police expect it. The superintendent . . . and' – he cleared his throat – 'she's a prime candidate for the new procedure. I'll be scheduling it with the neurosurgeon.'

Declan felt a heavy weight in his stomach; he rested a hand over it.

Doctor Malone was still talking. 'I won't discuss your behaviour with you again.'

A squeeze, painful and final, on his shoulder, and Doctor Malone veered away to a motorcar parked in a bay off the road. Declan followed the patients, unseeing, to the bus, herded along, shuffling, head down. He could have been one of them.

He stumbled up the steps; the driver said something to him but Declan didn't catch it, sliding into one of the front seats, scooting close to the glass that was spattered with tiny droplets. It had started to rain lightly; he realised his own head was damp. He hadn't noticed before.

Nurse Shaw stepped on to the bus a moment later and Declan looked up at her as she paused at the top of the aisle next to the driver. Declan became aware of the space beside him. Nurse Shaw moved past, not even looking at him, ducked into a seat on the opposite side of the bus. Declan dug his nails into his thigh.

Tom was walking up and down the aisle shouting for his medication. One of the attendants got up to deal with him, clamping his arms to his side, looking over at Declan for help. Declan did nothing, staring dumbly back. It was then he noticed Edith, towards the rear, alone, her eyes closed, her head rested back. He lurched backwards as if he'd been stung, head striking the glass window.

As the bus bumped back along the road, the buildings and turrets of Seacliff rose up over the pine trees to his left, he knew with a sinking feeling that all his efforts were hopeless. He couldn't stay at Seacliff, he couldn't help Edith, couldn't loosen the power Doctor Malone wielded at the hospital.

Over the past few weeks he had felt flashes of real confidence that had lain dormant within him rise up, spill out of him, a belief he could make a difference. It was checked, stuffed back down: he could do nothing but watch. His fingers gripped his thighs tighter; he felt the marks forming on his skin. He remembered lines from a patient's notes, the explanation as to why she hurt herself, slicing thin lines along her arms, the top of her thighs. Declan could understand it now, the need for release; or else he might open his mouth and never stop screaming.

How could he help if his hands were always tied? How could he ever hope to do anything in the shadow of Doctor Malone? And if he continued to try to speak to her, he would be leaving anyway; Malone had made that abundantly clear. All these thoughts remained as they turned through the gates and headed up the driveway, sweeping past the front lawn, past a fencing gang back for the day, the attendants carrying the tools they had been using, given the damage that could be done with a shovel.

He moved as if sleepwalking through the corridors to his office, letting himself in and pacing the room, the same thoughts on repeat. He leant against the window frame, one cheek resting on a cold pane of glass, the outside a blur of dull greens and greys, the rain a little heavier now.

He had promised to help Edith but he found himself constantly blocked. He thought of the notes he had, confused, gaps he didn't understand. He thought of the medication she had been given, higher doses in recent weeks; the insulin, the electric shock treatment when she was doped and under. He thought of the new operation she was scheduled to have and couldn't bear to imagine her on that trolley being wheeled in for that more permanent solution.

He bent his head over his desk, shut his eyes and slammed both hands down on the surface. Then, inhaling slowly, he drew out his chair and sat down, pulling a piece of paper from the ream in front of him, seizing on the fountain pen lying on the blotter pad. He wrote quickly, to the nearby hospital, to towns further away. By the end of an hour he had written five letters enquiring as to other jobs. He couldn't be there to see it. If he really wanted to help people he needed a new start, away from the hospital, somewhere that was just his, somewhere he could reinvent himself: do something.

He piled the envelopes up on his desk, the addresses written in his clear, round hand. Even his handwriting made him feel a fraud: childlike.

Chapter 36

BEFORE

Mother has had her baby and lots of the ladies from Dunedin have come to see her. He's a boy baby, Peter, and I'm a big sister again. They've brought him presents: a wooden rattle, a blanket, a woollen cardigan, booties. I think it's funny that some babies get lots of presents and some get none. Mary would have loved the rattle; she used to drag a kerosene tin round on a string to make it make a noise. She loved noise.

We are sitting in our living room with the two pale-green sofas with no back, just one big curved side, and Mrs Clark has served tea and I am dressed in my best dress, the one I normally wear to watch Daddy in church on Sundays. Outside it is sunny, the sky blue with no clouds, and I want to be running in the garden around the honey pear trees. I still miss when I was the other girl and I was allowed to go and run through the plannies, shoes sinking into the thick pine needles which hid all the holes that the rabbits lived in, and dipping my feet in the creek where I saw the cat who'd cacked it in a sack.

'And how is the little man behaving?' one of the ladies asks, looking at me. She's got curly grey hair and a grey woollen dress.

'He's not like my sister. He cries all the time,' I say. When I think of Mary I get an ache inside still; her face is the most clear, her wispy baby hair fine, not like Peter's dark head of hair, her wide-apart eyes following me from her spot in the basket in the scullery. Then when she was older, her too-skinny legs, poking-out stomach, her fine, light-brown hair a tangled mess. Following me around even when I felt too old to play.

A couple of the ladies look up, eyes wide, the talk stopping.

'Your sister . . . ?' The grey lady licks her lips and looks quickly at Mother, who is holding the baby to her chest.

'We haven't . . . Edith, her imagination, you see, she is a very fantastical child . . .' Mother isn't looking at me now, her words all jumbled and funny.

'It is confusing for children,' another woman in a pink cardigan says, picking up a knitted hat and returning it to the small pile before smiling at me.

I'm not confused; I know about babies. I used to hold Mary, and feed her, too. 'You can't have a baby unless you get your month-lies,' I say proudly, remembering. I don't notice all the ladies are quiet again, just remembering how my other mother had shown me how to pin pieces of bath towel back and front to my singlet when I bled and I hated it because I swore you could see them. 'Before, when I was big, I was one of the first ones to get my monthlies.'

'Edith.' My mother's voice is different now: short, loud. It makes me stop and look up at her, my hands moving quickly together on my lap.

The other ladies aren't looking at me or Mother; their eyes move around the room. One murmurs, 'Honestly.'

'I'm sorry, she picks things up, muddles things.' Mother is looking at each of the women in turn, her voice rising.

The lady in the pink cardigan is the first to speak. 'You've cho-sen a lovely name,' she says, and I can see Mother jumping on the words, wanting me to be quiet. It makes my head hurt, as sometimes I forget what I shouldn't say and I feel the sadness that I should be somewhere else with my other mother and sister but I'm not because I'm in the cave and now I'm here and I like my new family too.

The ladies don't stay long and Mother and I move into the hallway as they put their coats on. One of the ladies leaves the house, clutching her bag as she walks up our pathway, head close to the other lady, her mouth opening and closing quickly. She turns her head and catches my eye and I know she is talking about me.

I turn around and Mother is sitting on the bottom of the stairs. She has started to cry and is rocking Peter. I freeze in the hallway, the door still open, the ladies now gone through the gate.

'Why do you keep saying these things?' Mother says. She hasn't noticed the baby has started crying again.

'They're true.' I don't know what else to say.

'How do you know about them? Where are you hearing them? It isn't right; it isn't godly.' Mother's voice is really high now and she is jiggling the baby up and down. His little face has gone very red.

I don't know what she means and I don't understand.

'You can't keep saying things. Shocking things. You can't know about these things. It has to stop.' She is shouting and Mother never shouts and tears prick into my eyes and I want to cry too, like Peter.

We don't see Father walking up the path and into the house until he is in the hallway, and Mother can't hide the tears quickly enough.

'I'm sorry, darling, I didn't see you there. You just missed our visitors.' She brushes at her eyes with the back of her hand.

Father is quiet, looking from Mother to me and back again. His fists curl and, looking at me, he asks, 'What did she do?'

I feel ice inside me as Mother stands up, talking over the baby's crying. 'Nothing, I . . . she didn't mean to.'

Father steps closer and bends down so he is looking at me straight in the eye. 'This will stop, Edith. Rest assured, I will stop this.'

My mouth is dry and I can't move.

He stays, unblinking, in front of me. 'Go to your room.'

It is a second before I can feel my feet and legs and then I squeeze past Mother and the baby, up the stairs and I run, run, run away from them all.

Chapter 37

NOW

Declan felt invisible: moving from work to his room to work and back again. He ate alone, or skipped meals, losing more weight so that now when he removed his shirt he could see individual ribs, a concave stomach. He'd lost his hunger, the desire to fill himself.

The date had been set for a few weeks from now. Edith Garrett would have the new operation.

He avoided eye contact with the attendants and nurses he knew, not wanting to engage anyone in conversation. He stopped attending orchestra practices, made excuses to the conductor as he hurried past him. He saw his regular patients, kept the sessions timely, referred them for treatment, assessed the effects, changed their medication as if from a distance, barely registering their words.

Audrey had just left his office: committed after a failed suicide attempt, two weeks after her mother had died. She had tried again. Was she insane? Declan had wondered. Are desperation and madness the same? That thought should have tormented him more as he'd sent her down to have electric shock treatment, administered to patients capable of violent outbursts. Instead he signed her notes with a heavy hand, ushered in the next patient.

He was alone in his office, staring at a file in front of him. He picked at a piece of skin next to his nail, a small searing pain as it came away. A dirty cup and saucer from days before sat next to the file, a white film across the forgotten liquid. Nurse Shaw didn't bring him coffee any more and when he did see her in the corridors he was quick to change direction, his keys clashing on the ring as he escaped through another door. He stood up, moving over to the window, placing one hand on the cold glass.

His eye was caught by two figures crossing the lawn together. Doctor Malone, his hands interlocked behind his back, was talking to the superintendent, a grim expression on his face. There was something about the way they moved that made Declan frown; the superintendent was careful to glance over his shoulder as they approached the ground where the ward had stood. They seemed to be inspecting the area, their heads bowed together as they spoke and Declan watched as Doctor Malone gestured with two hands.

His fingers splayed on the glass, hiding the two men. What did it matter what they were discussing? He turned back to his desk, sinking into his chair, unable to get comfortable. The hands of the clock seemed to freeze on the same number as he stared, unseeing, at its face.

If Doctor Malone was out there, that meant he wasn't in his office.

Thinking about Nurse Shaw had reminded him of something she had told him when he'd first asked for the files of Martha and Edith: he knew where the rest of the notes were, the answers that could help him. He was done with sitting around on his hands, waiting for the axe to fall. As if gripped by madness himself, he stood and headed straight to the doorway.

Declan felt the beat of his pulse in his neck as he moved down the corridor towards the nurses' station, empty; the nurse was in the dayroom with the patients. He could feel his limbs tingle as he unlocked a cabinet, reached for the large rattling hoop of keys, glanced over his shoulder.

Everything alert, he left the room, his rapid footsteps loud on the stone.

He was about to break into the office. He had seen them outside a moment ago but it wouldn't take Doctor Malone long to get back here. Straining to listen for footsteps, the familiar bark of Doctor Malone's voice, he fumbled with the keys, trying each one, cursing under his breath at every wrong turn.

Then it happened: a sudden click and the door opened, swinging into the room. For a frightening moment Declan expected the great man to be sitting in his chair, an angry twitch of moustache, but the room was empty, only the hawk on the shelf giving him a steely gaze.

He lingered in the doorway, a noise unmistakable: someone wheeling a trolley. They crossed the corridor, down to another ward. The sound of another door opening and closing; they hadn't looked his way.

He had time to change his mind, to return the keys. If Doctor Malone discovered what he'd done it wasn't just his job that would be over, it would be his career.

A head of curls, a pale face, a promise made; he stepped inside.

He moved across to the large filing cabinet, relieved to find the drawers unlocked. 'G,' he muttered, pulling at the drawer that slid towards him revealing rows of different-coloured folders. 'Garrett' was thick, filled with wads of paper, some yellowed, some lined, some stamped, some formal, some written with a typewriter, by hand, newspaper clippings: a treasure trove. His heart almost burst from his chest as he hugged the bundle close, shut the drawer with a nudge of his hip.

Another noise outside; footsteps approaching, two indistinct voices. Declan could feel the hairs on his arms stand to attention.

He moved silently to stand behind the door, praying it wasn't Malone, praying that whoever was there didn't wonder why the door to the office was ajar. The voices grew louder and Declan felt his whole body tense. Then, a bark of laughter and the sounds were fading.

He moved as if in a trance back to the nurses' station, returning the keys without a word to the attending nurse back in the room, his breath suspended as he placed them inside the cabinet. The nurse barely glanced up as he locked the cabinet; who would question a doctor in a white coat?

His eyes were drawn to the haphazard pile in his arms, papers sticking out at every angle. Was this where he would discover the proof he needed? His whole body buzzed in anticipation as he left the room, as he rounded the corner to his office.

Tom was waiting outside, Franklin the attendant rolling his eyes at something he'd said. Declan retraced his steps quickly, knowing he couldn't waste time with another patient; waste time with anything else. Careful not to make a sound, he darted left, then right, into the warren of corridors and doors, the papers hot and urgent in his arms. He had to read them now.

Locking his bedroom door behind him, breathless from the circuitous route, the climb up the turret steps, he laid the pile on his bed, sitting next to it and pulling the first page towards him. His eyes scanned it, left to right, moving down, already turning to the next page, searching for something, anything he could use.

His eyes bulged as he read, turning the pages sideways to read smaller lines in the margins, corrections scratched out in ink. He felt his body jerk with every small discovery. Edith had told them so much about the supposed other girl: the house 'Karanga' in Oamaru, the name of her mother, her sister, the abuse at the hands of a stepbrother who had come to live with them. Declan couldn't help but wince at the words five-year-old Edith had used when she

228

described Primrose being hit, molested and worse. Cigarettes, sex, violence, blood: so much that surely might have made any doctor pause, ask how a small child might have known these things.

He felt the skin on his arms prickle. He scrabbled for a small notepad on his bedside table, started writing down information. The treatments she had endured made him flinch; time and again she had told them the same things, time and again they had sent her for electric shock therapy, changed her drugs, given her sedatives to calm her. Over a two-year period she had been reduced to a shadow of herself; Declan read her measurements, imagining a thin, broken young girl.

He didn't know how much time had passed, how many appointments he'd missed. One entry leapt out at him. He stared at the words, trembling at the account, at what that boy had done to her.

Her other mother needed to know she was there, Edith had cried.

Edith had been adamant. She needed to be told. She'd be missing her.

No one had believed her.

It was so exact, Declan knew precisely what he needed to do. Impossible, and yet he remembered the feeling he had standing in that house. The same feeling that washed over him now as he read the details with his own eyes, as if back in the consulting room with the child. He had to go back there, to this place. It would be the proof he so desperately needed; it would be the way to get her out.

Chapter 38

NOW

He had barely slept. He set off early, sunlight leaking over the horizon as he took the coastal road, marvelling at the sky streaked with pink and orange and pale-blue ribbons, the wide, blue ocean on his right. Winding his way round lush green hills, sheep grazing at the side of the road, he felt an excitement bubble.

He left the truck on a road above the harbour, removing the bag he had brought, a thick handle sticking up out of it as he swung it on to his back. Even higher up, the air still smelt of seaweed; below him he could make out fishermen hauling up buckets of fish, nets opened, men skirting bollards carrying their loads, small boats bobbing up and down on the clear water, the sun reflected on its surface. Nearby a boy in shorts and braces raced after a pigeon whilst a girl in a straw hat had her shoes laced up by a laughing mother.

He moved out of sight of the harbour below, following the marks he had made on a map of the area, back up the road he'd followed before towards the house with the rusting roof: Karanga. Cutting away from the road, he took a path that led him into a nature reserve, trails leading away from him, pine needles thick underfoot. He was wearing sturdy boots and could feel sweat prickle at his neckline as he walked, sticking to worn paths, feeling a growing unease.

He strained his ears, hoping to hear the sounds of the sea, of waves crashing against rocks, but the still calm of the day meant that all he could detect was the rustle of insects in the leaves around him, the occasional cry of a bird. He rolled up the cuffs of his shirtsleeves, his arms pale, the hairs dark against his skin. He could never be mistaken for a man who worked outside.

His footsteps crunched over fallen branches, drying patches of mud. The air became more stifling as the trees grew closer together, the sky almost hidden by the thick canopy of leaves above him.

Eventually, he emerged through a thick curtain of foliage, the sound of the waves loud as he burst into the space close to the cliff edge. The wind picked up, buffeting him from all sides as he moved along a coastal path, peering below at intervals. He wasn't confident he would know what he was looking for, but he was fortunate that the tide was out. After only a few minutes he felt his body tense as he spotted the telltale row of three boulders a little way out at sea, the tiniest sliver of sand below. The rocks he had seen on the map. He looked about him, able to make out a route down to the thin piece of beach. He felt his heart beat faster as he started to descend.

He landed heavily, feet sinking into the sand, coating his boots, droplets of wet sand spattering his trousers. He barely noticed, moving towards what he thought he might never find, staring up at the small entrance to a cave. He thought of the notes he had read and felt a genuine thrill rush through his whole body. What else had Edith been right about? He shivered, despite the sun above him.

Moving into the mouth of the cave, the stench of rotting sea-weed overwhelmed him as the temperature plummeted, the shadows becoming thick as he picked his way inside. He placed his bag down and removed the shovel, wondering where to begin. The cave wasn't big, but it reached back as if it might burrow right below the forest. The sloped rocks suspended above him made him feel as if the whole lot could come crashing down, burying him forever. He inched forwards, the air cooler still, dank with damp, light not reaching the corners. He paused next to a large rock jutting out of the shingle where the cave narrowed. He was deep inside, more than thirty feet from the entrance, and for a moment he craved the outside space, imagined running straight out of there, back out into the sunshine, clambering back up the cliffside.

Instead, he pushed the shovel into the sand and started to dig, knowing he had to start somewhere.

He wasn't sure how much time had passed, but he dug holes in different points all along the back of the cave and in the area behind the flat rock at intermittent points. He was thirsty, his flask empty and the paltry sandwich he had brought long gone. He felt his stomach growl but wouldn't stop, desperate for answers, for proof. He was aware the sea was nearing the mouth of the cave, that he could be trapped there at high tide, and that thought made him dig faster. He could hear the waves now, rolling relentlessly in, back and forward, back and forward, the strip of sand disappearing, soon probably not visible from the cliffs above.

He finally looked up, sinking the shovel into the sand and resting on the handle, surveying his work like a farmer looking over his crops. The back of the cave was a series of large shallow holes and he was feeling his own stupidity wash over him, the logical part of him shaking its head at his foolishness. Had he convinced himself up there in his room, surrounded by the notes? Was he going mad?

The damp had seeped into his clothing, the sweat meeting in his back, his muscles aching from the exertion. He looked over his shoulder, knowing he didn't have long left. He imagined remaining down here as the water slowly moved in, cutting off the exits, forcing him to stay as the sky darkened and night rolled in, the sharp smell of salt and seaweed around him.

He stepped into one of the holes, wanting to dig deeper for a few more minutes. He owed her that. He was her only hope. Someone had to listen to her.

He lifted the shovel and brought it back down, pushing it deeper into the sand, and frowned as it stopped on something hard. He bent down to feel what he had struck. He felt a smooth edge, bigger than another pebble or stone, and longer. He felt a roar in his ears, a tingling in his fingers as he wondered if he had done it.

He pulled the shovel out and sank it in again, next to the original spot, pitching forward as the shovel resisted. Then, gentler now, he sank it next to that spot. He licked at his dry lips, feeling everything tense as he made his way round the obstacle. Finally, as the shovel slipped easily again into the sand, he dropped to his knees, reaching his hand down and feeling for the edge with both hands. It wasn't possible. It couldn't be what it felt like. The cave was even darker.

Something became unstuck and he fell backwards, water seeping into his trousers, which he didn't feel at all because he was staring at a long bone flecked with sand.

He scrabbled backwards, stunned. What he was seeing wasn't possible. She had told them. She had told them all those years ago. It was true.

He stood slowly, moving across to the opening of the cave where it was lighter, turning over the bone, inspecting it before returning to gape back down into the hole as if he had conjured it from nowhere. He fell to his knees again, his hands moving along the space, faster now, feeling, digging. Impossible.

◆ ◆ ◆

The bone was long, still fleshy in some places. He felt around, felt others, stared again at the first. His clothes were sopping with water by the time he emerged, his trousers heavy, the bone now in his bag.

The tide was high as he reached the truck above the harbour. The sun had sunk below the horizon and he knew he should get back to Seacliff, but he couldn't leave her down there alone. It felt wrong to go. He thought of what the young Edith had said: that no one would ever find her. He imagined her lying there, the tide inching towards her now as she lay in the darkness of that cave, finally uncovered after all these years. He had never wished for a new day to begin as fervently as he wished it then.

He found a boarding house: a man in a cloth cap, his socked feet up on the counter, one toe poking out, a beer in his hand. He stared at Declan who had brushed fruitlessly at his trousers. Declan paid cash and was pointed up the stairs to a dirty single room with a narrow, lumpy bed and a small, smeared window covered in curtains so thin the moonlight still shone in.

He lay fully clothed on top of the blankets, everything still leaping and fizzing inside him. The moon disappeared behind a bank of clouds, but he lay wide awake in the darkness. What did this mean? What could he be sure of any more? He could smell cigarette smoke through the wooden floorboards, imagined the old man below him. He couldn't sleep, slipped his damp boots back on and let himself out of the room, creeping down the stairs.

He walked, Oamaru eerily silent, the enormous limestone buildings looming on corners as he meandered seemingly without purpose. It was only after a while that he realised where he was walking: back along the road that led up the cliff, pausing at the fork that led down to the trees and the cave beyond. So much had changed since he had walked that way that morning. He couldn't see the trees or the sea beyond, just a cloudy sky, a few stars spattered in the gaps between them, the faint lights of houses behind him, lampposts along the harbour.

He moved up the road, thin lines of orange pulsing around the edges of some upstairs windows, people still awake. An animal streaked in front of him, scuttling across the dust, kicking up tiny stones. He paused, a hand to his chest. He was jumpy, picturing his bag in the truck; he had lingered for an age, wondering what to do with the bone. It seemed wrong to leave it in the truck, but he had.

He kept walking, lights now almost gone below him as he moved to the end of the road, to the house that he had visited before.

He expected to look up to see the boarded windows faintly in the dark, the chimney lost in the inky blue sky. He stopped in front of the house, wondering what had happened there, wondering what had come before. He wondered if the girl, Primrose, had really lived there. Frowning, he squinted for a moment, wondering if his mind was playing tricks on him. He took a step forward, sucked in a breath as he stared at the window to the left of the door, the glow from behind the boarded-up windows, faint light squeezing between the thin cracks.

Someone was home.

Chapter 39

THEN

She never slept deeply any more. Deputy Matron had made her return her mattress, had threatened to send her to Matron if she saw it on the floor one more time. So she was back in her bed, staring at the door, imagining every footstep, cough, scrape was the moment she would come.

The nurses' checks were erratic, the gaps between them longer; sometimes they didn't come at all for hours. She wished the war wasn't on, that the nurses were patrolling when they should be like they used to.

She knew, knew it was her when she heard the creak on the fifth step. A hush. Whispers. Footsteps padding, the night shifting around her. Edith held her breath, her blanket drawn up to her face, her eyes straining in the dark, the tiny sliver of moonlight through the crack of her shutters not enough to help her see the outline of her own door; the blackness only making every sound louder, repeat over and over in her head.

'Edie, princess.' Crooning near the gap in the door.

Edith couldn't help let out a small whimper of panic, her knuckles clutching the material around her. No. They couldn't get in. They wouldn't get her here. Something in the lock; a scraping sound of metal in wood.

Someone giggled: Martha? Shirley?

'Shh.'

'You want to wake up the whole bloody place?'

Edith felt her body tremble. She knew she needed to get up, but she seemed incapable of moving, stuck in this position, every muscle taut.

She thought of dragging the mattress across again but what would Matron do? Send her to Doctor Malone? She couldn't be sent to him again; he would sign his name, take her to the white room.

Silence, and then the sound of the latch, a slow movement, a whisper of a breeze.

Edith lifted her head an inch. Faint grey silhouettes in the darkness. Another giggle. They had done it. They were here in her room, about to step inside. Metal turning again. Locked in with them. Her nose felt clogged with the smell of them: cigarettes, porridge, sweat; she thought she would choke on it. She squeezed her eyes tight, hands over her face, feeling the years drop away, as if she were back in her bed in one of her nightmares. They were coming closer. The monsters were here.

Weight at the foot of her bed, a scrape and the sharp scent of a match, a glow in the dark, smoke blown between the fingers covering her face.

'Surprise,' said the voice.

Her eyes flew open. She scrambled backwards but there was a hand gripping her, another over her mouth.

'Shut up,' Martha hissed. Edith stared up at her, feeling her eyes roll back in panic, her lips pressed into a damp palm.

Her chest rose and fell, rose and fell; this wasn't her imagining. What would the nurses do if they found them there? She thought then of the bathroom, Nurse Ritchie staring past her, Nurse Shaw's eyes sliding away guiltily. She felt a tightness in her chest, a scream stuck somewhere inside. Martha removed the hand from her mouth. Had she realised she wouldn't cry out?

'We were so bored in the dormitory,' Donna said, leaning back against the wall as if it were totally normal, as if for a moment they were friends in this place, telling each other stories in the dark. 'So we thought we'd come and play a little game with our favourite pretty patient.' She moved her head to the side and lifted the cigarette to her lips as she observed Edith. 'Do you want to play a game?'

Martha was still standing next to the bed, not quite sure perhaps whether to sit, eyes darting to the door, something resting on the floor that Edith couldn't make out.

'I don't want to be long,' she said, her voice soft, a whisper; another look at the door.

'Stop being such a fucking spoilsport. Now,' Donna said, barely lowering her voice as she stubbed out her cigarette on the wall with a small hiss; Edith imagined the black spot in the morning, a reminder she hadn't imagined it all. Donna crouched over Edith. 'Told you she'd be excited to see us.' Her face was delighted as she glanced at Martha.

A thin smile back.

'So, Edie,' Donna said, using the name Nurse Shaw had first used for her, it sounded all wrong in her mouth. 'Now we're here you don't want to ruin our fun.' She pouted, her groin pressing down on top of her.

What could she say to stop her, make her go away?

'And for our little game to work well we need you to be a good girl and lie down, all still . . .' Donna said, leaning forward and blocking Edith's view completely until there was just her face, the badly-cut fringe, her thin lips. 'Then' – her breath on her face, stale smoke – 'we're going to need you to take off that nightdress.'

Edith could just make out Donna's pout in the dark before she started to laugh.

Edith's eyes darted to Martha, who was fidgeting next to the bed, her hand up near the broken shutter, weak moonlight on her palm. 'Let's get on with it,' she said in a burst.

'Don't rush me.' Donna's head snapped to the side; Martha was quickly silent once more. Her focus went back to Edith. 'So come on, lie down now, I've got something for you.'

Edith felt her breathing quicken again. If she did what she was told it would be over. Patricia had never done what she was told. She wriggled down quickly, pausing for a second before reaching to pull her nightdress over her head.

Edith lay, pale in the dark, her fingers itching to snatch the blanket back. Donna held her breath, as if she was waiting for something.

Martha had moved across the room and for a second Edith thought she was leaving. Then she returned, something dangling from her left hand.

'Head down,' Donna instructed before Edith could see what it was. A rope? The panic spread again, her insides lurching.

Martha leaned across her now, the item a strip of some kind of cloth, like a man's tie, and covered her eyes. The dark room disappeared into nothingness.

'Good girl,' crooned Donna, stroking the inside of her arm so that Edith felt nausea swirl inside her.

Every sound seemed louder; the pressure on the mattress, the movement by the bed; she strained to hear and feel it all. What would she do to her? She imagined the fingers in the milky water of the bath, on her chest.

Something soft: a whisper on her cheek, tickling her flesh, making goosebumps spring up on her bare arms. Breath caught in her chest as the tickling moved from her face down her neck, like a soft feather duster, along her collarbone.

'We knew you'd like your present,' Donna said, her voice sounding wobbly as if she was about to burst with the next words.

Then, with no warning, a weight on her chest: heavy, furry, stiff, sticky. Edith gasped, hands flying up to remove the blindfold, her whole body bucking to remove the thing. A hand pressed it to her, something dug into her skin, scratching her. A smell, a terrible rotting smell. Bucking, bucking, get it off, get it off.

Laughter.

A worried voice: 'She's too loud.'

The sounds faded as everything became about the thing on her chest, on her stomach. Wet liquid, the smell. She was whimpering, she knew it.

'Donna.' A hiss.

Fur, claws. Her insides about to explode with the fear.

Then suddenly the weight was gone, a hand over her mouth, another pulling at the cloth over her ears. 'Shut up.'

Her chest rising, falling, rising, falling.

'Stop fucking breathing like that.'

'Donna.' A hiss.

A footstep.

From outside the room. The mattress lightening, figures melting away.

A bunch of keys jangling and a lone voice. Then the latch clicking, a torch shining on to her bed, Edith staring wide-eyed at the beam, sweat beading her top lip, her hairline. Reaching for her blanket to cover herself up.

Where were they? Silhouettes pressed into the corners of the room. What if she shone the light there?

'You making that noise, Edith?' Deputy Matron's voice.

'I . . .' What if she shone a light in the corners? What would happen then? Would they all be in trouble? Would she help her? 'I . . .' She swallowed, feeling the panic rise, clutching her blanket. 'A bad dream . . .'

'Get back to sleep.'

The torch moved away, the door closing, Edith's fingers still clutching the bedclothes as the latch clicked, signalling the missed moment.

They all waited in the dark, Edith wondering for a second whether it had been a nightmare, a hideous nightmare that Deputy Matron had interrupted.

Then she heard the whisper. 'Let's go; I can't get caught.'

'Relax.'

'I want to get out. I've only got a few years left, my boy will be . . .'

'Shut up about your boy.'

Silence.

Edith still lying there, too frightened to shift position, to call out. Would they cover her eyes again? Where was the heavy weight now?

A figure loomed over her, making her cringe back into her pillow. 'Well, this has been fun,' whispered Donna, one finger running down her cheek.

Then she was gone, footsteps on the wood, Martha exhaling as she moved, too. A key turning, a slight breeze and then a few words drifting into the room as they left: 'Sleep tight, Edie, hope the dead cat doesn't bite.'

Chapter 40

NOW

Declan's head was crammed, heavy with facts and lack of sleep as he drove back along the coastal road towards Seacliff, the sun low, a weak orange, about to be lost behind a thick bank of cloud sitting stubbornly on the horizon. The shadows lengthened as he drove out of Oamaru, his whole world altered. It had been the longest day.

He was still replaying the moment he had pushed into the local police station first thing that morning, approached the desk where a man sat groggily cupping a cooling mug of coffee in his hands; the policeman's expression shifting as he reached into the bag and gently lowered the bone down on to the counter, morphing from an early morning sleepiness to wrinkled confusion to revulsion in a few seconds. He looked at Declan with narrowed eyes, scraping his chair back to stand up.

Then it had been a whirlwind of activity as he had explained what the bone was, where the rest of the body could be found. The policeman had picked up the telephone, holding the receiver to his mouth as he was connected to his superior. Declan had yet to explain how he had known where to dig. There was a pause as he imagined the man arresting him; it hadn't occurred to him that he might be a suspect. That he might be leading them all to his victim. They had been in a motorcar moments later, Declan sitting next to him in the front.

They were met by another motorcar half an hour later: three more men, a pathologist and two other policemen. The group shook hands and Declan spoke quickly to them before leading them into the cluster of trees, the policemen exchanging looks as they followed Declan in silence. One of the older policemen remembered the case: a runaway, case closed, but some of the family had made him wonder.

The tide had been high and they struggled to make it down to the mouth of the cave, picking their way round rocks, water spraying over their ankles as they clutched the edges of the cliffside.

'We could wait an hour or so, for a lower tide,' one of the policemen said, but Declan pressed on, dropping on to the strip of sand and hurrying towards the mouth of the cave, his boots, already wet, sinking into the soaked sand as he did so. For a crazy second he imagined approaching the back of the cave, the flat rock, and seeing nothing but a smooth surface of shingle, no evidence of anything at all; or a series of holes, all empty, as if the day before had happened only in his mind. Then he remembered the weight of the bone in his hands that morning. He approached the rock, saw the handle of his shovel sticking up in the grey morning light.

Slowly he approached the grave, noting his hurried attempts to cover it again when he had left the day before. He could make out a long, dark clump of brown hair he had missed. The rest of the policemen gathered behind him, a small, silent semicircle. One man removed his hat. They were still for a moment, all contemplating what they were looking at. This wasn't petty theft, break-ins or their usual fare, and Declan felt a momentary flood of sympathy for them. This would be something none of them would ever forget.

The pathologist placed his bag on top of the rock and started issuing instructions. One policeman had stumbled to the mouth of the cave clutching his stomach, was being sick into the shallow water. Another glanced nervously over at him. The pathologist raised an eyebrow at Declan, a look between two professionals: Declan realised he was a long way from the scared student he had been before. There was no nausea now, not when the remains were the very proof he needed to free her.

Once a large part of the torso had been revealed, Declan turned to the pathologist who was recording notes on a pad, squinting in the poor light.

'When was the body buried?' Declan asked him.

The pathologist shrugged. 'Very hard to tell at this stage, but the sand is damp so decomposition has been slower. You can see places where the skin is still intact, the clothing is brittle, but there . . .'

'Would the end of the Great War sound right? Early 1920s?' Declan asked, attempting to keep his voice light.

All the policemen looked up at that, and Declan tried to focus only on the pathologist's face.

He was shrugging. 'That might not be a bad estimate,' he said. 'But obviously I'll know more when we take the body back to examine it.'

Declan spoke to the policeman he had driven over with and they moved away, giving a simultaneous breath of relief as they ducked under and out of the cave. The tide was further out and they managed to get back up the cliffside with relative ease, largely silent for the walk back to the motorcar, sand sticking to their shoes, the hem of their trousers, watermarks on the material.

Signs had been erected already, an ambulance to transport the remains had been summoned and the area was sealed off to any wandering hikers. A local journalist had appeared next to the haphazard arrangement of motorcars and was already asking questions: there were rumours, but no one seemed to have any idea who the body could be. Declan asked to speak to the chief superintendent, or whoever was in charge.

The chief superintendent, a portly man with a shiny head, had in fact been waiting. He asked the policeman to brief him and got another to show Declan into a holding cell and bring him a drink. Declan sat in the windowless grey room that smelt of piss and tobacco and sipped at the milky coffee in a paper cup. In the distance he could hear a shout, a telephone ringing, footsteps. He wondered how long he would be left here, and then couldn't help a smile slipping out as he thought of the irony of him being locked up. A bark of strange, high laughter. So this is what it felt like.

The chief superintendent appeared in the doorway, apologising for leaving him in there for so long: procedures to follow. He was mumbling a little, clearly this scenario wasn't in the handbook.

He had some questions: did Declan mind? Did he want another cup of coffee?

Declan shook his head, cut him off with a hand. 'I believe the body will turn out to be the body of a teenage girl. I believe she will have been found to have died by a blow to the head in the year 1922 at the hands of her stepbrother. I believe she lived in a house on Seaview Road called Karanga, the one at the end. I believe she was called Primrose.'

The policeman stared at him, pen poised over his pad, unable to tear his eyes away.

Then, as if the spell had broken, he dropped his pen and placed two hands on the table in front of him. 'But how do you know this information? Who are you?' He was angry, seemingly on the verge of arresting him, fingering the handcuffs that fell from his belt. But his face was puzzled, the questions obvious: how could this young man, who couldn't possibly have been any older than a toddler in 1922, have been able to murder a young girl?

'If those things are true, I can tell you more, but please, for now, I need to get back to Seacliff. People will wonder where I am; the truck isn't mine.' Declan felt dazed, wet, exhausted, his body drooping now that others had taken over things; the adrenalin leaking out of him.

'You can't leave,' the policeman said, face aghast. 'We've got a lot more questions for you.'

Declan reached into his pocket and drew out his wallet. 'I work at Seacliff Institution. Doctor Declan Harris. This is my identification. I have to go, but if you attend this address there is someone who will help you with your enquiries. Please.'

He left the police station, feeling years older: a different man.

Chapter 41

BEFORE

I am in my bedroom lying on my bed looking at a picture book. It has been raining all morning and little drops slide down the window, pause, drip more. All I can see in the street below are the tops of umbrellas. When I was big, before, I remember a day with fat grey clouds when it rained on the beach, hitting the top of the sea so you didn't know where one ended and the other began. Here it bounces off pavements, drips from rooftops and flows down the streets.

The bell goes and Mrs Clark appears in the doorway.

'You're wanted downstairs, Edith,' she says. She has taken her apron off but her day dress still has floury marks on it.

Before I leave the room she holds me by the shoulders and wipes at my face with the bottom of her skirt, tries to smooth my curls. 'Need you to look nice now,' she says. Her voice makes my heart beat fast.

Father is waiting for me in the doorway to the sitting room that is normally reserved for guests.

Mother is standing on the other side of the hall. Peter is crying in his basket next to her but it is like she doesn't notice. I want to go to him and hold him but Father told me I am never allowed to touch the baby now. I feel sad because I know I can make him smile by tickling his nose with mine. I used to do that when I was big before, with Mary, and she made the same gurgle.

'Edith.'

I stare back at Father.

'Can you come inside, please, Edith,' he says as I hold the bannister on the stairs.

I swallow. Someone is standing behind him but I can't see who it is. There is a wet umbrella propped up by the door, a little puddle already underneath it.

I pull on my skirt as I cross the hallway. Father turns his back on me and walks into the room.

The curtains have been drawn and all the lamps are lit and there is a man there, older than Father, dressed all in black. Father doesn't look back at me as I wait in the doorway, not wanting to go inside, looking over my shoulder. Mother takes one step towards me and then one step back.

'Edith.' Father's voice, low.

I don't want to go into the room with Father and the old man. 'I . . .' I know he'll get angry if I say that. It looks different though, dark; the rain is louder too.

'Edith.'

Looking back at Mother again I bite my lip.

Father clears his throat. I don't want to be a bad girl. I shuffle forward and Father moves round me to close the door to the hallway.

'Edith, this is Reverend Peck.'

'Hello,' I whisper.

The old man holds out his hand and I look at Father before taking it. It is huge and dry and I don't know what to do, so I just leave my hand in his as he moves it up and down.

I wish the curtains weren't closed and Mother was in here too. Everything smells of mothballs.

'How do you wish to begin?' Father hasn't looked at me at all and my head moves from him to the old man as if I am my jack-in-the-box.

'I think it would be best if she lies here,' the old man says, pointing to a long green sofa. He moves across and looks at me expectantly. 'Edith, would you lie here, please.'

I think he might be a doctor as well as a church man like Father, as Mother always needed to lie down when she was being looked at by the doctor. I'm not ill, though, and I don't want to lie down.

I step back over to the door. 'Please, I don't . . .'

Father puts a hand on my shoulder and I freeze. 'Now, Edith.'

I blink quickly, don't know what I can do to escape.

'Please, Father.' I spin round to look at him, one hand reaching up to him.

He turns me back round and I find myself moving across to the old man, climbing up on to the sofa to lie down. I don't remember to remove my shoes; Mrs Clark will be cross if I get marks on the cover.

'My shoes . . .'

'Lie down.' Father's voice is different: loud, sharp, and I do as he says.

Reverend Peck moves to stand at my head and I twist to try and see what he's doing. Father is staring at him standing above me.

'Let us pray.'

Father dips his head and I know that when those words are said in church I am meant to do that too, and I close my eyes but I don't want to. I look at the door. What would happen if I ran out? I hear a sound and realise it is coming from me.

The old man speaks over it, leaning down so that both his hands hover over my body, so close I think he is going to touch me. Only Mother and Mrs Clark touch me, not Father. I stare at the hands and try to press into the sofa away from them. Father still has his eyes closed and I try to stay as still as a statue. The old man is praying, asking God and the Holy Spirit for things. Father is repeating some of the words and I don't know what to do so I lie there and try to look at the lamp behind Father, at the light. I try not to make the noise but I can't help it; I sound like a hurt animal, a scared animal. The old man doesn't stop. Father doesn't open his eyes.

I make the noise again and I am back there: the other girl, making the same sounds as I watched him from the flat, wet rock.

He had stepped inside the cave, slowly. He had followed me there. He was angry. I remember now that I had threatened to tell them: to tell his father and my mother what he'd done to me in the plannies, that it had hurt. He was holding something in his hand. I tried to ready myself for him. I had to fight back this time.

He grabbed for me and I twisted, found the flesh of his arm, sank my teeth in.

He howled. 'Bitch.'

He pulled me up by my hair. I screamed as he grabbed my shoulders.

Damp sand clung to my skin and clothes as I thrashed. I tried to reach out to grip the stone, to get back on my feet.

'Bitch.' He said it softly, repeating it as I scratched and clawed at him, wanting to tear the skin, wanting him to hurt, to be frightened like me.

It all happened so fast. I saw him lift the rock above him. Raised my hands, the first blow smashing my knuckles, the crunch of bones, the feeling of things shattering inside, then the pain. A pain I'd never known. Someone was moaning, a terrible, keening moan and I realised it was me.

I had to get out. I clutched my broken hand to my chest. I spun, trying to turn towards the blue, the way out. Then, an explosion in the back of my head, my teeth clashing together, a shock of white and hot. Agony as it happened again, again and I felt myself falling, my body hitting the shingle below: wet and hurt and sticky blood and—

I am crying out as I lie there and I am back in the room with the old man and their faces are leaning over me. It seems forever until it is finally over and the old man is shaking hands with Father and saying that whatever is inside me should be driven out. I stay lying down. I can feel my hands are all sticky now, and above my lip is too. My body is shaking, the noises leaping and jumping out of me.

Father shows the old man out but I can't stop lying on the sofa. Father doesn't come back and I am alone in the room with the lamps and I don't know what to do and I know that I have something bad in me and the reverend doctor was telling God about it. I feel warmth leak out of me and I know Mrs Clark will be angry but I can't stop shaking and I can't get up.

Mother is in the doorway and then she is next to me. I don't talk to her about what happened but she sees where I have wet myself and she calls Mrs Clark who doesn't get angry at all but half carries me out of the room. She changes me as I stand in my bedroom and I don't speak as she lifts me on to the bed even though I am frightened the old man will come back and I curl myself up so tight to make myself disappear.

Mother brings me down later to say goodnight to Father and I whisper it quietly but can't look at him at all. He doesn't ask me to read with him; he hasn't done that for weeks.

'What have I got inside me?' I whisper to Mother that night in bed when her hand is just next to my lamp and she is getting up to leave.

She turns off the light, but she doesn't say anything. 'Goodnight, Edith.'

That night I dream. An old man, a cave, it's wet, I'm lying on the sofa, I'm lying in the drift needles in the plannies, I'm lying in the ground, everything is in my mouth, gabbled words I don't understand float over me. Something is inside me. I'm me but I'm not me. My head hurts, so much, I'm falling. I want to go home, I need to tell her where to find me.

Mother is there in her nightdress shushing me and Father appears in the doorway, calls Mother away and then closes my bedroom door behind me. I am left alone in the bed. I feel the warmth of my pee in between my legs again and I don't sleep for the rest of the night and I don't move and although it smells I don't want to leave or shut my eyes in case it makes the dream happen again.

Chapter 42

NOW

The next week seemed to Declan to be interminable. They were building something on the site where Ward Five had been, machinery digging at the ground, enormous sacks placed nearby. Something to ensure no one would think of the fire, of the place where so many women had lost their lives. Time moved on, the seasons would change. Edith would stay but she would be changed soon: different. His patient Tom Barton had missed his last appointment after an argument in the yard that had ended in him and another man being restrained and removed. He had been added to Doctor Malone's list. The date of Edith's operation loomed in his mind and he rushed daily to check for telegrams, for news from Oamaru.

A few days ago he had received an offer of a job, a place at a smaller asylum in Wellington; with the war continuing, the shortages, they were keen for him to start as soon as possible. He picked up the envelope, turning it over, thinking . . . wanting to leave Seacliff, not wanting to leave Seacliff: not wanting to leave her. He looked at it again now, knowing he must reply soon.

Then an urgent telegram arrived from the chief superintendent from the Oamaru police department.

◆ ◆ ◆

He had been planning it all night, had barely slept; woke already slightly shaking with the anticipation. He knew Doctor Malone recognised authority, that he would need to throw everything at it. He pleaded with the chief superintendent. Mildly irritated, but ultimately too curious to refuse, the man agreed.

He felt his stomach grumble and twinge with the anticipation of everything that was to come. He needed it to go smoothly, realised how illogical it might all sound. That he might be the one in the straitjacket by the end of it if he failed. He swallowed, his mouth dry, peering at the clock once more, knowing she was due to arrive on the 10.34 train. That it would take her a little while to make the walk up from the station.

It seemed an unending wait, his eyes constantly drawn to the window and his view of the driveway, looking out for a lone woman, panicking that she wouldn't come, that he would be humiliated. He licked his lips, forced his eyes back to the article he was reading by a journalist in America that months earlier he might have scoffed at. It mentioned the commission set up by Gandhi a few years before to look into the case of Shanti Devi, a four-year-old in India at the centre of a compelling case for reincarnation. Even this couldn't hold his interest; he must have read the same sentence three times. He glanced again at the driveway, at the carriage clock, at the driveway again, jumping at the rumble of a trolley in the corridor beyond. He got up from his seat, moved across to the window as if he could conjure her.

The minutes ticked by and he noted a motorcar appear, the chief superintendent stepping out, craning his neck as he looked up at the soaring building, Declan felt sweat pool under his arms, break out on his palms. What would he say? He couldn't prove anything unless she was here. He needed her to support his theory. He rushed to pull his coat on, as if the white material could give him a layer of authority. He thought he might vomit as he turned the doorknob of his office, his plans all dissolving around him.

The policeman was waiting in the foyer, the receptionist fussing around him, asking if he would like a tea or a coffee. He was waving her away with a hand, the buttons on his waistcoat straining with the movement.

'Doctor Harris, I assume all this cloak and dagger won't be a waste of my time.'

Declan felt a familiar sense of fear as he looked at the man. He had forgotten the size of him, a hat covering the bald head. Declan felt like a boy next to him. He opened his mouth, closed it again, trying to think of another reason he had telephoned him so urgently. His mind was a blank, he simply couldn't think of anything to fabricate. An attendant wheeled a large trolley past and Declan wanted to run and disappear under it.

'Thank you for meeting with me. I know you have plenty of questions so I thought it best to show you . . .'

And then, pushing her way through the heavy oak door of Seacliff came the woman he had been waiting for; under a pink felt hat and a worn coat, she looked up at him.

'Miss Wilson.' She looked startled as Declan took her gloved hand, the relief making his handshake so forceful she winced as he gripped her. 'Thank you so much for being here, thank you for getting here this morning.' He could have kissed her.

The policeman gave Declan a sharp look. 'What is going on? What has this place to do with anything?'

Declan held up a hand. 'Let me explain. Do both follow me.' Turning to the receptionist, feeling confidence rise up within him, he asked her to ensure patient Edith Garrett was brought to Doctor Malone's office that moment. She hurried off and Declan tugged at his tie, nerves bouncing around him. This had to work.

He coughed and turned. 'Shall we begin?'

'Please do, Doctor.' The policeman was trying to hide his exasperation.

'I believe there is a very good reason for you both coming here today. I thank you, sincerely,' Declan said, quiet but firm. He looked at them both. 'Now, if you follow me.'

The three of them moved down the corridor towards the office. Declan was aware of the everyday sounds and smells of the asylum: a shout from an attendant, laughter and talk from inside the dayroom, the smell of cabbage as they neared the kitchens. Miss Wilson was staring around, her eyes wide apart, both rounded, her nose wrinkled a little, clutching her handbag to her with both hands. Her dress seemed a little big, as if it had been made for someone larger. The policeman had fallen into step beside Declan, intermittently looking over his shoulder at the woman.

Declan licked his lips as they stopped outside the office door. 'In here,' he said, his voice breaking a little. He knocked on the wood. This was the moment. There was no going back now.

He strained to hear the familiar voice and felt his resolve waver in the face of no response. He stood hopelessly outside the door, turning to the two people in the corridor.

'I'm sorry, if you could wait here I will see where Doctor Malone has got t—'

'I'll tell you where Doctor Malone has got to.' Doctor Malone stood at the end of the corridor, his face set in an angry line. 'I don't like being ambushed by my own staff, Doctor Harris.' More words petered out as Declan saw him take in the policeman's uniform, the female stranger. 'I . . .'

256

'Doctor Malone, please, I have invited a couple of people who I think can help us with a particular patient.'

Doctor Malone forced his mouth together, his colour growing as he moved stiffly towards them, produced a bunch of keys from his pocket. Declan swallowed down his instinct to appease, to kow-tow as he stepped aside, watching Doctor Malone unlock the door.

'Oh please, Doctor Harris, do show us the way.' Doctor Malone waved him in with a theatrical flourish and Declan knew that his days in the job were numbered. He imagined himself packing up his things that afternoon, making the long walk down the driveway, looking back at the turrets and stone, humiliating his father and wondering if he would have done things differently.

He moved into the room, clutching the folder stuffed full of paper, better organised now, knowing this wasn't about his job any more; it was about something much bigger.

Doctor Malone moved behind his desk, his bulk silhouetted in the windowpanes. 'Well, Doctor Harris, you have us all here; what is it that you wanted to tell us?'

Declan turned to the woman in the felt hat. She looked ner-vous, casting frightened glances at Doctor Malone who was stiff with tension, bristling with energy. Her pale face, pinched with worry, blanched as she met Declan's eye. He steered her gently towards the leather-studded chair and invited her to sit down. Opening the folder on the desk, he pulled out the top three sheets, things he had copied out in a neater hand for her to read.

'Here.' He handed them to her and she rested them in her lap, reaching into her handbag for a small pair of spectacles, blushing up at them all as she fumbled. 'Please take your time, Miss Wilson,' Declan added, hearing Doctor Malone huff behind him, while the policeman, unable to tear his eyes away from the young woman, waited.

She removed her hat, her light-brown hair flattened, as she hooked a pair of spectacles over her ears and lifted the first sheet of paper, glancing quickly at the other two men, clearly loathing the unexpected spotlight on her actions.

He knew Doctor Malone and the policeman were watching her every movement as she read the three pieces of paper. Declan had underlined certain passages in them. Her lips were moving as she read, mouth moving faster as she turned to the last page.

'I don't . . .' She looked up at him, a bewildered expression on her face, then back down, scanning the last sheet, her forehead a series of furrows.

It seemed the carriage clock was louder with every second that passed, that everyone was waiting for the moment she would finish. Declan felt every muscle strain, his fingernails biting into his skin as he waited, body buzzing. Miss Wilson eventually stopped, looking up at Declan, her expression one of abject confusion. 'But . . .' One of the sheets slipped from her lap on to the floor as she stared at Declan. 'I don't understand?'

A knock broke the moment, Declan leaping a little at the noise.

'Doctor Harris,' came Matron's voice.

'Come in,' Declan called over his shoulder.

Doctor Malone threw both hands up in the air. 'Bloody circus,' he said as Matron pushed in, a terrified Edith in her wake.

'You asked for Edith to be brought here, Doctor?' Matron was brisk, looking curiously at the group in the room.

Doctor Malone started to bluster. 'I did no such . . .'

'Thank you, Matron, I did.' Declan stepped across the room, taking control of the situation, blocking out the protests from Doctor Malone as he ushered Edith into the room. 'Thank you for seeing us, Edith,' he said, a wide smile on his face, wanting to relax her, trying to hide his shock at her diminished appearance, her skeletal frame; her red-rimmed eyes, unfocused, scabs on the skin around her temples. She wasn't looking at him at all, her gaze fixed to the floor: didn't react to his words.

'That will be all, Matron,' Declan said firmly, watching Edith edge along the wall of the office, her eyes never moving from Doctor Malone, like a cornered animal. She looked impossibly thin, her white blouse too big for her, her skirt slipped down her hips. Declan felt his body ache at the dramatic change: lacklustre hair, a light gone from her eyes.

'This, Miss Wilson, is Edith Garrett. And you are reading the things she said when she first arrived here fifteen years ago.'

Miss Wilson was staring at her too, curiosity coupled with alarm rather than recognition on her face. She looked back down at the notes in her hand, picking up the fallen piece of paper from the floor.

'I . . . but . . . how?' She stared more closely at Edith.

Doctor Malone had clearly had enough. 'What is all this, Doctor Harris? What kind of show are you running here? I do not appreciate being left in the dark.'

This was the moment.

Declan turned to face the woman in the chair, not responding to Doctor Malone's blustering. 'Miss Wilson, may I ask. What have you read?'

'I'm not sure,' she began, the words slow, removing her spectacles and staring up at Declan.

'The notes you have just read,' Declan explained, 'were from statements made in interviews with Edith when she first came to Seacliff, when she was five years old. Can I ask you, Miss Wilson, do you know Edith?' He indicated Edith with a hand.

Edith jolted upright at the mention of her name, flat against the bookshelf.

The woman stared at Edith, at her lank hair, the curls limp, at her worrying at the sleeve of her blouse. 'No,' she said, with a small shake of her head.

'Did you know her family? They lived in Dunedin. Her father was a pastor there; she had a younger brother, Peter?' Declan asked her, his voice loud, clear.

The woman shook her head. 'I've never heard of them. But then . . .' She looked, puzzled, at the pieces of paper in her hand.

Declan took a deep breath. 'What are you wondering, Miss Wilson?' He felt his whole body tense, suspended, desperate for the answer.

The policeman shifted on the spot, head moving left to right, from the woman back to Declan. Even Doctor Malone was quiet now.

Miss Wilson lifted the pieces of paper. 'How did she know all this?'

Declan felt an enormous wave of relief flood through him, that she had clearly read enough, that the woman had recognised it all. That Edith hadn't been lying all those years ago.

'This is Primrose,' the woman went on, waving the papers at them all. 'This is my sister.' Then she burst into tears.

Chapter 43

NOW

The chief superintendent confirmed that the body found in the cave was that of fourteen-year-old Primrose Wilson. That she had been killed by a blow to the head. He read Edith's statements about how Primrose had died, and it matched the injuries found. Miss Mary Wilson, Primrose's little sister, had been six at the time. She'd never believed Primrose had run away, had left her. She returned to the house, Karanga, in Oamaru, always in the hope of finding her there. She told Declan, through fresh tears, that her stepbrother had died in a bar fight in 1928, that he had abused them both as children, that Primrose had always protected her.

Declan listened to all this as if from a distance, staring over their heads at Edith who seemed to have collapsed against the wall, her mouth a rounded 'O' as others spoke. The only one who remained silent was Doctor Malone, fists curling and uncurling as he kept his back to the room and looked out over the front lawn. Edith's eyes darted over to him time and again until Declan finally steered her out of the room, not wanting her to become even more overwhelmed.

They stood for a moment in the corridor outside Doctor Malone's office. Edith had a faraway expression on her face, one hand reaching up to the stone wall for support.

'Will you be all right?' Declan asked, his voice soft.

'That was my Oamaru sister,' she said finally, looking back at the door that was now closed. 'But I don't remember her now. Why don't I remember her now?' She stared up at him, suddenly a lot younger than her years.

Declan bit his lip. Should he tell her about similar stories? About children who lost these memories of past lives when they were five or six years old? It was too much. He held her shoulders firmly in both hands, forced her to look at him. 'Do you know what matters, Edith? You weren't lying all those years ago.'

'I wasn't,' she said, shaking her head quickly in response.

'You were telling the truth,' Declan clarified. 'But now *they* know that. Doctor Malone knows that.'

Edith's eyes rounded as he said his name. 'So your diagnosis,' he continued, 'the multiple personalities, the schizophrenia. That can't be right, Edith, can it?'

Edith shook her head again, slowly. 'I never thought . . .'

Declan released her, smiling as he saw the information finally starting to sink in; some colour seemed to already be returning to her cheeks.

'Will I still have to have the operation?' she asked finally, her voice almost a whisper. 'They say it's next week. I'll be like Patricia.'

'I will try everything in my power to stop that,' Declan said, feeling the strength in his own voice and trying to transmit it to her.

'Would I . . . would I ever be allowed to leave?' The smallest flicker of something appeared in her eyes.

Declan recognised it as hope. He didn't want to make promises he couldn't keep. 'I hope so, Edith. I really hope so.'

She clasped his hands then, quickly, Declan surprised by how cold her skin was, the strength of her grip. 'Thank you, Doctor, thank you for helping me,' she said. 'Bernie always told me you were kind. I knew you were kind, that you would help me if you could.'

She let his hands go and headed back along the corridor towards the dayroom. Declan watched her leave, her feet light on the flagstones. He knew he still had a fight left to go and he needed to ready himself for it.

The chief superintendent offered to drive Mary back to Oamaru and Declan walked them back to the foyer; so much had changed since that morning. It had started to spit outside, the lengthy gable-lined windows of the foyer dotted with rain.

Mary moved towards him, her head down, confusion etched on her features. Then, as if deciding, she reached for him quickly, hugged him tightly to her. 'I always knew she would never do that . . .' she said near his ear, then drew back, held him at arm's length. 'That she wouldn't have gone without saying goodbye.'

She blew her nose and stepped away, under a black umbrella the chief superintendent was proffering just outside the entrance-way. They disappeared into his motorcar. Declan remained in the open doorway, leaning against the frame, one hand up as the vehicle moved down the driveway spitting up stones as it went, until it turned through the main gate and disappeared.

He knew what he needed to do now.

Chapter 44

THEN

It was Visitors' Day. Some patients were combing their hair, straightening clothing. Bernie was lying on her back on her bed in the dormitory, the blanket beneath the bed empty, a flattened space where Misty had lain.

Edith swallowed.

The moment the darkness faded that morning she'd seen Misty under the bed, pushed there, eyes glassy, blood dried; the smell worse, filling the small space, forcing Edith to cover her mouth and nose with her scrunched-up nightdress as she wondered what to do with her.

When Edith approached, Bernie tucked her knees up, a small ball on the iron bed. Edith sat on the mattress next to her. Should she tell her?

Further along the row of beds was Joan, who didn't speak at all. She was reading a book from the library. Her hands were always a deep shade of red from working in the laundry. Rosa was in the corner bed, rubbing something into the bow of her violin, utterly oblivious to anything else as she wiped, wiped, wiped.

Edith fiddled with the collar of her blouse, her fingers still remembering the fur, her hands the cold, stiff weight as she'd stuffed the body under the staircase.

'Bernadette,' Nurse Ritchie called from the doorway, her voice bored-sounding. 'Visitors for you.'

Bernie didn't react at first; then, in a whirlwind, she unclenched, sat up, eyes wide as she reached for her comb, pulled it through her hair.

'They're waiting,' Nurse Ritchie said, tutting as she did so, muttering something Edith couldn't make out.

They were here. Edith felt a flash of something, imagined herself hearing the same words, combing her curly hair for visitors who she could tell things to, who might talk to the doctors. Bernie was smiling, pulling on her cardigan, straightening the collar of her blouse.

'Edie, will you?' She held out a ribbon.

It felt slippery in Edith's fingers as she went to tie it to the end of Bernie's plait.

'I can't believe it. They came, I thought . . .' Bernie tailed away. 'Come on.' She was on her feet.

Edith didn't want to go, but she didn't want to be alone either. So she followed.

They walked through the dormitory out into the corridor, past the nurses' station and into the dayroom. Bernie wavered in the doorway, her eyes on two figures, backs facing the door; both stood next to an empty table looking out of the window at the sweep of lawn, neatly mown in front of them. Bernie approached them shyly, the man turning and holding out a hand for her to shake. She almost bobbed into a curtsy as she took it. Her mother stayed looking out at the lawn for the longest time before joining them both at the table.

The room filled and Edith sat on a hard bench, the only person not in a group. She stared round at the walls, noticing the mark in the plaster where Patricia had thrown the chair, the smear on the glass of the nurses' station, the white plimsolls that Nurse Ritchie always wore, the laces double-tied, looped over a hook.

Then she saw her. Donna was sitting at a table by the barred window in the corner, her legs twisted together, ankle over shin, as if she was in knots. Her face was pale, her eyes narrowed underneath the wonky fringe, the tic evident as she glared at the person in the seat opposite. Edith felt her insides freeze as she thought back to the night before: the feel of Donna's legs clamped round her.

Donna wasn't focused on her now, though, and Edith realised that she had a visitor for the first time. The woman opposite her had newly washed grey hair, the ends curling on her collar. She was holding her hand out to Donna and talking in a low voice; Edith couldn't make out any words. The more she spoke, the more Donna hunched her shoulders, folding into her seat. Edith couldn't seem to look away as, unbelievably, she saw tears leak out of her eyes. She watched her face slowly collapse, as if she were a building they were demolishing.

Edith was distracted then by noise at Bernie's table. A gleeful squeak, Bernie launching herself across the table at her mother.

'Thank you. Thank you . . .'

Her father watched, patting worriedly at the pink spot on the top of his head.

A nurse stepped forward, realised there was no problem, encouraged Bernie back into her seat.

Bernie's smile was so wide as she turned to grin at Edith. Her mother produced a handkerchief from her handbag as she dabbed at her eyes, a leaky smile at her husband.

Edith flicked her eyes back across to Donna who was furiously wiping at her own face as the lady with the grey curled hair continued to talk. Donna scraped back her chair in one violent move and stood up. Edith had never seen that expression on her face before.

She looked like a child, younger than Bernie in that moment, hopelessly lost in the cavernous dayroom. Tears streaked down her face and the sleeve of her cardigan couldn't wipe them dry.

Where was this Donna last night?

Then, as if she could feel Edith watching, Donna looked up and across at her. Her expression shifted the moment she laid eyes on her, her chin up, eyes small slits. She walked away as the grey-haired woman continued to speak. She didn't look back. Straight past the nurses' station and out of the door.

Bernie's parents left soon afterwards, too, and Bernie moved across the room wordlessly, holding something small in her hand that her mother had given her before they left.

'They're taking me home. Doctor Harris wrote to them, Edie, Doctor Harris told them I was better . . .'

Edith's head was swimming as she took in the words.

'In a week or so, I'm leaving . . .'

Edith couldn't answer. Bernie was leaving. She would stay.

'Mother gave me this. To keep me company while they arrange things. Isn't that kind, Edie? It's a little cat like Misty . . .'

She opened her fist; a small porcelain cat sat on her palm.

Edith blinked and looked at Bernie, trying to remember what she should say. She moved away, down the corridor, back to the ward, Bernie trailing her.

She wasn't concentrating, hadn't realised how Donna would react. She should have thought about it. Donna was waiting for them both when they returned, standing right next to the dormitory door, slamming it when they were inside. The other girls melted away, Rosa lingering to watch from a safe distance on the other side of the room. Joan had put her book down, turned her back to them as she lay on her bed. Joyce started slapping the walls. Donna told her to shut it. Martha and Shirley stood nearby, ready to be summoned.

Edith jumped as Donna pushed her back against the wall. 'No visitors of your own? Just want to watch?'

Edith swallowed, trying to think of something she could say to stop this. She didn't want to be any trouble; she knew where trouble led. An image of the white room flashed into her mind. She swallowed again.

Donna stepped backwards, her chest rising and falling, the tic in her eye more pronounced as she looked at her. 'Who'd visit you, anyway?'

Bernie was silent, looking over her shoulder, aware of Martha and Shirley standing to the side. There was a hush in the room as Edith tried to think of an answer that would slow Donna's fast breathing, calm things down.

'I . . . please, Donna, I didn't mean to see. I . . .'

She hadn't expected it, halfway through, her hands out wide to reason, Donna launched herself. Edith put her hands up as she came. A fist winded her. She bent over, pain shooting through her as a hand slapped the side of her head.

She stumbled, tried to find her feet, her balance. She felt Donna's grip loosen; someone started to scream and Donna looked over her shoulder at the noise. Edith saw her chance then: her nails, cut by Nurse Shaw the week before, were blunt on her face but she was raking, felt skin beneath her fingers, not caring what she was clawing at, just wanting to get her to stop.

Bernie was leaving.

The weight on her chest: fur, liquid. That smell.

Donna stumbled backwards and she realised she was winning. She felt a surge of something as she grabbed at a clump of her hair, pulled hard, listened to Donna scream out. There were more people calling, bodies around them, eyes everywhere, faces blurred as Edith felt blood pound in her head, the whole room indistinct and unreal.

Legs clamping her tight in the dark: the key turning in the lock.

Then she felt two hands underneath her armpits, someone pulling her off, Bernie planted in front of her, mouth wide open, another pair of hands around hers as they prised her fingers, one by one, from the hair she was clutching until she was dragged backwards, only thin strands left in her closed fist, Donna holding her head as Edith realised Shirley and Martha had hold of her. They didn't do anything, waited, held her tightly as she writhed and bucked, as Donna looked on. Her face shifted into a smile and she blew at her fringe as she stood up.

'Hold her still,' she said as she aimed a kick at Edith's sides, and she groaned as she felt Donna's foot crunch against her ribs.

Edith looked up, at Bernie a few feet away, just watching; saw as the porcelain cat slipped from her hands on to the floor: a small tink as she cried out. Edith thrashed anew, twisting her whole body, shaking her head, feeling the snap of her ponytail on her cheek.

Martha lost her grip and with her free hand Edith flailed and scratched, not letting them hold her. Then suddenly both hands were free. She didn't hesitate, not thinking, not caring, just launching herself on to Donna with a snarl, shouting every unpleasant thing over the pounding in her own head.

Stale smoke on her face: kneeling over her in the dark.

Maybe there was a call from nearby, a new voice, but all she could see was Donna, her aching body thrashing and fighting and wanting to hurt, barely acknowledging that Donna wasn't reacting, was letting her do it. Then suddenly there were more hands all over her, lifting her right up so her legs circled pointlessly in the air. She saw their uniforms, saw Donna being held down too as she felt the cold, sharp jab of a needle.

Then the room swam and she fell to the floor; a crunch, something sharp, her head hitting the floor, a tiny porcelain head severed from its small body: a grey cat like Misty, broken in two.

Chapter 45

NOW

Doctor Malone had clearly been watching the motorcar leave, too, was standing with his back to the door in his office, all his muscles tense. Declan stood in the open doorway, swallowing as he almost changed his mind. Then Doctor Malone turned, face purple when he saw who it was, his whole body quivering, his Adam's apple moving up and down.

'Doctor Malone . . .' he began, starting forward.

'Don't you dare.'

Declan had never heard him shout so loud; the whole room seemed to shake with the sound.

'I need to speak with you.' Declan focused on keeping his voice calm, refused to be intimidated by the older man.

'I don't give a damn what you need to do. I have never been more humiliated in my life: to be ambushed like that, to have my practices questioned, to have the whole institution brought into disrepute by a nobody, by someone with minimal experience, almost a teenager. To think I allowed you to stay on here when I should have wiped my hands of you the moment I had the chance . . .'

Declan stood, body still, hands held behind him, waiting for the diatribe to end.

Doctor Malone was pacing, spitting words out. Then, gradually, when he had started to run out of steam, when he had not incited a reaction, he faded, the sentences shorter, until eventually they petered out and he was left, hands clutching the back of his chair, staring Declan down.

Declan didn't flinch, although the expression was so hate-filled he wondered he didn't drop down from the look alone. But he had been used to loud, angry men all his life. He thought of his father, the teachers he'd had over the years; he would not cower in the face of it any more.

Feet planted in the middle of the room, Declan spoke as clearly as he could. 'I will be leaving this office to write to a number of publications, medical journals, newspapers and suchlike, with details of this case. I am planning to make numerous claims about the way in which Edith's case was originally handled and the treatment she has suffered at your hands . . .'

He could see the whites of Doctor Malone's knuckles as he spoke; a vein was pulsing in his neck. He wondered that he didn't combust.

'I don't have to do these things,' Declan added, slowly and quietly, feeling for the second time that day that everything hinged on what happened next. This had to work. He thought back to Edith earlier, reaching to clasp his hands. He had planned this; he knew he could do it. He just needed to hold his nerve. 'On one condition.'

Doctor Malone opened his mouth, shut it again. Had he heard Declan? He removed his hands from the back of the chair and stood up straighter. 'What do you mean?' he asked slowly, eyes narrowed, waiting for the trick.

Declan took a breath. This was it. 'I won't tell a soul about what has happened here if you agree to cancel the leucotomy on Edith Garrett immediately and sign release papers for her, make proper arrangements to ensure she will be allowed back into the community . . .'

Doctor Malone looked across at him with an expression of utter disgust. 'Impossible,' he scoffed, moving around from behind his desk. 'Need I remind you, Doctor Harris, that Edith Garrett has been a patient here for fifteen years.'

Declan interjected, his voice firm, refusing to move as Doctor Malone stood in front of him, inches away. 'And she was committed for simply telling people – telling *you*, Doctor – the truth.'

'The truth is preposterous, it's . . .' Doctor Malone was almost talking to himself, pacing in front of Declan as he spoke. 'How did she know? How is it possible . . .?'

Declan spoke quietly over him until the older man was silent. 'We might never know. When things are calmer I would be happy to show you the research I have found on the matter. There have been other cases, Doctor, where children appear to have been able to recall past lives, violent deaths.'

'Absurd,' Malone sputtered, his jowls wobbling, his face reddening.

'Be that as it may, it was the truth,' Declan stressed. 'You heard it yourself. Yet she was told she had multiple personality disorder, schizophrenia. Underwent extensive treatments, had God knows how many drugs.'

Doctor Malone stopped, the stuffed hawk on a shelf above his head. 'But we can't just let her go. It would be admitting . . . no, no, we could never.' He was flailing now. 'And how can you even entertain this? Children have fanciful thoughts, they say fanciful things. How can you be certain this wasn't a story she was told, that she hadn't visited the town? What you're suggesting beggars belief.'

He was gabbling. 'She can be manipulative. She can be emotional, unpredictable . . . violent.' His eyes wild, he scanned the room as if for answers.

Declan felt a flash of anger at the man's selfish desperation, his nostrils flaring as he stepped forward. 'If you can't see your way to doing this,' he said, emphasising every syllable, 'I will be writing up this case. I will state that Edith, a five-year-old child at the time, was simply telling people truthful things. That she was taken from her parents under your recommendation, that no enquiries were ever made to follow up what she was saying. That you deliberately mis-diagnosed a child to keep her in the asylum. That a body has been found. I will ensure that Seacliff, and you personally, are utterly humiliated.' He had crossed off each sentence on a finger, his voice clear and strong. Then he waited.

'I'll refute it,' Doctor Malone said, his voice thin, his energy fading.

'I have the notes detailing the case: all of the notes.' Declan stressed the last part.

Doctor Malone didn't say anything, his whole body still, hands dropped to his sides as Declan stood there, breathing heavily, his chest rising and falling, trying to swallow down the fear inside him, that he would be caught out, that Doctor Malone would never agree.

'You . . . you wouldn't . . .' Doctor Malone began in the small-est voice, barely a whisper.

'I have already made enquiries,' Declan lied, 'and have received some very real interest, I assure you.' He hoped the bluster would distract Doctor Malone from checking the facts.

Doctor Malone didn't speak. Declan waited for him to react, to pace once more, to throw his arms around, to shout, to swipe at objects in the room. Instead, after a few full minutes of silence had passed, he saw the older man droop, his shoulders rounded as all the anger melted out of him. He nodded slowly, stepped back across to the chair behind his desk and almost fell into it, his head in his hands.

Declan moved towards him, pressing on; he knew he had to finish this. 'You will agree to halt the plans for the operation, to release Edith Garrett. You will ensure she is given the right support to help her back out in the community. And you will apologise to her,' he added as an afterthought.

Doctor Malone nodded dumbly, his head moving in his hands. Declan could see a small coin of flesh where he had lost his hair on the crown of his head. There was something very human about it.

The older man looked up at Declan. Perhaps he was going to explain? Perhaps he was going to apologise?

'I will,' he said.

It was enough.

Declan tried to swallow down the surprise that he knew was all over his face as he nodded, leaving Doctor Malone and walking back to his own room. Closing the door behind him he sagged against it, feeling tears prick at his eyes. He rested his head back, closed them.

He had done it.

Chapter 46

THEN

The walk from the white room seemed a painful blur: body jittery, a head full of clashing voices, footsteps, whistles.

Matron stopped writing and looked up as Edith entered the room on shaky legs. Dismissing Deputy Matron with a hand, she motioned to a chair.

'Sit down,' she said, neatening the pages with a decisive bang on the desk.

Edith jumped. She walked unsteadily over to the chair in front of Matron's narrow desk and slowly sat, gasping as she did so at the pains in her thighs, her stomach; the skin under her hair throbbing, one eye sticky, half-shut. She tried to focus, swallowed fruitlessly, her throat scratchy and dry. Was it hours after the fight? Days? She'd woken a few moments ago, strapped to the bed. Deputy Matron had unbuckled her, brought her here.

Matron was watching her now, her face screwed up as she scanned her face and body. She was wearing spectacles, her eyes bigger behind the lenses, a chain around her neck. Edith crossed her arms in front of her chest, unfolded them and let them hang by her sides. She wanted to ask Matron why she'd had treatment; she hadn't been any trouble – it had been Donna – but all the words stayed in her head, plugged by the sour expression on the older woman's face.

She had a different-shaped hat to the nurses and there wasn't a hint of hair around the edges, as if she was entirely bald underneath. In all her years at Seacliff, Edith had never seen Matron without her hat.

'I'm disappointed to be seeing you, Edith.'

The words hit her harder than if she'd raised her voice. She found herself feeling choked by them. Looking down she saw her knees trembling and placed her hands on them, pushed down, trying to remember words, words she should say.

'I had thought these episodes were in your past?'

'They are.' The words exploded out of her as she looked up, loud in the small room, surprising herself.

Matron's eyes widened so that Edith could make out all the whites around the pupils. 'That is not what Doctor Malone thinks. He thinks you have become a problem again. After all this time, Edith.'

'No, I'm not, I'm not, I'm sorry . . .' She rocked once forwards and backwards before remembering to stop, to be still, to be silent. All those things she must remember, from so long ago now; but she must do them again. She didn't want to be back in that room. She didn't want the yellow pills that made you not notice if things were sped up or slowed down, she didn't want to be put in the coats that tied endlessly round you so your arms were squeezed by your sides until you lost the feeling in them, lost your balance.

She shook her head, slowly, carefully. 'I'm very sorry, Matron, I won't be a problem, no, I won't be.' Her hands were in her lap now; there was blood underneath the nails on her right hand. She didn't know how it had got there. She covered the hand quickly with her left.

'I would like to hear your version of events,' Matron said, pulling out a fresh sheet of paper.

Edith swallowed as she watched her waiting, her pen hovering over the page. She took a breath, scrunched up her face, images returning in chunks: what things should she say?

She started to speak, haltingly, feeling as if she was swimming through a murky lake of pictures as she recounted the events that had led to her being there. She was getting confused, felt her palms dampen as the words got tied up in her mouth, tripping over themselves; she tried to go slower, the sentences weren't making sense.

'I saw her crying, that's why . . . no, before that she was waiting for me, after Bernie's parents . . . it was . . .' She could feel herself grow hotter, fingers tapping at her knees. She wasn't sure how long ago it all was; it could have been weeks, not days or hours. She needed to get it right. She wanted Matron to write it all down correctly. She wasn't a liar. 'She came to my room . . . she came and then . . .'

'Slow down, slow down. Take a moment, now start again. I was told you started a fight. You bit Donna,' Matron said.

Edith stopped short at that. 'I didn't . . .'

Did she? Did she bite Donna? She imagined the feeling of Donna's flesh in her mouth, sinking her teeth down hard, not caring what it was. They think she bit her. If she said she didn't bite her they'd think she was lying. She might have bitten her.

Matron was looking at her and she licked her lips, tried to start again. 'She was angry because I'd seen her, in the visitors' room. She waited for me in the dormitory. She can get into my room now . . .'

'Edith.' Her voice was a warning.

It wasn't coming out right; she knew it didn't sound right.

'She waited for me,' Edith started again. 'After the visitors left . . . Bernie was there,' she burst out in a rush. 'She'll tell you what she did.'

'Bernadette couldn't recall anything.' Matron glanced over at the pages in front of her. 'Two other patients agree as to the order of events. It is clear you attacked Donna and what I want to know is, why? We will obviously need to ensure there are no more violent episodes in the future.'

'Violent . . .'

'This isn't the first occasion recently where you have lost control, had to be removed from the dayroom. Deputy Matron tells me you have been seeing things again, moving furniture, and of course I don't need to go into your history with you.'

Edith's knees were quivering; her hands couldn't do anything to stop them. Goosebumps were breaking out on her arms. Her voice was fading in and out as the panic seized her. This felt like the times when she was younger, when she couldn't make them understand.

'Doctor Malone feels that you can't control your emotions. We've had others who can't control their disorder, allow themselves to be taken over . . .'

Edith tried to get her breathing under control, needed to reassure Matron that she was not one of those people. That she could control herself. Her head was full of clouds, like thick sea fog, and the words weren't coming. Her bruised body seemed weighted down, brain sluggish. She knew she needed to say something, but the more desperate she was to speak the more she struggled to do so.

'Doctor Malone feels that further treatment will have a limited effect.'

Edith looked up, hope lighting in her eyes. She wouldn't be having more treatment. Was that really true? Her hands loosened their grip.

'There is a new procedure,' Matron continued, 'that could settle you. Doctor Malone is now considering you for this procedure.'

Her mind raced as Matron said the words: the new procedure. Then with horror she thought of Patricia, her dull eyes, no longer caring the furniture wasn't straight, the chairs all in the wrong places: not noticing any more. She scratched at the back of her hand, feeling her skin itching, itching as she watched Matron write.

'No . . . I . . . Matron . . .'

Matron wasn't looking at her, just writing. It was all upside down and Edith wished she could read better; she could only make out the letters on their own with her finger under them, struggled to remember what they meant when strung together. What had she written there? What might Doctor Malone do?

'Please, Matron, I . . . please . . .' She wondered if she kept saying it whether the other words would come, whether Matron would realise Edith wouldn't do it again, wouldn't do anything again. She had to find the words. She scratched again, feeling the skin break under her nails.

Patricia but not Patricia.

'You'll be returned to the ward, but I'm looking at your privileges now, Edith: unlimited grounds access will be revoked – that will include your time with the gardening gang, the ability to go on outings off-site, your own room. These things will not remain in place and I will be moving you to another ward in the next few days to prepare you for your operation.'

Edith couldn't focus; everything was too much. Her walks with Bernie, the garden, pressing the soil into the ground, the scent of the flowers. She closed her eyes, her throbbing body suddenly impossibly heavy. It was as if all the last few years of good behaviour meant nothing to them.

'Now, can I see that you return to the ward without starting a fight on your way, or do you need someone to escort you back? And Edith—'

'Yes, Matron,' she whispered.

'Doctor Malone will see you first thing.'

She didn't hear her, didn't hear anything apart from the noise in her head, the voice trapped inside that couldn't speak aloud; that voice was getting louder, raving at Matron, moving out of its shadowed place where it had been hiding. She felt her whole head fill with it, her fists clench as she strained to keep it inside.

'Edith . . . Edith . . . ?'

She realised she was being dismissed.

'Edith, do you need someone to take you back?'

She held her head in her hands, shaking it. 'No, Matron.'

'Right, then.'

She lifted a hand and Edith knew she had to leave now. She had to think, to get away. She stumbled as she got up, one hand on the desk before leaving. Moving down the corridor, clutching at her ribs, her chest felt tight, her breath shallow as pain swept through her. She felt the nausea as she arrived back on the ward, placed a hand on the cool stone wall and breathed out, hunched over, before she stepped inside.

She wanted to run through the line of beds in the dormitory but her body just wouldn't let her. It was evening now and everyone was milling around; all eyes swivelled to Edith as she walked slowly down the aisle. She wasn't sure if it was the evening of the fight or weeks later. Everyone looked the same, but she could never be sure.

Bernie was lying on her side with her back to her. Edith thought of what Bernie had told Matron. That she hadn't been sure what had happened. Other women were watching her from the walls, floor, beds of the room. Joan was reading a book as if no time had passed at all. Joyce stopped patting the wall with the flat of her hand as she passed, waggled a finger at her, a little giggle escaping.

Edith didn't pause.

She wanted to get down the stairs, get down to her room, get into her bed. Her head was still thumping a dull beat and she could feel the tug of drowsy sleep on the edges of it all. If she could just lie down.

Martha, knees tucked under her chin, watched her as she passed. 'Edith,' she called out.

Edith didn't stop as she passed.

Shirley sat on the bed opposite. 'Donna's going to be m-a-d when she's back,' she said, her mottled body bent over as she secured a bandage on her leg.

Edith kept walking, to the stairs and the safety of her single room. It was only then that it really hit her: her room wasn't safe. She would spend every night lying open-eyed, clutching at the sheets, waiting for someone to do something to her; they would come back, and if she said or did anything, what would Doctor Malone do to her?

There was howling and laughing as Edith turned to head down the stairs, and then a small hand grabbed at the back of her tunic. She spun round, eyes wide, a sharp pain as she lifted her arm, heart racing. It was Bernie: her face red, her eyes puffy. Edith lowered her arm, her breath released, her lungs burning.

'I'm sorry,' Bernie whispered, casting a look over her shoulder. 'When Matron . . . I didn't . . .' She was the same height as Edith, standing on the first step. A smell, something below the stairs: matted fur.

'It's fine,' Edith said, her voice low too, one hand on the wooden bannister. 'I know you couldn't.'

Bernie was frightened of Shirley and Martha; there was no way she would have said much to Matron.

'I should have,' Bernie said. She darted her head back towards the room, leant in closer. 'They told Matron you started it,' she said hurriedly. 'They told Matron you've had it in for Donna for ages. That you're always starting fights with her.'

Edith flinched at that, knowing it would be hopeless to try to tell Matron anything else.

'It's OK.' She gave her a gentle push, a small smile. 'Go on.'

Bernie turned reluctantly and Edith walked slowly down the stairs, one hand gripping the bannister until she was on her floor, the doors to the single rooms shut, hers left open.

She felt the remnants of her energy leak out of her the moment she lay down on her bed, grimacing as she shifted. Her eyelids closed, even if she had wanted to stay alert, watch the door. The ache in her head thrummed as she heard the sound of the room above. Was Donna back on the ward too? She forced her eyes open, strained her ears. She could make out a nurse doing the rounds, shut her eyes again. The door opened, torchlight cast over her; the sound of the key being turned. Never again the relief of feeling that for a few hours, at least, she was safe. She would never be sure.

Chapter 47

NOW

The day was finally here. He couldn't believe it. He was driving her there. There was sunshine in a wide, cornflower-blue sky. He felt his insides flip.

The arrangements were in place. A halfway house in Dunedin and a place on a secretarial course three days a week. Her parents' money had been saved, enough for her to buy a small house, somewhere by the sea was what she had said, and the estate had been turned over to her. Edith had seemed tiny signing papers in Doctor Malone's office, the fountain pen shaking in her hand. She had stopped, a drop of ink bubbling on the end as she went to practise her signature, something she had never needed before. She left the office clutching the sheet filled with different versions, giggling and showing it to Nurse Shaw who had smiled faintly at her, looking at Declan over her shoulder.

Edith had been moved into another ward, given her own room as she waited for arrangements to be made. She had lessons in cookery, laundry, housekeeping, sewing. She had a visitor now; Mary would come and they would sit for hours, Mary telling her more and more about Primrose and their childhood together: about running through the plannies in the pine needles, splashing in the creek, lying in the meadow at the back of the house, about the way Primrose would curl round Mary at night. How much she still missed her.

Edith would regale Declan with updates when they met over tea and biscuits in his office. No need to talk about notes or the past but simply for Edith to be excited about the future. She was always checking when they were leaving, when she would be free. It made him grin stupidly at her, his stomach bubbling, daring to hope that he had time to get to know Edith away from Seacliff, away from that place. They would be two people, two young people with different upbringings and experiences but something extraordinary uniting them.

Declan had undertaken more research in the field, different theories competing in his head: the power of the mind, the nature of the soul, the possibility even of reincarnation. He wasn't sure what he believed, but it had transformed the way he viewed the world; suddenly there were possibilities in everything: magic everywhere.

'I've never even been in the front of a motorcar,' Edith said when he spoke about the plans for her release.

Declan smiled at her, thinking then of all the many firsts that Edith would experience; how she would have her first home, first pet, first dance, first kiss, and he found himself flooded with a happiness for her, an excitement. Imagine seeing the world for the first time, knowing she could travel anywhere, eat, cook, dance, walk whenever? She was free. He felt a renewed glow, a contentment. The best thing he had done.

He had turned down the job in Wellington and had given his notice to Doctor Malone too. The senior doctor was still in shock and struggling with the investigation into the fire. Martha certainly wasn't going home now. Declan didn't want to be in that place any more. He wasn't sure what the future would bring; he just knew he was leaving with her. He had one more night in Seacliff and then who knew what next.

◆ ◆ ◆

Now it seemed surreal that she was beside him, that he was staring across at her sitting in the passenger seat, her curled hair whipped backwards by the breeze from the open window, her cheeks rosier, her face fuller. She looked healthy, itching with excitement as she craned her neck to peer into the distance, taking in the passing landscape, staring out at houses on the side of the road, a cart selling vegetables, the stretches of iron-grey sea they could glimpse in the distance.

'Am I really going to have a new life?' she asked as they drove along the coast.

Declan turned and looked at her, feeling his head swim. *We both are*, he thought, feeling his stomach swirl for the future.

'In my own house,' she said slowly and quietly, 'where I can look up at the sky. See shooting stars,' she added with a grin. Then she grew serious again. 'And I won't have to go back to Seacliff, not ever.'

'Not ever.' Declan laughed at her wonderment. He hit the steering wheel with gloved hands, happiness suffusing his whole body. 'Not ever.'

'Not even if I say things?'

Declan shook his head from side to side. 'Nothing, Edie' – the name new to him, a small thrill at using it – 'nothing you can say will ever send you back there. You're free.'

He stressed the words, desperate for her to really understand that it was over, that the nightmare was finished.

She laughed then, high and excited, resting her head back on the seat. 'I never thought it would happen. I thought I would just have to make things safe instead . . .'

Declan was still smiling as she spoke, the road ahead clinging to the side of a hill, sheep grazing in the long grass to his right, oblivious to them moving below.

'. . . that I would have to stay there forever. But then you promised. And you'd got Bernie out so I knew you would do it. And now—' She held out a hand, indicated the road ahead.

He snuck another glance, saw the widest smile as she rested her head back once more. He felt another glow that he had done this.

'This will be much better. Before, I thought I'd be safe because Donna had gone. That was why I did it. To make myself safe. I had to do it . . .'

Declan couldn't quite keep up, concentrating on the winding road in front of him, still making plans for later that day. He was going to take her out for her first meal in a restaurant. He had made the reservation over the telephone, picturing a white tablecloth, a candle, a small vase of flowers and Edith sitting across from him in a dress that fitted, her flushed face happy.

'There were lots of matches for the cake. I knew no one would notice if some were missing. And I knew I could get out because the shutter in my room was broken, you see. Martha must have known too, she must have got the key, got out. It was a shame Bernie was up there though. I didn't want her to die . . .'

It was as if he hadn't heard the words; the sounds of the wind, the motorcar's engine dulled, the scene in the restaurant dissolving as he repeated them in his head, repeated them again, over and over. He felt his foot slipping on the pedal, his eyes leaving the road as with the slowest turn of his head he looked at her, sitting in the passenger seat beside him, her eyes closed now, her curly hair a wild halo around her and the smallest, satisfied smile on her lips.

◆ ◆ ◆

I'm Edith.

I was a patient.

I was a loony.

I'm guilty.

I'm free.

AUTHOR'S NOTE

The Seacliff fire

The Seacliff fire on 8 December 1942 was the starting point for this book. Seacliff was the largest building in New Zealand when it was first built in its isolated spot on the Otago coast, forty kilometres north of Dunedin. On a plot of about a thousand acres, the building was modelled on the Scottish baronial style and included spires, turrets and a fifty-metre observation tower. By 1942 it was home to hundreds of patients and staff.

Ward Five was a two-storey wooden outbuilding attached to the main building at the end of the nineteenth century, made up of single rooms and one twenty-bed dormitory. There were thirty-nine female patients housed in the ward. They were locked inside their rooms and the windows were also locked, only openable with a key from the inside.

The fire began at around 9.45 p.m. and was incredibly aggressive. In 1942, during the Second World War, there was a shortage of nursing staff and no one was on duty that night; checks were made by other staff from different wards every hour. There were no automatic alarms and by the time the fire had been noticed by a male attendant, it was too late for most. Only two women survived the blaze. The building was reduced to ashes in a few short hours.

Arson was considered; rats biting through wires was another theory, but the cause of the fire was never determined. Most believed it to have been caused by earth movement, but arson was never ruled out. When work began on the building in 1878 there was real concern about the site, which was found to slope ten degrees towards the sea, but the architect refused to consider a move. The main building hadn't even been completed when pieces of plaster started to fall and noises from the timber in the roof were reported. There was a major landslide three years after completion, which led to partial collapse. By 1954 it was deemed unfit for purpose; patients were moved out to nearby Cherry Farm and Seacliff was finally demolished. There is barely anything left of the opulent buildings if you visit the site today.

Children who recall past lives

I became fascinated by this topic after reading about the research undertaken by Dr Ian Stevenson, who studied the phenomenon for fifty years and wrote numerous books and articles on the subject. He studied children who claimed to have lived before, who recalled details from another life, and he sought to verify these details. Most of the children seemed to lose these memories by around the age of six.

One of the most notable examples reported in the media is the story of James, an American boy who began to have screaming nightmares just after his second birthday. He would cry out, 'Plane on fire, little man can't get out!' He repeatedly hit the propellers off his planes, spoke about the crash that had killed him, included details about the Corsair plane he had flown in the Second World War and the friends that he had flown with. After some research his family visited the surviving relatives of a Second World War pilot, James Huston Jr, who had died in the way that two-year-old James had described. The family were so convinced by the little boy that they accepted him as the reincarnation of their family member.

Another child seemed to be able to recall numerous details about the Hollywood agent Marty Martyn. Ryan answered more than fifty questions correctly about Marty's life, including verifying his correct birth date, which differed from the incorrect official birth record. In other cases, like Shanti Devi, mentioned in the book itself, children were able to identify family members from their past life, and on some occasions children even identified the people who had killed them.

The theories on this subject are varied and controversial. Many of the children appear to be recounting deaths that were very violent, and some believe these to have left a mark on space and time. Others believe in reincarnation, even demonstrating that some of the children have interesting birthmarks at the same site as the injury sustained in the previous life. Whatever my thoughts on the matter, it was a topic that drew me in and I wished to explore the idea in this book.

ACKNOWLEDGMENTS

This book was such a passion project and I could not be more excited to work with such a dynamic publisher as Thomas & Mercer.

To Jane Snelgrove, who loved this book from the start, thank you. To the whole team at Amazon, thank you for such a warm welcome and for being so professional and fun to work with. To Jack Butler for his endless enthusiasm and good humour. To Laura Deacon, Hatty Stiles and the countless others who work hard behind the scenes. To Emma Rogers for the fantastic cover design and Laura Ranftler for the original image used. That burning house is so powerful.

Thank you to my literary agent Clare Wallace at the Darley Anderson Agency for the countless things you do. A particular thanks to Tanera Simons and Emma Winter, too. Your early feedback on this book gave me the confidence to push on and I am very grateful to you both. To the cracking rights team at Darley Anderson, Kristina and Georgia, led by the exceptional Mary Darby – thank you for selling my books abroad. To Sheila David for working hard to turn my books into film or television projects.

If there are any errors in this book they are down to me, but lots of kind people helped me along the way. Thank you to Dr John Ferguson and Dr Tamara Gall for medical facts; to Kate Meyers Emery for some rather gruesome facts about decomposing bodies;

to Susie Hill and Catherine Campbell; to Keith and Bron Petrie for some brilliant New Zealand jargon – we miss you guys.

A debt of gratitude to some early readers who helped steer me: to Bree Oliver-Moss for killing off Warren (!) and to Joanna West for such helpful feedback. To my sister Naomi Billington – the book is dedicated to you, Superfan!

Thanks also to the Christchurch Library for sending me such great online resources. A few books helped me in my research, too. Susan Tarr's *Phenomena* and Janet Frame's autobiographies helped me build up a picture of life at Seacliff. Various books by Dr Ian Stevenson, Dr Jim Tucker and Mary and Peter Harrison all helped me explore the idea of children with past lives.

An enormous thank you to some incredibly generous authors for reading and providing quotes: Kate Riordan, Cathy Bramley, Roz Watkins, Amanda Jennings, Vikki Patis, Susanna Beard, Rachael Lucas, Cressida MacLaughlin, Angela Clarke, Rona Halsall, Maddie Please, Anna Mansell and more. To the BookCampers and Lady Novelists for being endlessly cheering and supportive in person and on our endless WhatsApp threads.

The book blogging community takes such time and care to read and review books. I am always amazed by the generous way in which you shout about the books you love. The support I have received in the past with my earlier books, or as Rosie Blake, has been humbling. Thank you for saying such nice things about my writing. Thank you to the many readers who buy my books and go on to review them online. You help others to find my books and I am so grateful to you.

To my parents, David and Basia, for always encouraging me. To Rosie and Dena for, quite literally, holding the babies while I write. To my husband Ben and wonderful children: Barnaby, Inessa and Lexi – I love you all.

And to anyone I have forgotten – and there will be someone – please forgive me.

ABOUT THE AUTHOR

As an ex-history teacher, Cesca has always been fascinated by true stories from the recent past. She has written three novels; her debut *The Silent Hours* was described as a 'moving debut' by *Women and Home* magazine and *The Times* called Major 'a talent to watch'. Her third novel *The Other Girl* is a historical thriller set in an asylum in 1940s New Zealand and is inspired by a terrible true story. Cesca has vlogged about the writing process for *Novelicious* and the *Writers and Artists* website. She has also presented shows for ITV West and Sky. She writes other books under her pseudonym Rosie Blake. She runs writing retreats twice a year in the West Country and teaches creative writing for the Henley School of Art. Cesca lives in Berkshire with her husband, son and twin girls.